Duke
of
Egypt

Duke
— *of* —
Egypt

Margriet de Moor

TRANSLATED FROM THE DUTCH
BY PAUL VINCENT

ARCADE PUBLISHING • NEW YORK

FIRST NORTH AMERICAN EDITION 2001

Originally published in Dutch under the title *Hertog van Egypte* by Em. Querido
Uitgeverij, BV

This is a work of fiction. Names, places, characters, and incidents are either the
products of the author's imagination or are used fictitiously.

Library of Congress Cataloging-in-Publication Data
　　Moor, Margriet de.
　　　[Hertog van Egypte. English]
　　　Duke of Egypt : a novel / Margriet de Moor. —1st North American ed.
　　　　p.　cm.
　　　ISBN 1-55970-546-9 (hc)
　　　ISBN 1-55970-661-9 (pb)
　　　I. Title.
　　　PT5881.23.O578 H4713 2002
　　　839.3'1364—dc21　　　　　　　　　　　2001045788

Published in the United States by Arcade Publishing, Inc., New York
Distributed by AOL Time Warner Book Group

Visit our Web site at www.arcadepub.com

10　9　8　7　6　5　4　3　2　1

Designed by API

EB

In memory of my husband, Heppe

And how was the voyage?
And the heart that cracked without breaking?

Marina Tsvetayeva

Duke
of
Egypt

Part One

1

*T*here are a goodly number who claim that they realized immediately what was happening that afternoon. They remember him coming into the pub, good-looking, in a homburg hat, and everyone agrees that his nomad's eyes scanned the drinkers until they picked out Lucie.

In fact, it had been raining all morning and I was the only one who took any notice of him, the only one, I say, because even Lucie hadn't looked up when she accepted a cigarette from him and thanked him with her usual smiling, absent gaze. We were in The Tap at the busiest time of day before the new road was built. So when Joseph came in he attracted scarcely any attention, partly because the truck drivers had started discussing some campaign or other and were having to yell louder and louder to make themselves understood. While they ate their sandwiches at the bar, tempers were becoming frayed over some collective wage agreement, or over student militancy, or possibly over nuclear tests. It was the 1960s, and in those days people were getting pretty worked up about such things.

Joseph completely ignored the noise. He went over to the right-hand corner of the bar, motioned with his hand, ordered a Coke, and turned to the telephone hanging on the wall just behind him. His kind talk loud. Although his face was averted, I could hear his voice above the political discussion, but it was impossible to tell whether he was cursing or begging, since he was speaking their language, making expansive gestures with his arm and somehow creating the impression that he was talking into the wind to someone on the other side of a meadow.

But when Lucie discovered that she was out of cigarettes, he was leaning against the bar again. Lucie is strange. She stares. Lucie's one of those people who couldn't keep up at school, and she's got the kind of metallic red hair that makes you understand at once why she was made fun of in the street as a child. At the time we're talking about, she worked in her father's business, the same job that she now does together with Joseph, but back then, at twenty-one, it was she who was responsible for the stables, reared the horses, and knew what a yearling might fetch at the Delden market. The farm is on the road to Benckelo. If I close my eyes I can picture her easily, in boots beneath a summer dress, lunging a gray foal. With dramatic concentration the animal repeats the circuit of which she is the irresistible focal point.

She patted the pockets of her jacket. A lighter and an empty cigarette pack. Then she looked down and saw a thin hand with a twenty-carat gold watch on the wrist, offering her her favorite brand. She calmly fished out a cigarette, smiled briefly, and lit up, ignoring the man, who soon afterward paid and left. As I said, it was raining. Joseph had pushed his hat down and crossed the street in front of the pub. It was only then that a few people noticed him through the rain-wet windows.

"They've been camped in the field next to Smeenk's factory for a week."

That was then. That was a minute before they saw Joseph gliding past The Tap in that big fat car for the first time. Afterward everyone got used to the Chevrolets and Mercedeses in which he would invariably appear in the village as soon as the leaves started falling, on his way to his wife. Yes, he came and he went. He arrived from the east between two faded fields of corn and left heading south down a blooming avenue of chestnuts. I always understood that restlessness of his. Houses and streets are beacons that we've placed in our own heads, like calendars and clocks and written stories. But in Joseph's memory there are a few other things, wheels and horses and barking dogs, all clamoring to depart. Is it the call of open space? Woods, church spires, fields; in short, freedom? Joseph's space doesn't call out loud, but quietly chafes between his skin and his clothes. What's so wonderful about being dumped across the border, almost immediately after your birth, as happened to him in 1936? It was December, there was a blizzard raging, but even in such weather children like Joseph were born out in the open. The following morning a team of about ten gendarmes slithered toward the wood on bikes, with dogs, to where a *kumpania* of three caravans was camped. Freedom, or disruption? If life were fueled only by what instinct had always known, Joseph would never have stayed cooped up in a house for entire winters. But life also consists of omens, and when Lucie gratefully took one of his cigarettes that afternoon in the pub, it was preordained that for the next sixteen or seventeen years he would drive through the village with her in his jalopy, first with just her, and later with two or three kids in the back, and often with a trailer attached in which a couple of nervous horses had to be transported to Delden or Zwolle. In those cases he drove slowly (by his standards), since horses have an unerring sense of speed and hate anything over forty-five miles an hour. And then Lucie would start singing about Tom the piper's son, and Joseph would be sitting there with a slight grin on his face, he'd be catching the meaning of the song a lot better than Johan, who was two at the time, or Katharina, who was only five months old: Tom, Tom the piper's son, stole a pig and away did run. That's the way it is, and who's to say he's wrong?

These days there's something about them that makes me uneasy.

They've grown silent. And in the left wing of the farm a couple of people sleep in till eight o'clock. Lucie's father, who lives under the same roof, has been up and about for ages by then. He has invested in chicory, and every morning he checks the barn, where through the use of hydroponic gardening there is an idiotically quick harvest in the making. Today Lucie has just had time to close the door after her children as they go off to school. She has put on coffee and lit a cigarette, when Joseph says to her, "I'm getting rid of the mare."

He doesn't look at her as he says this. He looks at the dogs by their empty bowls. He's wearing a dark brown suit, a sweater, his feet are still bare. Lucie also is staring straight ahead, and even if she were not, she still wouldn't see that Joseph is turning into a different person, his face bonier, his hands whiter.

"What mare?" she asks stupidly.

He takes his coffee from her and walks across to the windows.

The kitchen is spacious. There is a dining table with chairs, a sofa covered in cushions, and a dresser containing a group of statuettes of the Virgin Mary, all of them brought by Joseph. While he sees a thin dividing line of sun above the landscape of barns and hillocks in the far distance, she looks at the statuettes. She is reminded of the past; he had the Virgin of Mostar with him nine years ago, she calculates, when he came home. Bellaheleen had just had her first foal then.

. . . It had been at the end of an exhausting afternoon. Whether it was because Lucie had sold the young stallion the day before or for whatever reason, the mare hadn't wanted to have her hooves trimmed. They had been working on her for hours when Joseph's car drove into the yard. After an absence of four months he got out, gaunt, his eyebrows and mustache still raven black, and as he approached the group by the stables, he did not say a word, but with a motion of his head he made it clear that they were to leave the horse to him. He took hold of the mare. Scratching her front leg a little he started first cajoling her and then, without any transition, cursing her, using the pathetic sounds that had dominated his tongue in the past few months. The animal stood listening in a trance, not moving an inch, and quite docilely let him have his way. When he finally raised his eyes, the look in them was guileless. "Let's agree . . ." Searching for Dutch words, he proposed to Lucie, her father, and a casual laborer that the offspring of Bellaheleen no longer be sold, and although they knew that something so absurd was out of the question, the father and the farmhand nodded. As for Lucie, she had looked from his neckerchief to his shoes and her pale gray eyes blinked. . . .

So all that remains is his superfluous answer to her superfluous question.

"What mare?"

"Bellaheleen."

He turns away from the window to put on his socks and boots, a jacket, and finally an old hat, before venturing out into the pouring rain. A little while later, by the time he is standing out in the field whistling to one of the horses to come to him, Lucie has finished the kitchen and is on her way to the stables past the beet waste and a rusty piece of agricultural machinery to talk to the farmhand about the work.

The stable boy is noting down on a blackboard which horses have been fed.

"They've been inside for too long," he says, pointing to the two bays that have been fighting behind the paneling of the stall. Just then Joseph arrives in front of the stables with Bellaheleen. He puts the thirteen-year-old mare under the sheet iron lean-to in order to give her a quick extra grooming, preparing her for the intended sale. Lucie helps. She uses a metal comb and a brush, she rubs the wet skin with clean straw, and suddenly everything is as it used to be, as it used to be at a time that's gone for good. She and Joseph move in comradely fashion around the body of the gray-brown animal. But when Joseph flicks his cigarette butt into the rain and coughs convulsively a couple of times, Lucie goes into the stables to get the horse cloth and it's the stable boy who looks up. Joseph notices.

With contempt in his voice he says, "Breathing seems to have to hurt these days."

The boy grins in embarrassment. "It's November," he says.

Lucie puts the blanket over the horse. She bends down to pull a few wisps of straw out of the tail. Then, as she straightens up again, she is caught unaware by a memory: Joseph telling her about the time they drove through the rolling landscape of Silesia in a group of eight caravans. She stops in bewilderment. She opens her eyes wide and remembers that special way he has of telling a story, theatrical, for effect, which, though it is etched in her memory, now, after months of silence, terrifies her.

"That's the Tornowitz plateau," she hears him say. "After a burning hot day like this you can expect it to rain tonight, pig rain, it turns the whole camp into a swamp, but it doesn't kill you. I was sleeping like a log one night, when all of a sudden I woke up with the feeling that someone was blowing in my ear in the dark."

Lucie, with the wisps of straw still in her hand, looks at her husband in alarm, because she knows how the story continues.

"Good God, Joseph!" she cries.

He drops his arm. "What's wrong?" He and the stable boy are about to trim Bellaheleen's mane.

"Nothing," says Lucie. She buttons up her coat. A moment later, as she crosses the yard by the gate, she hears, less than three feet from her right ear, "Jesus, Lucie, do you know what it turned out to be! There was a rat crawling over my face."

What do you make of that? Joseph's voice of a few years ago, and that encampment on the plain? Lucie often sees shadows, I know, improbable things that dart away at the last moment, but she's seen them. All morning, from the November countryside of Twente, Lucie looks out over a summery Silesia, at fields full of rapeseed and cowslips that stretch as far as the encampment in the bend of the Prosna. At noon she is still floating in that twilight, but everything is paler now, slightly farther away. She bumps into her father in back of the house.

"Whoa there!"

The old man steps back in irritation. They look at each other for a moment.

"You're supposed to have ordered some peat moss."

"Oh, I did. Yes, I'm sure of it," she says.

"Where is it, then?"

"They'll bring it this afternoon. You mark my words. They're delivering a week late again. Do you remember those stacks of firewood?"

Once you've turned seventy most things are fixed.

Fixed in the past. Gerard is a widower. He lives in the right wing of his ancestral farm. He has sold off their land a little at a time. When his wife gave birth during the war, he was hoping for a son, but instead got the red-haired daughter who was to remain his only child. Meanwhile, this most precious blood relation has given him a son-in-law and three other descendants. Gerard leads the way into the back of the house. Two yellow Labradors leap up to meet him. In the kitchen, filled with blue smoke, he finds his son-in-law involved in one of his noisy telephone conversations. Fuming, the old man sits down.

"I don't call that talking," he says to his daughter. "That's raving."

She picks up the breadboard and the bread knife. He's a bit different these days, she thinks vaguely. Contemplating her father's very recent filthy temper, she starts cutting the bread.

It's a business conversation with passionate proprietorial interest. Joseph is offering to sell a thirteen-year-old pedigree mare with a very pleasant nature.

"Yes, sir," he shouts. "This is the horse you're looking for. Yes, noble. Yes, fiery. I'll be right there."

He slams down the receiver and goes off to sell off his favorite horse in grand style.

Lucie and her father see him go down the muddy path, hat pulled down to his eyebrows. Gerard snorts with dislike. Then he mutters something. Lucie, who's used to the generally good relations between her husband and her father over the years, isn't quite sure, but she thought she heard "Gypsy!"

2

I don't understand them, and yet I do. In the summer I understand them. In the winter I don't. Skirts, earrings, hair loose — yes. A woman with her grandchild on her lap sitting staring at a couple of burning tree trunks — okay. There's nothing to understand about that. When the woman laughs you see a mouth full of gold. I have no problem with those caravans either. They are places full of furniture and statues of the Virgin and artificial flowers, crammed cubicles, incomprehensible, but marvelous. They mark coordinates across the map of European history. Even those ugly white caravans can beautifully broaden your mind. Don't forget that the world is an old family domain, where you must be able to sit and chat with your relatives in the farthest outposts. Other things I don't understand — that shouting, those bare feet, those buttoned-up vests, and all in the *rain!* Looking back, I have the feeling that it rained the whole of that summer of 1963. They said that they wanted to stay near Smeenk's factory for the time being. They'd got the outside faucet working again.

Naturally everyone stared when that sky blue eight-cylinder vehicle glided past the windows. The truck drivers had left, and the regulars, suddenly more at ease, felt they could talk about, for example, the insurance premiums on those old jalopies, which, for types with droopy mustaches and romantic eyes, were pretty steep. This village is in agricultural eastern Holland. Most pub regulars from before the war remember that the horse dealers always appeared just at the right moment with a cob or a plow horse, and after a lot of arguing would get down to business in a surprisingly flexible way. They were people with a wonderful knack with animals and tools. After the silence following the war, why shouldn't they gradually return to their old haunts? The atmosphere in the pub mellowed. Louis Armstrong could be heard on the radio and in the back a couple of men were playing billiards. I wondered why somebody started in about the women who'd been fortune-telling in the church square that morning. Why is that regarded as indecent? I happen to know what it's like when your path is blocked and someone looks you deep in the eyes. She takes your hand. You suddenly become dead serious. When she turns the palm to the light she's already fully sharing your grief. "You long for passion, but love seems hesitant." She gives a stimulating inventory of your future, a future that obviously means nothing to her personally.

He drove out of the village. The light of the sun about to break through hung low over the fields. He looked at the line of treetops and turned off toward Benckelo. Soon this would be a path to the factory. Now it was where his family lived in six wagons and caravans. His family who, as he would soon discover, had had another visit from the police. The driver's window was open. The dank smell of wet nettles was familiar to him. A lot of water had flowed under the bridge since then. The area, which had experienced the occupation and liberation, the Marshall Plan and various governments with Euro-American leanings, was becoming more prosperous. Farmers' children bicycled to the high school. In the fields the combine harvester had appeared, so that farmers, *if* they still kept horses, could let their Gelderland cart horses out to graze while they focused on racehorses crossed with thoroughbreds. A lot of water had flowed under the bridge, but Joseph remembered the area. A gust of wind shook the poplars. He adjusted the windshield wipers, and thought of his father, who until 1942 or 1943 must also have passed by here. In those days a farmer would sometimes have twenty horses in his stable. Those who used ten for the deep plow could bring up a good three feet of soil. It was quite common then for farmers to search far afield for men able to work with such a team of horses. Joseph's father and his five brothers and fourteen cousins, blacksmiths and traders, were such men.

He passed Gerard's farm. He didn't see the gnarled sign on the oak by the gate. Two wavy lines crossed by a third were at eye level for a horseman. After about a mile came the path. Through a hedge of brilliant green he reached the factory site, where a familiar scene awaited him. A scene that, allowing a margin for time and place, had been the same for as long as he could remember. On one side, the caravans, a muddy field, steps with children on them. On the other, the police.

It was a wet summer, the summer that Joseph and Lucie met. Rain and more rain makes a camp like that look anything but thriving. But those endless muddy routes lead past plowed fields and orchards, under warm suns, under cool moons, they point where you can stretch your arms out and look into a pair of kindred eyes. How's your father? How's your mother? And those dreadful aunts and uncles? The annual fair, the scrapyard, over the centuries you have become adept at a very quick presentation of your person.

Unfortunately your greatest achievements lie outside

world culture. There is the square where the audience loves to listen to a pair of demonic musicians. You stand under a blossoming chestnut tree with a Stradivarius. You are one of the exalted. With a cool head and ironic fingers you play variations on the theme of melancholy, while your eyes flirt. There are people who remember their earlier softness, their true selves, and they can almost feel the tears coming. So be it. Let them enjoy their fit of melancholy, you must be on your way. Fairs. Lions' cages. There's not a circus where the lion tamer isn't one of you. An expert in the dialectics of logic and rapture persuades not only people.

But on that patch of green next to Smeenk's factory, little could be achieved with persuasiveness or anything else. The policemen pulled out a document: *According to official reports we have received, you have stationed six caravans on this site.* Joseph parked, got out, and walked over to the police cars where two of his cousins, Branco and Sanyi, were talking to four policemen. Branco had a letter in his hands which he gave to Joseph with a look that suggested he'd read every word without the slightest problem. Politely, but with no trace of a smile, Joseph greeted the authorities. He explained that he'd requested an interview with the mayor at the town hall. The policemen looked at him stupefied. Then, a shaking of heads.

"I'm afraid we've got our instructions."

Joseph flashed an accommodating smile. "With a temporary residence permit . . ."

This time the shaking of heads was accompanied by a flicking gesture toward the letter in his hand, as if a mosquito had to be shooed away.

But Joseph knew that an order did not apply until it had reached the eyes or ears.

"This place is suitable," he said calmly. "We can work, no problem. We're basket weavers, car mechanics, grinders, fortune-tellers, musicians, horse trainers, horse buyers, chair caners, traders in fancy goods, dealers in accessories, dealers in carpets, blacksmiths, and acrobats."

He spat out the rest of his cigarette. His pride, round and gleaming, hung among the last raindrops falling from the poplars.

"We have money."

There was a moment's silence. Still energetically acting as family spokesman, he turned to the policeman who, from his insignia, was the highest in rank. "Can I have a word with you in private?"

Under the canopy of one of the caravans he assumed a soulful expression and told the officer in lengthy sentences that the health of an old man in their company was deteriorating daily. As he talked his eyes wandered from the purple-tinged sky to the caravan where Nikolaus, a cousin of his father's, lived. Old, he said, sick. He gave the authorities no further information, and that should have been sufficient. "Old and sick" should be enough to grant a man who, like any other, had wanted to be the hub of his own little universe, yet who all his life had been pestered by people in various uniforms, bothered for papers, for passport photographs, for fingerprints, for stamps and numbers, including the one searing number that had been stamped on his arm permanently — to grant such a man a short respite at the end of his life.

His name was Nikolaus Andrias Plato. He was Dutch, born in Arnhem in 1909 while his parents were passing through. To call him old at the beginning of the 1960s was no exaggeration. Men and women of his age were considered ancient rarities at that time in Continental Europe if they had olive-brown skin, gold teeth, steely blue hair, or the eyes of a burnt-out acrobat. If their appearance was the kind that made civilizations prepare the stake.

These things always start insidiously. A bit of nuisance, a bit of antipathy, and then suddenly there are signs everywhere saying that all the charlatans known as Bohemians and Egyptians must leave the country. We are now in the sixteenth century. Humanist Europe is building, draining, opening up new territory. This new Europe is looking askance at these strange people who require constant and more police. The bizarre lot flees to a neighboring country but are rejected in the same manner. From now on they are branded and flogged. The right ear is cut off and, if anyone dares to show his face again, the left one too. From now on, in the centuries that follow, there is talk of a "Gypsy problem." France sends them to the galleys. Prussia strings them up. In the Dutch Republic, after eighty years of war, people are finally free to take matters into their own hands. The down-to-earth border provinces of Gelderland and OverIJssel start talking to their neighbors about a radical solution, and Cleves and Münster are prepared to cooperate with an elimination plan.

The chosen people are not the only people to have been chosen; there is a younger brother, an artful dodger, a dangerous marginal figure. The Wandering Jew does not journey alone; he is accompanied by a tramp with bare feet, gifted, exceptionally musical, though alas totally illiterate. By Spinoza's side walks an anonymous fantasist holding forth about the uncreated universe in which one day God appeared, with his companion the Devil next to him, and about the fact that both are mere words: the eternal story of good and evil. Berlioz listens to a *rakóczi* on the violin. Freud is accompanied by an old woman, a *puri dai* who interprets dreams. Among the masses that have to pass through the gate with its inscription about how work liberates, there are a number of freebooters who are scarcely surprised to be welcomed on the other side by an orchestra playing a fine tango by Malando. Nikolaus Andrias, his parents, and his whole family were arrested by the Dutch police on May 16, 1944. They lived on Bilderdijkstraat in The Hague.

Joseph took out his cigarettes, offered the policeman one, and lit up. Behind him in the doorway of the caravan stood two little children. He looked the policeman straight in the eye.

"I can offer you a sum of money."

It was too late. A regretful gesture of the head. The man either didn't want or was unable to take him up on his offer. It was too late for any kind of accommodation. The letter, which spoke of this article and that clause, warned about the penalty charges that would be imposed if the caravans were not removed from the municipality of their own accord within twenty-four hours.

Twenty-four hours. You might just have had time to hang out the washing among the trees after all that rain, when that patrol car appeared again to check up. You might have promised a nearby farmer four tubeless tires to put his Opel nicely back on its feet, no problem: how unpleasant when that twenty-four-hour countdown started again. Twenty-four hours — sometimes forty-eight — then you left. Toward the evening of the third day the Andrias family started tapping water again and stowing the gear firmly in the caravans. They left in the morning. Four caravans, two old Culemborg vans, and six cars crammed with men, women, and children. Joseph, at twenty-seven still without a family of his own, was carrying two nieces in the front of his car and in the back "his uncle" Nikolaus and Nikolaus's wife and one of his sons, Sanyi.

I'm thinking of that rocking caravan. Of the drowsy atmosphere in those cars. It was just starting to grow light. Six in the morning. The path led past a meadow where the heads of the cows protruded above the ground mist. I only need to stand by Gerard's farm and in the distance I can see the point where they turned onto the road. Joseph drove carefully. In the mirror he occasionally looked with concern at the face of the old man, who had had a miserable night. His mood was that of someone who, when he sees a tree, thinks only of a tree and, when he sees a pothole, thinks only of a pothole. So when he happened to look up at Gerard's oak tree and his eye fell on the Gypsy sign, he thought of nothing except those two wavy lines crossed by a third. I heard him shifting gears as he drove past — very handsome and serious — and I believe that he didn't even know that those lines, which in more mythical times had meant a welcome, were a sign from one stranger to another reassuring him that decent people lived here, people with whom you could eat and talk. I doubt whether he knew, because you hear the craziest things about those magic signs and, as for truth, you never really know it.

There's something else I'm not entirely sure about: whether Joseph, shifting into third gear, had a sneaking intuition that in the course of that same year his suit would be hanging over a chair at night at this address and that his low-heeled black shoes would be placed under the bed of the red-haired daughter of the house. Who is to know? Anyway, something had been prepared for. What had been prepared for was the theme of Joseph and Lucie, which in a friendly but resolute way would supersede another theme in his life: Joseph and Parasja.

It had been about thirteen months since she left him. After six years of marriage that had never been considered a real marriage because no child was born, Parasja had been taken back by her family. She wasn't reluctant to go. They had met each other during a long summer in the fields of an abandoned Serbian monastery near Banja Luka. Parasja, slim, strong, glowing in a meadow full of horses, defied her grandmother and her uncles. As a result of an old dispute, they did not eat with Joseph's family. They had ridden off one night when the stars fell clean through the fields of corn. When they returned, no permission was granted for their union. Having still not conceived after six years, Parasja began to think of the imprecations that must have been uttered at the time.

They were surrounded by the police. Once they reached the outskirts of the village, they were hemmed in by two patrol cars. A policeman stepped out of his car.

Kata, Nikolaus's wife, was in a bad mood. "May your father's bowels and those of your mother and your brothers shrivel up," she began. "May your grandfather's stupid head . . ."

Joseph rolled down the window ready to reply to the kind of questions he had been familiar with from time immemorial:

"Where are you going?"

For an instant, pressing on the gas pedal and feeling the friction of steel seemed the only thing to do.

"We're taking A35 toward Almelo."

As usual they had an escort. A white car in front, and another behind the convoy, a service of the Netherlands state. Joseph, accustomed to unexpected official action in his life, had his mind on other things. Having been jolted awake, he thought: Parasja, I'm going to forget you. I'm going to forget all about your hair, your head, your chin, your lips, which all seem to be fixed in a permanent smile. I'm not going to remember a thing — not a single detail. I swear that by God the Father.

That's what he thought as they approached the municipal boundary and the Benckelo police peeled off.

Do you think that I want to go on seeing you and your gold bracelets in the years to come? And your shawls, and your sacred panties with that flower design that you always hang out to dry under a towel but which, of course, I've seen anyway? How many nights in the course of his life do you think a man can lie tossing and turning, thinking: Come here now and crawl in beside me?

At the Delden traffic circle the column of caravans kept so close together that there was a minor traffic jam to the right of them. At IJssel a police van was waiting.

He lost patience. Christ, Parasja, that scolding and hounding of yours! You don't think I'm still in love with you, do you?

"A very good morning to you! Can I see your papers?"

Joseph handed over his documents. He felt a nervous pressure in his chest.

How many places did we go to in six years? Must I go on seeing the suburbs of Gdansk, or Berlin, or Budapest, or the cornfields, or the vineyards where the women worked? During the storm over Reims you defied every law by continuing to walk around bareheaded with thunder and lightning around you. What good to me are our little Dutch fields? In a place caught between space and confinement, we're allowed to make our Gypsy commotion for twenty-four hours?

At last the papers were in order. The group owned a collection of the most beautiful passports and visas. And then came the question.

"And where are we driving to?"

Joseph started up, became silent for a moment, then again mentioned Almelo.

But all right, all right, Parasja, you mustn't joke about family! A distant uncle of mine called a distant uncle of yours a louse.

They pulled away from the embankment. The cars merged with the rest of the morning traffic. The police van in front left little doubt about the nature of this transport. A little farther on, there was a brief stop at a shop open at eight in the morning. What group of women is served at such lightning speed with bread, pastries, and Band-Aids and then shown to the door with such fretful care? Between Zenderen and Almelo there was a provincial road. Where the developed area was marked off by a railway line was where the concrete path to the caravan site began. The police had disappeared. After an hour of costly negotiations with several other camp dwellers, the Andrias family were parked together with their wagons and cars. Behind Nikolaus's caravan there was room enough for his imminent death.

On the earth beneath you a mattress and a couple of thick pillows. Above your head a piece of canvas that doesn't let a single raindrop through. In cold weather a fire at your feet. I think the tradition of fleeing your dwelling in your final moments is beautiful, but I don't understand it. Gentle hands lift you up and carry you off while you're still alive. The mourning has already begun. From all sides the eyes of your family look at you encouragingly. As darkness falls, you sometimes hear consoling lamentations. In a while they will be certain to put a bunch of hawthorn on your fresh grave, because no soul wants to be haunted by your *mulo*.

Nikolaus Andrias died one afternoon in summer. The camp was full to bursting. The family that had flocked together bought a grave, asked for a chaplain, and summoned the village brass band to play the Radetzky March or anything at all. Their pained lament amounted to a final pact with the dead person: These were the tricks we played on you, you probably played plenty on us. That's all right. We forgive each other.

To depart as you came. Without possessions. Without debts. A legacy makes no sense in such a situation. After the funeral meal, which despite two downpours lasted for the rest of the day, the wood fire was revived as the sun flared up one last time. The scorched smell of Nikolaus's suit, his shoes, and his socks and hat dissipated toward morning when a new storm erupted over the camp.

"The Andrias family? What? Gone again?" was heard two days later at the town hall in Almelo. They didn't understand why the Gypsies had left, because they were now on a *legal* site. Discussions had actually *begun* about work in the cattle-feed factory. How were Social Affairs supposed to understand that since a recent death something burning hot, something unbearably chaotic, lingered about those drenched poplars? There *was* no way of comprehending the sound the night began making, which, until then, no one had noticed.

For that matter, the family itself made no effort. They left after that death, and there was no reason why, rather some sort of wild reflex of memory. Language and dreams. The true story takes place on that level, and anyone who writes down any of it takes possession of it. But *those* people don't write anything down! Three days after the funeral Joseph began packing, and so did Branco, and Kata's three daughters. What is not written down never becomes a text but remains an image. Kata sat at the table in her kitchen. In her hand a crystal glass with a gold rim. Nothing is ordered in time. She took hold of a lemonade bottle in front of her and looked in astonishment at the label. Cause and effect have no fixed position. She couldn't read what it said. There is no composition. She poured and brought the glass to her lips with a trembling hand. The image, completely clear and resolved, corresponds with life itself; we're leaving here tomorrow!

Is it proper to write about people who themselves don't do it on principle? Am I allowed to sweep up the glass that the inconsolable Kata has accidentally dropped from her hands? And in one of the slivers, crooked, pointed as a dagger, accidentally see something of my own features?

Joseph didn't stay with his family all summer. His cousin Branco was man enough, so Joseph, single and with his own car, was free to go where he wanted. Free, for example, to drive to Alsace via Limburg and, via Vierzon, to Limoges and then on to Toulouse. And free on all these journeys to make contact with friends and relatives whom he sometimes knew only from the stories.

Who else but I should follow him? Should ride with him in his Buick, gazing out beyond the big front windshield? It's nice to merge with a wonderful blue landscape full of undulations at forty-five miles an hour. Joseph whistled through his teeth and thought peacefully of nothing. Towns, campsites, and parties in the evening. It's worthwhile attracting the glance of the pipe-sucking, chatting Joseph from behind a bonfire. They told each other stories. Over the next fifteen years Joseph heard all kinds of anecdotes about his vanished parents, his vanished uncles and aunts, and occasionally he almost crossed paths with Parasja.

That was good. That was right, absolutely. Still, though the sun might go on rising and setting again in streaks of red, sooner or later Joseph would be pulled over. His papers would be examined testily between four fingers and at a moment like that I was definitely no longer a bluish landscape but was up to my ears in a compromising skin that I didn't like one bit. "You can't stay here. What's your destination? Disperse, please, folks. Those are the regulations" — and then I felt ashamed to the depths of my soul and I knew that

I must also be concerned with the friendly policeman who wanted to do everything by the book. But why did Joseph remain so good-natured when confronted with this gentleman? Did he know that the man's ancestors had been drivers of the plague carts at the time when his own ancestors had been playing with young brown bears in the eastern Balkans? But no, amenability, polite looks, I don't understand and perhaps I *can't* understand. Your head may be hidden under a wiry copper bush of hair, and because of that you may have been pointed at by every Tom, Dick, and Harry, and especially teased by an angelic girl at elementary school, but that's definitely not enough to understand what centuries of police checks do to your feeling of reality. To your daily repertoire, your eternal now that is sometimes nice and intimate, with kitchen utensils and eiderdowns, and at other times terrifyingly distant, with an ice-cold wind over plowed fields where birds circle overhead. I like the fresh air, but even more I like a solid table between a pair of brick walls.

"That's your *gadjo* soul," says Joseph later to Lucie.

3

*G*erard is angry. It started more than a year ago, quietly at first, when Joseph and Lucie decided to cut down the oak by the gate.

"Why?" he had asked.

"Search me," said Lucie. You could see her thinking. "To give the trailer more room on the bend."

He got angry. "You two have gone nuts."

"No, not at all. We're waiting till the rain's over and then the hollow side branches will come off first."

Three days later it was still raining and from the kitchen window Gerard saw the stripped branches falling. Pitiful streams of water splashed from the holes and drenched the man hanging on to the trunk. Joseph, ghostly pale, filthy from the mud, had a chainsaw in his hands, which, as the morning progressed, started droning more and more unbearably.

"Fool," mumbled Gerard around noon. He turned to the sideboard, groped at random, poured himself a drink, gin, poured another, and stood there looking out, helplessly, with the glass in his hand. Helplessly, I say, not rage. You'd imagine he would have loved to get his hands on his son-in-law, the foreigner, the heathen husband sent by providence to drive his daughter crazy, the deserter, but you could see clearly that the old man was only hunting for words to have something to do while his brain stood still.

"Dinner's ready," Lucie finally called. Johan of fifteen, Katharina of thirteen, and Jojo of almost eleven, had been hanging around the kitchen, eyes bright with hunger. Now they were served up a completely disastrous dish of peppers and garlic. "Just boil an egg for me," said Gerard in irritation.

They not only took down the tree. That same month they also sold Linda, Walton Beauty, and Viking and then forgot to book Experiment, that marvelous stud, to service Bellaheleen.

One afternoon Gerard was walking home up the drive when he saw Lucie slaughtering a couple of geese by the drinking troughs. Of course he'd seen her dealing with chickens and rabbits often enough, always very deftly, but now he was amazed. One at a time she pushed the two swan geese, which were originally Asian, to the ground, put a broom handle over their necks, and stepped on either side of it. It was true that the breaking of the neck was very quick, but Gerard, who didn't know the method, lost his temper, God knows why. He continued to sulk all afternoon, and at supper hunched forward a little to avoid looking at the face of Joseph. Joseph was playing around half-heartedly with his children, sitting smiling with the same dull eyes with which he'd come into the kitchen in the morning, no earlier than eight o'clock these days, in the rumpled clothes of a man who wonders why it's morning again.

November came. Snow fell early. In the third week the grain-storage barn collapsed and on the Friday afterward Gerard discovered a leak in the stable that could be repaired only a week later by a flu-ridden Joseph. Little by little Gerard, who felt that there was something in the air about which no living soul would inform him — something illegal? something hostile? something to do with betrayal? — became furious, carried along by something terribly depressing that for lack of any tangible cause followed a course of its own. Gerard began to be irritated by Joseph, by his oriental eyes, by his hooked nose, by his Balkan mustache, by his Slav signet rings, by his Bavarian jacket, by his black cigarettes, and by the barbaric zeal. That zeal with which one Sunday in February he completely demolished the rickety chicken run on wheels, once meant to be moved from stubble field to stubble field along with a hundred and twenty Barneveld chickens and a beautiful cockerel.

Finally Gerard became irritated by the way Joseph strolled into the chicory house at about eleven in the morning for a chat with his father-in-law.

"Hello, how are things?" he says, pushing aside the rubber curtain behind the door.

The other man greets him with a nod.

"Give it to me." Joseph walks toward the old man in the semidarkness.

"No." Gerard, busy fetching a load of roots from the cold store, doesn't turn around. "I can manage."

Joseph has already grabbed the crate out of his hands and put it down on the workbench. "Nice stuff," he says. "Where did you get these from?"

The light is gray, dimmed by the curtain. Chicory originally grows underground, which is why it's always dark and warm in their greenhouse.

"From the Noordoostpolder," says Gerard, and something spins in his head that makes him think: Why don't you just *go*, for all I care? Why don't you get into that great big fat car of yours and drive away past the chestnut trees? If you're so fond of leaving? He glances to the side. He no longer needs to examine the face. He knows that those features, now empty and exhausted, sometimes suddenly assume the form of a fabulous friendship of more than forty years ago.

Before the war Gerard was a young newlywed, and Jannosch Franz, alias Jan Andrias and alias a few other things, was only a couple of years younger and already the father of numerous children. The first sign that horse dealers had descended on the woods was always the two-wheeled carts in which they set out to tour the district. The Gypsies went to the farms and bought the horses on the basis of incomprehensible criteria. When Jannosch Franz drove into Gerard's yard late one August morning in a shiny painted two-wheeled carriage, he was making his first visit in person. But he knew the farm and its location through his family, whose trail went back via the Netherlands, Scandinavia, and Russia to Germany. At the end of the previous century they had bought German passports in the name of Franz, Schmidt, Otten, and so on.

Jannosch jumped down from the box. He pushed his hat back and greeted Gerard with formal politeness. Fifteen minutes later the two men shook hands on the deal. Jannosch had bought a chestnut gelding with a lame foreleg from Gerard for the tidy sum of a hundred and twenty guilders.

They sat down in the shadow of the linden tree and sealed the bargain with a gin or two. Gerard had already hinted that he found it really infuriating that the August market in Delden fell in the middle of the rye and oat harvest. The following day swarthy men and a battered troop of women and children appeared on his land. They hitched the horses to the mower in threes, they picked up the sheaves and put them into stacks, and the following morning they came back to talk about fair payment. After reaching agreement, they lifted the sheaves one by one with pitchforks and tossed them into the barn at top speed before a storm broke. On Friday Gerard was sitting in the café when the horse market had finished. Successful business was being celebrated with noisy exuberance by the uncles and aunts, brothers and sisters, nephews and nieces of Jannosch Franz, who — on the windowsill with a child on his lap — was now being called *tjawo* by everyone.

They saw each other again the following spring, and how! Gerard certainly found it strange, but Jannosch shrugged his shoulders about it afterward: This time the entry of the Gypsies into the village was accompanied by the state gendarmerie. Four caravans rattled down Brinkstraat at three in the afternoon. The Gypsy women who walked alongside laughing inappropriately and the host of children and the men leading their horses by their halters found themselves surrounded by authority and couldn't go anywhere except directly out of the village again. Gerard thought it was idiotic and also rather embarrassing because, guarded like this between loaded police pistols, his friends did indeed look distinctly criminal.

It must have been in 1937 or 1938 that the commissioner of the National Border Guard was given something more to send back than a handful of Gypsies. And yet for a good ten years all kinds of work had been done. Letters, ideas, plans, perhaps unnoticed by a farmer like Gerard, but which had struck many Dutch people as a matter of public order and state authority. They argued that mayors should simply stop issuing permits, that consuls should no longer grant visas, that district commanders should, where possible, pursue this race of nomads. A competition had begun between Belgium and the Netherlands, the point of which was for each to palm their Gypsies off on the other as deftly as possible. A serious plan was proposed by the gendarmerie to deport these offensive tribes to some distant country or, better still, to an island. Things did not improve when with his own eyes the commissioner saw four women begging in Parliament Square in The Hague at Christmastime.

Earning a living. You can open a shop, but some businesses need a little more space than others. How are you supposed to allow your twenty salable horses to graze despite Article 4? How are you supposed to do business in Woerden when you've been tied down in Leiden? How are you supposed to sell your fancy goods in Strijbeek when the police commander has taken public offense at your low-cut dresses in the local weekly paper?

Behind the caravans in the wood they are sleeping quite calmly on the ground under quilts. Among the bushes are the gendarmes. In long overcoats, sabers at their sides, they're putting in some late overtime. Gerard has read the following headline in the *Benckelo News*: GYPSY BAND SIGHTED. SHOPKEEPERS BEWARE. He talks it over with his wife. Within the hour he bicycles to the encampment in the woods and invites the whole group onto his meadow fringed with hawthorn and maple. I think he was angry and simply had the urge to do something, but I don't think he understood yet what it would be like to be wild game with the hunters after you. When he did, five years later, he and Jannosch Franz were in the same boat and were both arrested on the same night.

He makes a melancholy sound. With his hands on the workbench he looks at the chicory roots that have to go into water that afternoon.

"If we want, we can get this lot in in an hour, can't we?" he hears.

He knows that inspired tone. "Yes, yes, I know."

He sees Joseph starting to walk around a bit, starting to look at the shelves where the chicory is growing. He's merely a dark silhouette amid the bubbling and flowing of the water which is kept moving continuously through the PVC tubes. Gerard's eyes follow him hesitantly, do their best to understand that they've been in the greenhouse together so often. Naturally Joseph never had a very high opinion of old-fashioned soil tilling. None of them did, did they? Travel along, use what you need, and on you go! Yet immediately he had taken to this practice of tricking nature into growing something in three months that normally took a year and a half.

"I think it's fantastic, Gerard. What would a crop like that fetch? Five thousand? We'll start tomorrow."

For weeks he'd helped to get the whole system going with great skill. As he worked, he talked to himself a bit, involuntarily, in his own special language. Gerard wasn't annoyed then. Not at all. Actually, he was quite touched by those hoarse, muffled words. It was as if he understood that a human being is generally even stranger than an elephant imported from overseas and that you can't help feeling sorry for its legs and the eye that peers down at you with such a lost look.

So I wonder what's up with him at the moment. It may be just senility.

In some corner of their memory old men often harbor some grievance that has been lying like a dog on a chain, waiting to leap up blindly. Suddenly there's that trigger, and that slight spasm in the head begins. There's something not right, they don't know what and get angry. Their movements are no longer so steady. Now they've got two heads. One doesn't understand what the other is thinking. In that way sensibilities get confused. Does the law of reversal now apply? Beautiful becomes ugly, nice becomes insufferable. How can everything that you once appreciated suddenly look so vile? A feeling of guilt, even older than yourself, turns to blind rage.

"I don't want to nag," says Joseph. He pulls out a plastic loop with his fingers and looks at Gerard. "But like this the whole hose is going to the dogs. Are those pliers still there?"

Gerard leaves the barn without answering. He walks past the earth bank and takes the path to the apple trees, which are now bare. His watch says half past eleven. What will he do for a change? He thinks of the coffeepot in the kitchen, but in the end he feels more like simply standing by the gate for a while. There are toadstools with luminous edges growing on the stump of the oak. Without thinking, he looks at the other side of the road where the construction of a barn has been suspended since the autumn. Without thinking, yes, because the plastic, the rust, cement spots, and the rotting wood need not the slightest detour to deepen his foul mood.

Christ Almighty!

Morose he sure is, the old man. Furious expression, eyes screwed up under a cap. It's strange, too. Because this summer of all summers hasn't his son-in-law stayed at home like a model husband? Doing odd jobs for his wife? Spending time with Jojo and Katharina and Johan? Stopped traveling for God knows what reason.

4

*T*he bust-up with that woman? I don't know. I don't know what it really meant. At any rate, there came a moment when Lucie started lashing out with a riding whip in a strange house while Joseph, just roused from sleep, looked on.

Last year September arrived suddenly. Lucie hadn't had her mind on things all summer. Joseph had been wandering through Europe as always and she had resolved to tell him when he got back that she had started dreaming. Dreaming very seriously about an Appaloosa mare. Lucie had been longing for a purebred, American, whose breeding had produced a pattern of dark patches that overlay the light base coat all over its body. It was impractical, made no business sense at all, it was a childlike variation on what she understood by love. She made inquiries in the area. She asked fellow dealers to keep a lookout for her in the markets in Bremen and Antwerp and she gave a voucher for a considerable sum to Tattersalls' auction. One Friday after three o'clock as she sat in the sun imagining the patches of the tiger horse, she suddenly thought: Gosh, it's September. And from one moment to the next, restlessness took hold of her. It lasted for two days. On Sunday night she sensed that Joseph was close by, in her immediate vicinity, and wondered where he was. In the morning the telephone rang. It was a woman called Christina Cruyse.

"Hi, Lucie." No-nonsense voice.

"Hi."

A voice she had known and defied since childhood. And God knows why she wanted to talk to her today.

"How are you getting on with this drought?" A pre-amble, a game. "We've been spraying at full power for the last week."

Lucie didn't reply, but did see the huge jets of water above the sixty acres of fields and meadows of the firm of Koopman and Cruyse. To the left of the house was the gate-way of Second Eden, where since the death of her husband Christina Cruyse had run a profitable Frisian horse-breeding business, set up with her own money. The planted fields were managed by her brother.

"Listen, Lucie."

The voice was sharper now, almost snapping.

"Yes?"

"You were looking for an Appaloosa."

"What makes you think that . . ." she started slowly, and couldn't help her heart being swept along. She closed her eyes tight in disbelief.

"Well," replied Christina Cruyse. "There's one here. Please come before nine."

Lucie walked into the kitchen. Next to the clock lay her car keys and next to the coffee machine her cigarettes. The smell of the smoke distracted her for a moment from the chaos in her head. Absentmindedly she saw that the apples on the worktop were the variety she used on winter evenings to make a dish of stewed apples and potatoes. Then she left the house, stroked the two dogs in the shadow of the linden tree, and on the way to the car passed the tool shed, the door of which was open. As she walked along muttering aloud,

"What day is it today?" and "This is a disaster," her eye caught the saddles, halters, bits, ropes, whips, she took a step to the side, just one, and then selected a very old whip, a trophy with a silver-plated handle and organdy ribbons between the cords, won once by one of her forebears at a trotting competition.

It was quiet on the road. Sunlight hung motionless over the cornfields and over the farmhouses with bedding hanging out of the windows. Well before she drove through the gateway she had seen two things in the yard of Second Eden. The tiger-patterned horse. Her husband's Buick. An Appaloosa, Christ, yes, she thought after she had parked her car next to her husband's, and she looked at the majestic creature with almost peaceful light gray eyes and the ridiculous whip like a joke in her hand.

There was the threshold of the house. At a table in the center the owner sat waiting for her, her eyes cheerful, ironic. A cat was eating from a dinner plate on the floor. And a shirt of Joseph's, washed and ironed, hung over a chair. Lucie realized that this was the end of the glory of the Appaloosa outside under the trees, and that the animal had lived for nothing. She stood in the enormous kitchen. This is possible, she thought in amazement, and looked at the eyes of a woman who was determined to show her into the semidarkness of the side room — yes, there, go through there and look! — where her husband was lying asleep in the double bed. On his belly, one arm stretched out by his head, a dark haze over his cheek.

It was inevitable that a moment later she should be smashing everything to pieces in the kitchen and perhaps shouting as well. The cups broke, the tea caddies fell, the Delftware plates came down, the hanging lamp started swinging, the lid of a saucepan hit the tiles in a tumble that lasted forever, and finally the whip wound itself around an open tin of French polish that Christina Cruyse still had on her windowsill to keep away the flies: It thudded to the ground and the varnish leaped in dirty brown splashes onto Lucie's breast and neck — an effect that brought Christina Cruyse, open-mouthed in the corner of the room, to the brink of a giggle.

They drove out of the gate one behind the other, Joseph at the front in the Buick and then Lucie in an old station wagon, and it's certain that she didn't look to the side or into her mirror for a moment, because the tiger horse no longer mattered. Joseph would shortly start trying to explain to her that the day before, when he'd turned off Brinkweg dog tired, Christina Cruyse, all smiles, had stopped him and mentioned her concern about a horse, her most recent purchase, which was sweating a lot, and guess, it's not difficult, what was wrong with the animal? And Lucie would say, "You mean hemoglobinuria?" as she took his bag out of the trunk. And so you can see her walking ahead of him into the house, without a single thought, a Penelope reunited with her husband after a long absence, carrying his gear in one hand, and in the other a strange whip.

That whip. The fact that she grabbed it. Where did she get the crazy idea of doing that? You would almost have thought that she had received some good advice in secret. Nice, Lucie, always nice to get what you want with all your heart and soul, but think twice for a moment, because people are evil. She didn't think twice, she just breathed in deeply. Without knowing it, did she suddenly breathe in the air of her old classrooms, school playgrounds, village streets, autumn light, damp, cold, incomprehensible mockery, betrayal? Can she, I think she can, in that one second before stepping into that shed, return for a moment to her ruined schoolgirl days? Evil can look so wonderful that you long to be part of it. Christina Cruyse was blond, thin, wore white socks, knew her nine-times table, had a rich father and a beautiful mother, and it was a little while before Lucie, although she had had her heels trodden on and been called names in a hissing voice, started to worry about that mocking laugh.

Now it's September. Stubble fields or tall corn along the road, apples on the trees, there she goes, Lucie, and it doesn't surprise me that she drives so slowly because though her head may be in a haze, her eyes and ears are well aware and understand that she is being lured. At the crossroads she slows down, first a cattle truck, then the tractor, she greets the farmer in the local sign language, finger raised above steering wheel, and goes on. The urge to reach Second Eden is very strong. A white blouse, a white face with copper eyebrows and the matching coppery hair bunched at the nape of her neck, I'm in a position to observe her delirium from the side. Have that pair been married for sixteen years? Lucie is in love with her husband, a love that has been fanned gently all summer and is now, what's more, being redoubled by a horse. But it is not what you would call peacetime.

She shifts down a gear for the gate. Where is the Appaloosa, she is thinking, when she sees her husband's car and parks.

Now she has the idea of stretching time. What you don't see with your own eyes doesn't happen. Where, then? Where and when? For the time being she walks with total concentration past an animal bred solely for markings and color. She is amazed by the patches. She follows the line of the mane to the base of the tail. It's a very big horse. Obligingly she tries to appreciate fully the perfect arc where the withers are, and when I hear her sigh like that, I hope that she takes a little time, after all she's crazy enough to do so, to inspect and admire the mare more thoroughly, Lucie, to call out softly, to estimate her age, analyze her build . . . to dream up all the excuses that will allow this wonderful truth to be truth for a little longer before it turns into error. Lucie cranes her neck. She has noticed the light outlines of mouth, eyes, and genitals. As she turns to enter the house, she remembers that the American origin of this breed goes back to Spanish ancestors with Moorish blood.

Joseph's shirt. Hanging there exhibited in full view. Then that cat sitting wolfing meat off a dinner plate. Joseph is terrified of using the same plate as an animal, filthy, utterly indecent, didn't he notice this impropriety? You can pollute yourself unbelievably just by eating from the wrong plate. Lucie feels the eyes of Christina Cruyse resting on her as she surveys the whole kitchen in a flash, and then when she looks back and sees the triumph, the fine, well-considered hatred — something irrevocable happens.

She's never been suspicious, Lucie. She's never asked herself what seductive creatures her husband may have been tempted by in the countries he visited or whether he kept faithful to his marriage. Now she looks up and at a stroke has had enough of her innate innocence. In fact, she no longer needs to go down that passage on the instructions of her fellow villager, banging her elbow against a door with a coat hook on it, clumsily, no longer ignorant, because — what I mean is, at the moment when Lucie glances at her husband on that bed, where she has never had any business, she is no longer herself.

"Unbelievable! Really, Joseph! You and that bitch, you and that rotten fucking bitch!"

Then of course he wakes up. He opens his eyes and sees immediately where he is and hears immediately who it is he's hearing. Not far from here he could have counted on a reunion with warm tears or a lamb sausage rolled in puff pastry, now he's somewhere else and obviously not alone.

He throws his clothes on, the jacket goes over his bare chest because his shirt is gone. Then he's ready and what is he to do? What is he to do when he appears in the kitchen doorway with a startled face covered by a mustache and stubbly beard? He sees that a pathetic Lucie is being observed from a corner with cold pleasure. Should he carry her off with him quickly and then see what happens? At that very moment she slams the polish off the windowsill. He sees a precise jet spurt up, branch out, and now he and the other person in the room see that her neck and breast are irrevocably covered with ridiculous brown patches. Lucie drops her arm. And as they look at each other, a silence falls that is not a silence but a vacuum. Because for the first time in all those years they feel the longing, Joseph as well as Lucie, to finish with each other for good. Without paying any more attention to the third person, they leave the premises of Second Eden. Their cars are under the trees.

A Buick and a station wagon glide after each other through the Twente countryside, which in the autumn heat is still full of butterflies.

5

*B*ecause she scarcely pays any attention to him, I might as well. After all, I am the same age as she is, was born in the same village, and sat at the same desk as the one at which she looked at the pictures with drowsy eyes, faded pictures of plowed fields, without immediately seeing the didactic connection with the words below: field, ripe, scythe. After school I hung above her head like a bird of prey, fields and embankments, not in pictures now but real, I saw her walking down the road and, although I'm much more intelligent than she is, I really couldn't follow the twists and turns of her mind. Images and more images and between them just a pensive silence. How are you supposed to fathom someone like that? When she got to her house she went up the path. A dog came to meet her. In the kitchen a maid with heavy milk-white forearms was pouring tea.

Now I am close to her again. Wander about the yard with her, pushing away the climbing rose that's come loose with my arm, see her daughter Katharina, who's just come in from school, walking along the fence and suddenly bending down in curiosity. The girl, who looks like her father, is very beautiful. I put out a transparent hand and stroke her lank hair. "They haven't even got their cocoons yet," I hear her say. She's looking at the grubby chrysalises of a couple of yellow butterflies that have hung themselves from the branches.

"Are they still alive?"

"Oh yes," says Lucie. "I think so. Later, in April, they'll simply fly out again at the first touch of sun. How was school?"

And that sounds maternal enough, I would say, for a woman who for some time now has had the feeling that the world has gone off the rails, the chrysanthemums smell of sauerkraut, and drinking glasses simply shatter in her hands. I go into the house behind her, boots, wet clothes, and on the worktop there is a plucked chicken. When Joseph strolls in she has already stuffed and covered the bird with herbs and she is bending down to open the oven with a padded glove. "Hi," she says. "How were things with the pedigree people? Sometimes I think, where is it all getting us? What do you want to drink?" It strikes me that she doesn't turn around for a moment to look at her husband; of course she knows what he looks like, but even so.

A Gypsy. He has a throaty voice and nimble hands and often extends the right one formally, because he's a great one for good manners. These days there's something dull in his eyes that alarms me. At night I hear him sighing. I know that he sometimes wakes up with a feeling of thistles in his chest.

"Crossbreeding will always need new blood," says Joseph, and by that he means that that afternoon he has been sitting arguing fiercely in the offices of the Royal Netherlands Crossbreed Society about the Gelderland mare which when crossed with a thoroughbred produces the best jumpers.

Now he is sitting at the table, elbows on the cloth, and under the lampshade is looking in the direction of the windows, which look back crackling with the icy drizzle. Shouldn't his thoughts now really be with that other world, out there, where he also belongs? In this country the rule applies that if your parents lived in a caravan, you — however regrettable that may be in itself — are also given permission. On hard-surfaced sites in Best, Hoogeveen, Stein, Oldenzaal, Assen, the caravans stand next to each other in bays. Immovable wheels, toilet cabins, underground umbilical cords full of gas and light and water. Our wandering brother is enjoying pleasant living conditions. He'll soon renounce his errant doctrine. Everyone knows there's a mystery, but a bell and a nameplate belong in their fixed place. People who just turn up are such a pain. Merely for the harvest, to play the violin, or to cover the cathedral spire with lead, showing complete contempt for death: these heresies are best treated with kid gloves. A camp school is being built. Why should the spelling mistakes of the fathers be passed on to the children? Seated between the television and the icons that glow with a reddish light in the evenings, the Gypsy looks at the pen of the welfare worker. Forms, letters, permits, petitions, fines, bills, reports are properly filled out with care by Social Services. Species are threatened with extinction, what's new about that? Apart from the language and a chaotic origin there is the anarchy of no fixed abode.

I don't know why he stayed at home this past summer. When I think about it more deeply, I say: Not because of the argument with that woman last year, that was just one more thing. But it's not good, and it's not right either. An order has been abolished. When Joseph came into the stable early on winter mornings, Bellaheleen would turn her head to the side and growl softly. And somehow that made it clear to him that his idiotic system of leaving and coming back again was all right.

Now something is in decline. Bellaheleen is gone, so

are the geese, and a yellow rose, old enough to smell intoxicatingly on June evenings, has come loose and hangs like barbed wire over the boxes that used to transport eggs. In that house a couple now sleep in too long and get up with sleepy faces. The children don't notice. They receive their hugs and their sandwiches and on Saturday the eldest son goes into the village and Katharina and Jojo stay and watch television with their parents. Why should Jojo, cradled in an arm, worry about an angry granddad who an hour ago crossed the hallway muttering to himself? But Lucie is another story. She has cut a tart into slices and serves lemonade and coffee on a tray. What matters to her is the one deplorable moment when in the kitchen of Second Eden, in an atmosphere she couldn't make head or tail of, she had to endure that incomprehensible attack on her honor that she'll never ever be able to forgive.

She has tried, though.

"Would you like some more?" she asks one evening.

Katharina and Jojo nod and put out their hands without looking. Joseph does the same.

On television there is a film with lots of violence. Lucie has her knees together and feels anxious. She doesn't know why, but her body, through which something evil is flowing, does. While on the screen a woman runs down a street at night in a tube skirt, she is suddenly reminded of a car under a port at Second Eden — expensive, brand new. The engine with the still gleaming bearings and pistons won't be proof against a handful of sugar carefully poured into the gas tank with an icy heart.

"Where are you off to?" shouts Joseph when she grabs her keys.

She drives down the road. The headlights illuminate the familiar roadsides. I'm going to do it and I don't care if they catch me, thinks Lucie, born under the sign of Scorpio with a deeply hidden impulse — if necessary — to sink her deadly tail into her own body. On the bend close to her destination she has to slow down. There is a red triangle, a car, and a fellow villager whom she vaguely knows on the road. "Could I borrow your jack for a minute?" he asks when she has stopped. Fifteen minutes later Lucie and the man have changed a tire and said goodbye after a bit of talk. Things don't always go as you expect them to. She has to jockey her car forward and back a few times before she's able to turn and return home down the narrow road.

One night, when Lucie has fallen asleep against her husband, she wakes up bathed in a cold sweat. She realizes that it's not hers. You should go to the doctor, she says in the morning. He obeys and comes back with a referral form for an X-ray. We'll go tomorrow right away, she says. No, he says, not tomorrow and not the day after. They finally go one Friday. The week they've been through has been a strange one, with a red December sun during the day. And at night rainsqualls rushed past with the sound of a very long express train.

When they got up each morning, they already felt lazy, full of unusual thoughts that unfortunately merged without a transition into something absurd, something disturbing: The dogs had run away, a tractor fell into the ditch, a pipe — which had been rumbling for ages — had burst behind a tiled wall. This Friday they get into the car and turn onto the road with a feeling of relief. After this unreal week, full of chores that were mainly so ghostly that wrenches and tools had wandered off on their own accord and were never in their usual place, after this week full of searching and surprises, they put the car radio on. Warmth, cigarette smoke, and after some squeaking a familiar radio program on

Channel 3 that gives everything the necessary depth. Let there be no misunderstanding about this program: The eyes and ears of the two gradually become completely attuned to each other. At about eleven they say: It must be here. And: Let's park. And: Have you got the letter? And when they go in through the revolving doors, they notice that they still have that calm, shared orderliness, and that it matches the white hall perfectly, with its counters and neon lights. Why don't we ask here? Having been pointed in the right direction by an arm in a short white sleeve, they find the elevator and arrive, as if in a fairy tale where the rule of naturalness governs, in a room where Joseph lies down under a gleaming machine, which can slide upward and sideways without making a noise.

By evening they are home. Their children are in bed. While Joseph watches television, Lucie, having thought very thoroughly, has had the idea of doing something about the accounts. Now she's sitting at the table with her notebooks.

"That hoof oil, Joseph, that was paid for long ago, wasn't it?"

And when she looks at him, she does it so seriously, with such glazed eyes, that I have the impression that she wants to know what's happened to their secret.

"I think so."

What she really wants to say is that her whole life has had only a single rhythm: him, and the strolling gait with which year after year he turned on his heel, and later returned.

"And the concentrate?"

Why are they now sitting talking about mixed feed when they used to — and you know very well, Joseph, that when you were back in my kitchen, in unfamiliar clothes, we really had other things to talk about. Have I ever told you that your stories wrapped me completely in a cocoon and that I could see the details of almond trees, bonfires, hedge-hogs, fishes, water courses, perfectly with my reproducing eyes? So why are we talking about fences now? And about roller girths that need repairing? Why do I ask, "Shouldn't we order from Horseland?" And you say, "Why?"

"Because they're going to move. They're clearing everything out and I've heard that they're giving sixty percent discounts."

Go away again! Go away again and come back in the autumn when they're busy plowing up the stubble fields. Let everything be normal again. Leave me in May, be restless, very taciturn, leave me in the stables and fill up your gas tank so that you can start squabbling at borders. Forget me on those journeys. I'm offering you the chance of not having to think for a moment of how I'm doing. Drink, shout, get emotional. Take the liberty of not remembering me before the hour when the sun begins to sink in the sky and quite in line with tradition you start thinking about winter quarters. Are you back, darling? I spread a gingham cloth over the table, put both my elbows on it. My eyes have grown huge with curiosity.

Part Two

1

I'm leaving tomorrow, Lucie.
   I always knew well before she did. I had seen him tin-
kering with his car for weeks, seen him trudging through
the wet grass in flat shoes that were far too elegant, seen him
sitting at the bar in The Tap with a surly expression and
buying rounds with the air of someone who does favors but
accepts no thanks. "I'm off tomorrow." Lucie had gone on
calmly clearing out her cupboards.
   I take the view that a man belongs in the place where
his wife lives. When you walk up the path from the road,
past a couple of outbuildings made of planks overlapping
like roof tiles, you can hear the play of the wind among the
boughs of a small apple orchard. Fifty yards farther you
come to the farmhouse. There it smells of grass and work
shoes and even, still, of the cowshed that once stood here,
though at the time when this was taking place, thanks to the
rib of beef with onion rings that Lucie had on the stove in an
orange pan, it smelled mainly of very pleasant living conditions. Take it from me that those two loved each other. Under a sloping roof where you could hear the swallows at
night, they had a bed in which you automatically rolled into
the middle.

But why did she overlook the fact every year that April or sometimes even May comes around?

"I'm off tomorrow, Lucie."

He stood at the kitchen table and, without paying her any attention, drank his coffee at leisure.

"Why?" was her belated question.

He glanced at his watch.

"Business."

It was getting on toward ten in the morning. Through the window fell a cold shaft of sun, gusts of wind chased the starlings from the hedge. Something in the air makes someone like me, for example, think, I'm still alive, but may well make another person pull out a bag, dust it off, and set it on the stone floor of the barn. When Joseph went to put his things into it in the late afternoon, one of the dogs was lying with its nose under the canvas.

"Yes?" he said, sensing Lucie's sudden presence behind him with some unknown urgent errand.

"The buyers," she said. "Didn't they need to know today how much we're asking for Dusty?"

Kneeling in the semidarkness of the stable, he took a tin of shoe polish from the objects around him and shoved it among the things in his bag.

"Phone them," he said. "Say that they can have the foal for two thousand if they come and collect it late tomorrow afternoon."

"Tomorrow!"

Only now did he raise his eyes to where she was standing. In the dusk she looked at her husband's appearance in astonishment, and at his hand that pulled a passport from the inside pocket of his jacket and flipped through it quickly. In a flash she saw a character with a thin nose and deep-set eyes, one of those types who hold everyone up at the border because his mug alone is enough to have him singled out.

"Two thousand," she said a little later on the telephone, in a businesslike way but still with the astonishment, which for that matter didn't lessen any in the course of the evening. Not during the meal, when she found him cold and dark. Not when they were watching television, when she had lost every memory of him, and not later either, under the sloping roof, when everything she had experienced with him there in the past had abandoned her. Even in her sleep she was still astonished at the man who in a kind of love at first sight kept holding her immovable in his arms.

Then it was morning — it doesn't matter what morning — it was one of those mornings when one thing became completely clear to her. Let me be off, look how the sky is clearing.

She's standing in the grass, in the stinging spring wind. Joseph has got into his car, the engine starts up, he leans forward and fiddles around under the dashboard. A gust of wind catches her in the back. With both hands she grabs her hair, which has gone haywire, and sees him turning onto the road through the puddles. Her eyes stare as usual, and yet she understands quite a lot this morning. She understands that he won't look back. Why should he? What good is her gray dress to him at this moment, her red hip-length hair and her jacket? It'll always be there. When she turns around to get to work in the stable, she lets out a sigh that means nothing more than: Between this spring and next autumn there is only the summer. Which puts her back on exactly the same wavelength as her husband.

Who is saying softly, "Benckelo, Nijmegen, Venlo." His car approaches the village, he turns right before the milk plant, soon his house will have merged with fields and distant woods. If someone were to ask him if he didn't have some sense of farewell, his face would assume a thoughtful expression and he would say nothing for quite a while. Now he's approaching the border. I see him arriving there at about eleven, the barrier comes down in front of his bumper, there is the usual fuss. I see Joseph brake slightly to move into the right lane and get out in order to hand over his papers, those of a nonhostile nonillegal intruder, so that they'll have to admit him anyway.

Farewell? I mumble meanwhile. Is he venturing far from home, then? His relatives live all over Europe. They *are* Europe. They are the plateaux of the upper Rhine, the terraced fields of Lorraine, the Dalmatian coast with snatches of music from the cafés, they are the Silesian-Moravian corridor, the brown bears and the wolves of the Carpathian Mountains, the mirages above the great Hungarian plain, and they are also the villages and towns on that eternal route, the alleys, the squares. They're all of that, in a moving form, and farewells, ladies and gentlemen, have no part in that.

Nor does looking back, of course.

Are you still following me, darling?

Well, no. Not exactly. While Joseph has been allowed to go on his way with a nod of the head from the border guards, Lucie is sitting at the table with her notebooks. While Joseph with hair hanging over the collar of his coat looks in all directions, Lucie is stocktaking. Space, the serious stillness of the fields. It's all familiar to him. Joseph whistles through his teeth and knows that two hours from here there is a camp near Krefeld that he will recognize first from the crows above the landfill.

He looks, she does the books. Two hundredweight of concentrate. Twenty rolls of wire. The rain patters at the windows. On the floor her son is playing with a yellow Labrador. Tonight she'll leave her cashbook and in an old armchair covered with a rug open another book, a novel, compellingly beautiful. Lucie loves to sit and sob in a knitted pullover at the eternal dramas of the world which, checked in their flight, have alighted on the bookshelf next to a beautiful potted linden tree. Capital, invested in enduring paper.

Joseph will sit on an upturned bucket in the dark meadow.

Oblivious of space or of time. You've found lots of relatives in the camp near Krefeld. When it's dark, a fire flares up on the field enclosed by rusty wrecked cars. Beneath a deep blue sky full of scudding clouds, men and women who can be incredibly long-winded tell their stories. Does time pass? You wrap him around with so many words that he no longer knows if he's living forward or backward.

He looks drowsily around the circle at the faces. Of course he knows what it's all about, he's simply still a little dazed by the extremely circuitous syntax of his native language. The latest news changes imperceptibly into fables. A cushion of chatter is fluffed up and the first to snuggle down on it are himself and the little children who are staring at him. Now the bragging about distant relatives begins, they're long dead, may the Virgin keep your ghosts away from us, but your peculiar behavior simply travels along with us. Why should your antics be left behind in time?

He doesn't say much. He sits in the row of men and sleepily passes the bottle of liquor. Whatever is being talked about concerns his life, but tonight it's good just to test the warmth and the pulse of it all. He won't be staying here long anyhow. By the end of April he'll be floating in a hammock among the Yugoslav plane trees. In mid-May he'll be repairing harnesses and saddles in a marshy region. In June he'll be dealing in scrap in a suburb of a Central European city. In July and August he'll be lugging bales of hay weighing more than a hundred sixty pounds and sleeping in blossoming meadows. But most of all he'll be found on the campsites, well off the road, of a race of people with lungs so full of air that it simply has to escape: as lamentation and ranting, as song, as story.

Family and adventure novel. Everything centers around the campfire. Anyone who squats down next to the flames in a white shirt stays silent first for at least a minute. All those present feel a huge tension mounting that quickly moves closer as this person pushes his hat back and announces that it's time for the next person. When he then spreads his arms, they know what is coming. They start staring. For though the facts may be known, the words bring something to light that nevertheless starts reverberating, aloud, that starts rushing around humming incessantly on wings so huge they almost touch your shoulders.

At the edge of the wood an irrepressibly curious audience has assembled. It stares at the words, finds them marvelous, unsurpassable, and there are some who hear the restlessness in them and the hesitations in the text. The story is good, enough to make you almost die laughing, but in the hesitations you can hear something of police checks, of identity papers, and if you're sensitive you can hear the criminal code in them. Doesn't matter. The fact that you get the hiccupy staccato of your native language in the pit of your stomach is good for feelings of belonging, solidarity.

But emptiness is something else. Emptiness in a story can be filled up recklessly with images. At the edge of the wood there are a number of men and women for whom certain images have no words. Long ago these images entered through the eyes and now refuse to leave via the mouth. Such things leave gaps in a story, empty spaces that, contrary to reality, the reality of the time, began with such unambiguous place names: Biala Podlaska, Czestochowa, Warsaw, Lodz, Belgrade, Hamburg, Munich, The Hague.

For Joseph it began with 's Hertogenbosch.

It was the crack of dawn. Day had only just broken, May 16, 1944. He was woken by the voice of his mother peering out through a window of the caravan. "Holy God," she said. "Why have you got it in for us?" Only then did the tumult that he had heard in his sleep get through to him. Harsh voices, not German, Dutch voices, just the voices of the Dutch police. Pounding on the doors of the caravans. He was only seven and a half. From under the quilt next to him his sisters appeared. One of them was called Wielja, a quiet girl of five, the other Umay, three years old. With her round hands and her curls, she was his favorite. In a basket at the foot his brother Leitschie slept peacefully through it all. He heard his mother strike a match, a cigarette glowed. He watched the door till it flew open with a bang and a policeman climbed in.

"Here," said his mother, "here you are."

It was all very polite. The policeman shone his flashlight on his mother's papers and the inside of the caravan and he counted the children. Then his mother, Gisela Nanna Demestre, was told that she must hitch up the horse.

There were about six caravans in the convoy. The police had left the gentile travelers in the surrounded camp unmolested and rounded up only the Gypsies. There were about forty of them. In the early May morning they drove their caravans into town. There was the Graafseweg and the Zuidwal. The tall windows of the mansions on Parklaan gleamed in the first sun of the day. People who were already up would have seen the procession. Horses, caravans with decorative carvings were moving slowly, and on the driving seat an exotic couple, a man holding the reins. At the windows children's faces, swaying, white, impenetrable, barely distinguishable from the faces, outside, of the men wearing the black uniform of the Netherlands Home Guard marching imposingly beside the caravans.

Joseph Plato thought of his father. Sitting between his mother who was driving and his sixteen-year-old cousin Paulko who had come to keep them company on the driving seat, he wasn't frightened. Awake, he was daydreaming in the cool air and looking at the back of the horse as he used to when he was still a boy with his father who dealt in horses over a wide area. They were on their way to the station. He didn't notice people stopping on the sidewalks and cars and wagons pulling over to the curb for them. His father had disappeared earlier that year, arrested at an address in Benckelo, in an area where the family had been going for years. Weeks had passed. Gisela had begged and cursed at the police station, but no one had told her what she wanted to know. Then the winter came and she decided to go to relatives in Brabant. His little brother was born. The 's Hertogenbosch assembly camp was a spot singled out and organized by the authorities for undesirable elements.

Horse manure on the road surface. The bells of the episcopal city striking seven when the group arrived in the station square. The Gypsies had to park their caravans in as neat a line as possible under the chestnut trees which were almost in bloom and were given permission to pack clothes and bedclothes and even something to eat. Joseph felt like some bread with a slice of bacon, but Paulko said, "I don't."

"Eat, Paulko," said Gisela. When he replied, "I can't eat because of the train," she glared at him.

Later they all stood on the platform, the whole bunch of vagabonds, roused from their sleep and badgered, who nevertheless vaguely believed what they had been told that morning, that somewhere in the north of the country in a place where some of them had actually camped before, Westerbork, the men would be put to work, the children could go to school, and the women would be allowed to stay at home. The whistle of the locomotive came closer. The train from Eindhoven pulled in. It was an ordinary passenger train, nothing special, but the rear carriages were old rolling stock with lowered blinds. How full it is, thought Joseph when they got on. Are they all going to the north too? In the compartments and in the corridors, besides a group of gentile caravan dwellers, were all the Gypsies from Limburg and East Brabant. When the newcomers came in, there was a whole spectacle of greetings and the space was taken up again. The train left with two policemen at both exits of the carriage. Joseph sat between his relatives on the soft seat.

The light in the compartment was on. What a shame he couldn't look outside, he thought, but the shades had been nailed to the frames. Soon the train slowed down again, stopped, pulled away slowly and then, after a while, slowed once more. Paulko, who'd been sitting in the corridor without a word, got up to look outside through a chink at the side of the curtain.

"A station," he said. And then: "I'll just see if I can still buy some cigarettes." When he looked around he saw Gisela. She said, "Let Joseph go with you."

The two squeezed their way along the corridor.

"Cigarettes," said Paulko to the policeman at the open doors. He pointed toward the kiosk on the platform. The policeman, a lad with watery blue eyes, understood and nodded. Something that should never have happened, during that whole government operation to evacuate people in as practical and as disciplined a manner as possible from Beek, Best, Venlo, Sittard, Eindhoven, Zwolle, Amsterdam, and which needn't have happened, happened anyway.

Because of the nod of an absentminded young policeman, two Gypsies left the train.

They walked in the direction of the kiosk. It was busy on the platform. People had been waiting for a long time for the delayed train from Eindhoven and were now anxious to get on board. Paulko and Joseph walked in the direction of the kiosk, past the stairs, turned right, and walked along the other platform directly toward a brick building with tall windows and above the door, in yellow decorative bricks, a word that neither of them could read, *Stationmaster*. The door opened heavily. They were both surprised by the emptiness and the abundant warmth of the room. A stove was glowing. A desk with a telephone on it was deserted. Against the walls there were wooden benches like in a church. Joseph had let go of his cousin's hand. Something in that atmosphere of incomprehensible emptiness and warmth drew him to the windows that he could see out of the corner of his left eye. He put his fingers on the stone ledge, stood on tiptoe, and could barely see over the bottom of the window frame.

There was no better lookout post. Less than four yards away stood the train with its blinds drawn. Motionless, full of invisible life. The center of the world at the moment of departure. The carriage in front of him began moving. Umay, Wielja, he thought, and at the same moment a miracle happened, the shade went up. Joseph Plato stopped breathing because there, in an illuminated compartment, he saw his family.

At the back the uncles. Standing, talking contentedly with arms folded. Seated, the aunts with loosely hanging hair, between them his mother. The beautiful Gisela had her baby at the breast. Clearest of all were Umay and Wielja, who were sitting closest to the window. They're going, he thought, what a shame. I'd have liked to say something to them before they went. Why did I get off, damn it? Wielja was sitting yawning, he felt his jaws respond, Umay was fiddling about trying to unbutton her cardigan. I expect it's as warm in there as it is here. He felt as if time behind him was passing, whereas in front of his eyes it was the opposite. He had ample time to see the fingers with which the stubborn Umay, her chin on her chest, pushed the buttons one by one through the knitted material. Wormlike fingers, lowered eyelids, which were as white and round as those of a marble angel in the Basilica of 's Hertogenbosch. Then he saw his father too. Where did he come from so suddenly? Jannosch Andrias Plato had appeared between his brothers in the compartment doors which had been slid open. Bareheaded and in his blue suit with suspenders, he was staring intensely outside as if in warning.

A nudge to the arm. Paulko. "We must beat it." The last compartment was disappearing around the bend in the railway line as the two descended the stairs of the station. Joseph felt nothing and heard nothing. That compartment, that dull red compartment full of his kinfolk was still in his mind. When Paulko pulled him past the baggage-check lockers, he didn't yet know that that crammed compartment of all things could become a vacuum. They went into the bicycle tunnel. Joseph walked along blindly with his companion. He didn't yet know that that compartment was a ghost. A story whose words are smashed. Inevitable result: an emptiness in his throat that, from that point on in his life, he would never be able to rid himself of, not even on the most beautiful summer nights, not under the fullest moons. Nor would he want to. He would just like, after so many years, to stay in a world of walls in the winter, of sheds, chains, stables, and people who evoke feelings in him but inflict a different kind of sadness on him than the sadness he already knew. Every human being has his reasons for inexplicable behavior.

Many years later Joseph would feel comfortable with a woman watching him go through the orchard with a disheveled head of hair after having just blinked when he says: "I'm going tomorrow, Lucie."

They emerged from the bicycle tunnel. In front of the station people were walking along in the sunshine, talking and greeting each other.

And on top of that, she was pregnant the first time. Incomprehensible, isn't it? She had quite a belly when she saw him getting into his car in the cool spring weather for the first time and knew for certain — and I know for certain that she knew for certain — that he would have put her out of his mind by the time he reached the electricity substation. I can't creep under his skin. I can't get behind his eyes to see how green his landscape is, how golden his sun, how fiery red his blood. So I'll just stay with her. After all, she's the one who has shared his sleep for the whole winter, with arms and legs and everything, who with her knees pulled up has managed to find a hollow in which a farmer's wife and a vagabond fit perfectly. A miracle like that can make me cry. I'll stay with Lucie. Because look, though he may drive off wherever he wants, I'll be following him anyway. That may be by slipping into the car with him and looking at him from the side, his true face could well be like that six-month belly of hers.

When she took to her bed one afternoon under the sloping roof with the splendor of August outside a bay window, her husband wasn't there. He had been away for the whole summer. In the village people had talked about it, of course. Most of them had known Lucie since she was a girl, a creature with a strange character, and people had gradually assumed she didn't have any emotions and therefore couldn't suffer. There wasn't much to speculate about. How bad was a husband who'd run off as in her case? They'd liked the Gypsy that first winter. He went to The Tap. He had a way with animals. But nevertheless there were a lot of people who didn't realize until weeks later that he had abandoned their village. Only a few people sensed it immediately with a strange instinct.

The day after his departure Christina Cruyse was wheeling a cart of groceries out of the market when she saw Lucie walking across the parking lot toward her car with a box on her hip. Christina left her groceries at the door and made a beeline for Lucie, almost running, and greeting her like a long-lost friend.

"So he's gone, then?" she said immediately.

Her eyes slid probingly from Lucie's face to the long plait across her breast and came to rest by her belly. "I saw him taking the Hengelo turnoff yesterday. Shall I keep my fingers crossed for you that he comes back?"

Lucie looked at the other woman with her usual vacant stare. Instead of answering, she handed the platinum blond woman the cardboard box full of cat food that she'd just bought.

"Sixteen," she said enigmatically. "Sometimes twenty. Depends." She pushed the trunk of the car open with both hands and took back the box.

Three days later Christina Cruyse started phoning her. "Not back yet, is he?"

It was very early in the morning. Still asleep, she mumbled, "No, not yet."

A day later it happened again, toward evening this time. Had he called yet? The next afternoon: Hadn't he left any forwarding address? When she picked up the telephone on the seventh day and the infuriating voice asked whether he might at least have thought of the baby, she couldn't say anything for a moment because of a lump in her throat.

"Bitch," she finally said.

It wasn't anger. It was a simple reaction to the malevolence of her questions, they weren't questions but a tactic, a method of disruption with no other target than the small compass of her soul.

"You rotten cow," she said more precisely.

There was a perplexed silence at the other end of the line. Lucie was about to hang up when, as if a familiar sharp voice within her was dictating to her what to say next, "May the maggots get you," she heard herself say, "and may your ugly flesh rot if you call me again."

Greatly comforted, she hung up.

The summer was hot and full of thundery showers. Apples dragged the branches of the trees toward the ground. The horses were so fiery that extra schoolgirls were required to ride them and exercise them. She worked every day until dusk. By then she had washed tails, combed manes, scraped out hooves, then she had slaughtered chickens in the afternoon and put them in the deep freeze, and in between, growing larger and larger in her blue dress, she had picked up the telephone and ordered a number of glazed pots for the terrace so determinedly that even her father became convinced of the order of things and swallowed any objections to an absent son-in-law.

He already looked old then, bent, with impenetrable fierce blue eyes. Instead of modernizing as everyone had done since the end of the 1950s, he sold off, without apparent regret, large sections of the land of his forebears. There was something contrary about him, which according to some people was almost certainly linked with the loss of his wife, a very pretty girl from IJlst, whose warm, strong character had unfortunately lost the battle against her translucent skin in the winter of 1951. Gerard was left with a daughter of ten. Although he was popular in the area, good-looking, and had the reputation of a resistance past, he didn't remarry. He raised horses, grew oats and corn and feed beets with the help of casual laborers, and looked after the little girl, Lucie, with a succession of different servants, so that she didn't grow up without the care of a woman. This summer he was in a milder and friendlier mood than he had been for a long time.

He liked his daughter's girth. Why shouldn't he feel happy about his impending grandfatherhood? You could often see him standing and looking with his hands on his back. Do you see the bulging side of the stables? For three days he mixed mortar and built a new wall against a stretched rope, and then he went to The Tap, bought a few drinks and accepted a few, and on the way home stopped off at the supermarket on impulse to buy a six-by-six roll of film. A day later he wound the film into an old Ikoflex with a sticking shutter. They were silly snaps, of course, of a horse, a dog, a barn. You see that there is a thick stripe of gold over the cornfield? Yes, and of course he also took a picture of Lucie.

"Go and stand over there," he said, and pointed to the exuberant garden.

She obeyed. She peered willingly into the lens while her father started turning the light and timing rings. That morning he asked her, "Have you got a name for the baby yet?" Then he said she mustn't move another muscle and pressed the shutter.

The photo still exists. I saw it lying in a box of junk in Gerard's room. She omits the smile this time. Serious, arms at her sides, she looks at a terribly distant point and meanwhile thinks as hard as she can about boys' and girls' names.

Can you see the vagabond, perhaps, Lucie? He's not

thinking of you for a moment. And still he wants you to have a beautiful child. Can you perhaps see him with his typical Gypsy arrogance when he's about his business in the market in front of the pilgrimage church of Kobryn? His eyes have been intently calculating, now the deal is sealed, someone sticks out his hand, he gives it a firm slap. Really he ought to be home. Every woman wants to feel her husband's hand on the shuffling feet of the baby behind her abdominal wall. But yes, as for Lucie, you can't make her out. Of all possible worlds, she thinks her own little world is the best. Yet she doesn't get angry at someone who stays away from it for a month or so. Shortly Joseph and his friends will visit a drinking establishment on the market square. They'll tap ash off the ends of their cigars and order green bottles of beer. When they get back to the camp, they'll see that there's definitely something to celebrate. A *patsjiv* is the party that you give for an unexpected meeting. Drink, songs, family and friends, the sense of time must be completely disrupted! Life proceeds from reunion to reunion. In the evening there's dancing. Old and young men perform dances that start innocently but, under the hot sound of a violin, can soon become menacing. I'm talking about real irony here. Of course there's food too. You bake hedgehogs packed in clay in an oven of white-hot stones. The spines stick to the clay shell. You only dig out the guts at the last moment.

The shutter clicked.

"Katharina," said Lucie, "or Kattela. If it's a boy he'll be called Hanzi."

The baby was born without complications. The doctor lifted him up by his ankles. "A giant," he said. "About eight pounds." Lucie, still resting on her elbows, was completely lost. She had seen new life appearing through all kinds of birth canals since her childhood. The past hour was part of the darker side of the world that didn't fit anywhere and left no memories. They laid the boy in her arms. Some newborn babies have folds in their faces, as though they've already experienced a few serious things. "They'll go," said Lucie to a worried Gerard. "Really, Dad."

She wasn't wrong. When they heard a three-note horn four weeks later and the dogs charged onto the path wild with joy, the baby's cheeks were completely round and pink. There he is, she thought, yes, I had an inkling. She waited for him in the doorway. In another minute she would let that man back into the house, hand him the infant, and make sure that he supported its head with his left hand. Now she was still standing in the doorway and saw the Gypsy strolling toward her past the black plastic ground cover. It was an autumn like all autumns. With an eternal smell of grass and muck in the air. The perennial first fairy ring under the trees. As she watched him approach, her face was set. Not the face, you would say, of a woman who wants to know love. Who wants to meet the same man for the next fourteen or fifteen years, draw him to her with always the same — homeward-bound — look.

2

*L*ike the first time.

When Joseph's car broke down on A35 near Stepelo in September 1963, he was actually on his way to the caravan site near Groningen. The year before, his wife had returned to Bosnia with her family. At the beginning of August, Uncle Nikolaus had died, and after wandering through Silesia and Pomerania he felt the urge to go into business as a car-parts dealer in the Groningen area. Although the obvious thing was to go north from Haaksbergen, he decided on impulse to turn off just outside Stepelo and dive into the farmland where he'd been with his family at the beginning of the summer. He could then deal with a couple of urgent phone calls in a pub in Benckelo, with a telephone to the right of the bar.

After fifteen minutes the warning light showed that the temperature was rising, which could only mean a leaking radiator. He could have reached the gas pump at the crossroads, but he turned off down the path to a farm with the intention of simply asking for water. He got out of the car and two yellow Labradors dashed toward him barking, but immediately quieted down after a growl from Joseph. The farmhouse had four windows at the front, with the door at the side. He knocked. There was no sound anywhere. Inside he saw a clock and a vase of red flowers. His instinct told him that there was no one in the house.

He was right. Gerard had driven to the auctions early that morning in an optimistic mood. The harvest of his four acres of potatoes might, he thought, be as much as fifty tons. Lucie was in the last empty stall of the large stable turning straw. She was particularly busy. Now that the stable boy had failed to turn up to work for the third time, she knew that she could no longer rely on him. So she ignored the barking dogs, put the fork away, and walked over to the only horse still stabled indoors.

"And how are you, Timone?" she asked softly.

The horse, a golden-brown mare who had been off her feed for the last two days, pushed her neck down. Lucy felt her ears. They were no longer so hot. In the mare's eyes she saw a powerful longing for the herd. She opened the stall door, caught hold of the halter, and walked the animal across the concrete, under the lean-to outside, to the trees and the wind. The Gypsy, about thirty yards away, still among the asters of the farmhouse, suddenly heard stamping and snorting. He turned his head and saw a woman and a horse looming up from the stables on the other side.

He straightened his back. He saw a young woman with copper-colored hair that lay in a braid over her shoulder. A woman in pants and boots and a half-buttoned greenish blouse, coming out of the stall with a horse in a halter surprised by the morning light. The pair turned, the woman raised her arm — her face turned toward him — and tethered the mare to one of the posts of the lean-to. Then she again raised her soft white woman's arm, said something kind, unintelligible, and put her forefinger and middle fingers firmly inside the bottom jaw of the mare. She was counting. He knew that she was counting, she was counting the horse's heartbeats because there was something wrong with the animal and it was almost feverish. The moment she dropped her arm and was about to let her gaze wander off to be able to think, her eyes met his and her whole face froze.

He began walking toward her. Dazzled, and with a dullness inside that in fact was nothing else than the beginning of a lifelong shudder at the thought of a world, a possible world, without Lucie. He crossed the courtyard and walked over to the woman who stood waiting for him motionless with her face turned toward the neck of the mare. Paying no attention to the smile that appeared around her mouth, he focused on the horse. He took the head, looked in its nose, laid his hands against the lower jaw exactly as she had done and silently counted the pulses of the artery . . . forty, fifty. Then he looked at the woman with all the authority he could muster.

"She was no doubt lying on pea straw."

Lucie nodded at once. It was quite possible.

"That's right," she said. "That's quite possible. That straw lay in the field for quite a while, damn it. At first in the rain, you understand, then in the sun . . ."

She stopped, burst out laughing, thought, and frowned.

He said, "Moldy pea straw."

"And to think Daddy wanted to chop it up immediately."

They looked at each other, both swept along by a fit of hilarity in which you go so high that both of you can look down at the world together with the sun and the clouds. And what a sight! To climb is to be silent. Words are one thing, the dark side of a human being is something else. I see a man in black, with a hat on, and a woman, falling for each other from the very first second.

Again he heard her voice.

"And Timone is stupid, I mean she's young. But good blood, you know. Soon there'll be the competition in Enschede, so I'm training her already, you know, with a nice line on a trotting bar, cavalletti and then two galloping jumps away an oxer. And she goes over them perfectly. . . ."

He said nothing but looked at the hand with which she was gesturing.

"Yes," she said. "She's been lying on pea straw. You're right. And that means she's eaten some."

She untied the horse in order to lead it down the sandy track past her father's agricultural junk to the meadow. Joseph walked with her. While he kept a careful eye on the crates and the barbed wire and a peeling red tractor, his full attention was focused on the woman who told him that she would shortly have to trim two large riding horses because the stable lad hadn't shown up. Without imagining how or where, he knew that a moment was conceivable when his hand would follow the line of her neck and breast.

"Here," she said. She opened the gate. The mare was immediately chased into the farthest corner of the meadow by an older horse.

He walked to the meadow pump showing signs of interest. The woman told him that the thing had been put there in the previous century by her great-grandfather. He stared at the green-painted cast-iron pump. Purely for pleasure he pressed down the handle, and enjoyed the water splashing from deep under the ground into the concrete trough. A little later he hunted through his pockets for cigarettes and they both lit up. The tobacco smoke, the grass, and the water had a better memory than she did.

"I've seen you before," said Joseph.

She tried her inane laugh for a moment. Then she said, "I know. Yes, it was on the tip of my tongue just now."

Shortly afterward they were standing in the grooming shed trimming the two horses. Joseph was handy. He grabbed the struggling horse firmly by the lip, ordered it to be calm, and went over its neck with the small clippers. Lucie, working next to him, felt that she had to say something memorable.

"That horse is called Delaleen. Her mother is the heavy Gelderland mare that you must have seen by the gate."

Without interrupting his work, he said, "Then the father is wonderfully fast and has good shoulders."

Only now did she hear his strange accent. "A thoroughbred," she said. "Oh yes, an Anglo-Arab from Hengelo."

After that they said nothing more because the shed, fragrant with sweat and bay grease, into which sparse sunlight fell, changed into an enchanted world that demanded all their attention. They were trimming the horses, yes, and when they looked at each other they did so from the side. And yet for a whole hour that shed was filled with a declaration of love repeated from minute to minute. Lucie finished first. When she was about to put the strop away, and raised her eyes, she met a man's gaze that made the blood course through her cheeks. Was this the moment? Joseph thought it was, at any rate. We want each other, what about going over to that pile of soft gray horse blankets? He took a step forward, almost touched her shoulder, when she suddenly began laughing so stupidly again.

"Hey, it's coffee time. How about coming over to the house with me?" And she said it in such a way that he understood perfectly well that over there, in the farmhouse, it was really the coffeepot that was waiting for him and not the bedroom under the eaves with the swallows' nests. His face remained controlled, inwardly he was cursing, yet his pique was not serious. Walking back into the sun with Lucie, Joseph, though frustrated, thought in his heart it was wonderful that the woman he was beginning to be obsessed with didn't give in just like that. Because in his circles it simply isn't done for a woman who is adored to lie flat on her back at the first sign like some gentile lady.

How long will the game last? You don't know, Joseph, but if you ask me, not too long. A week. Then she'll be standing brushing out a tub in the pantry, and you'll just have finished with the feeding troughs. You will have kept bumping into each other that day, agonizing meetings in which you kept lowering your eyes and found it hard to swallow. At noon the two of you ate potatoes and salt fish with Gerard and the casual laborer who's operating the combine harvester. All the devils in hell can't stop you now. You knock at the door. You see her over your shoulder smiling at you and politely pointing you to the boot bench with the foaming brush in her hand. But with a motion of your head you order her to come with you.

The pair of you walk past the barn. One of the dogs comes up wagging its tail, and she sends it away. "Off you go! Good dog!" It's September. The leaves of the linden tree are already yellowing. The stinging nettles are already starting a second flowering. Is it September or April? All the animals are outside. In the distance a bilious green machine cuts a swathe through the grass, growling as it goes. There's no better idea than for the two of you to walk along the edge of the ditch behind the orchard, in single file. Around the bend an alder grove with an infinitely soft bed begins. Sink to the ground there. Can you feel the depth under you and the height above you leaping up? Intoxicating. Freedom. That's right, isn't it? Direct connection and you don't have to know with what. Joseph, after a week of pain and violence in his chest, pressed to the ground a woman who surprised him after all by sinking her teeth into his shoulder. When the fury in her eyes calmed, he loosened his grip a little. She half rose. He saw her bending over in her dress like a dancer to pull the heel of her boots off. It was Wednesday, about two o'clock. By six o'clock Lucie was standing in the kitchen cooking pancakes for her father and herself. Gerard was sitting at the table with his sleeves rolled up. He didn't know that his daughter, tossing pancakes by the stove, was a married woman, with a piece of metal hanging on a chain under her blouse. It was a very ancient example of traveler's handicraft, which, among strange signs, bore the image of a dark woman. She represented a Black Madonna, whose style harked back stubbornly to the original powers of Ana, the mother goddess who, through no fault of her own, gave life to a grubby white bird with two heads.

Time for coffee, she said. He followed her into the kitchen. He put his hat on the table and sat down only when she offered him a chair. Smoking, tapping his cigarette inconspicuously into the ashtray, he observed her as she let in the dogs and put water on to boil.

"Are you hungry?" she asked. "I won't be cooking for a long time, but I expect you're hungry. I'll get some bread."

"Don't go to any trouble, Lucie." She had told him her name and now he was practicing. "I'm happy with a cup of coffee."

He heard her rattling the cups. When she opened a cupboard, he smelled cinnamon. He saw her walk over to the windows and look outside with her hands on her hips while behind her back the water ran through the filter. I want that woman, he thought. I feel very good. Just a short while ago I had a lousy dream every night.

She pushed the dogs away with her feet and put the coffee on the table.

"Don't insult me," she said.

She meant the apple cake that she'd cut for him. His interest in her increased when she started talking about the business.

There had always been horses. Until recently her father tilled his acres with only a couple of Gelderland mares or geldings for the plow and the mower. Ever since she was a child she had loved the stables where, in winter, the very presence of that breathing, that warmth, had something pleasant about them and where, as the months went by, the light increasingly flooded the hayloft. In the summer there was the spectacle of work, of the stepping and turning of a pair of animals totally geared to the land and with a pulling power of twelve hundred pounds each.

Dreamily she waited by the wagon until the hay had been pitched on. She owed it to her father that by the age of twenty-one she was completely at home in the stud farm. He owed it to her that the stables began to make money, because she'd understood that times were changing and it was better for a horse to be fast, strong, and with a red-white-and-blue pedigree. This year a sister of Delaleen's with six wins in show jumping had been sold for sport to Germany.

She took a deep breath. "Damn it, Joseph! The stables could be expanded."

They could go on breeding from the line of Delaleen, she thought of the Holstein stallion Amor, and in addition there could be two new broodmares. She knew of a beautiful Courville mare with a filly by Furioso. They could first get a couple of foals from the young horses and then train them for jumping, and they would go very proudly to the shows. Did he know that a jumper could sometimes fetch as much as ten thousand guilders?

She put out her arm and asked if he wanted another cup. Then she looked at him. "But if you don't mind my saying so, no idiot is going to get me to stop using Gelderlanders."

They agreed that he would start the following morning at seven o'clock.

Because of circumstances it was twelve o'clock.

Twelve noon is when the sun stops climbing for a moment. Suddenly all the sounds fall silent. The shadows become pale. Time contracts. Trees and estates disappear in an infinite everywhere-and-nowhere that has its feet on the ground and holds heaven between its fingers. I know of people who say that this is the hour of the *mulo*. That the sun has stopped for a moment to allow the *mulo*, the person who is dead, the chance to interrupt his journey on the other side of the grave and pay a brief, silent, calm visit to the area where he was once at home. When Gerard saw the Gypsy coming toward the house, he confused him with the memory of an old friend.

"God and all the saints," he muttered in amazement. "It's Jannosch Franz."

A striking man walked past the windows of the house in which Gerard was having lunch with his daughter. Despite the hat his skin was weathered by the sun and wind. He had a mustache, wore a black ribbed jacket, and in his eyes there was a mixture of passion and indifference, focused on pipe dreams, which Gerard would recognize instantly in a crowd of a thousand people. Boy oh boy, how young he'd stayed! With a pair of worn-out boots in his hand he went straight to the side door. He knew the way. Gerard heard him say something to the dogs and appear in the doorway with a greeting.

"Afternoon!"

His daughter jumped up. She needed no encouragement at all from Gerard to fetch a plate and fork for his dead friend. I'm going mad, he thought. I'll be fifty-three next month and I'm already losing it.

During the meal the Gypsy started explaining something to him and Lucie. Gerard tried to look up from his soup plate with his usual expression to nod now and then. He had the feeling it wasn't working. Of course he knew about the new stable lad. His daughter had told him the evening before. But now there was a door ajar behind his back through which a great draft of breath and smell and sound swept over him. He was sitting, God Almighty, at table with the man with whom some twenty years ago he'd ridden on horseback in the darkness of a forest path behind a field-gray Mercedes. Trying to keep up appearances, he listened intently to the young man who was explaining that he couldn't get there earlier because the replacement of a leaky radiator had taken up the whole morning.

When Lucie and the new lad got up fifteen minutes later to start work, Gerard stayed sitting at the table with Jannosch.

Silence. "Care for some gin, Jannosch?"

"Good idea, Gerard."

"It's been a long time, Jannosch."

"I felt like coming this way again for a change."

"That was a good idea. I imagine you've seen that quite a few things have changed hereabouts?"

"Oh, that's the way it goes."

"Horses have had their day in the countryside."

"What can you do?"

"Come on, let's have a drink!"

"I'd like nothing better!"

"We don't see you folks here that often anymore."

"Do you want me to tell you where we've all scattered to?"

"In a while. First of all a glass."

"Right, cheers!"

"Your very good health!"

"That's right, make me jealous! I'll drink to yours, old brother. May your blood go on flowing till Judgment Day. May your possessions double. What's over there in that vase on the cupboard?"

"Ah, you've got sharp eyes, Jannosch. Those are your wife's flowers, they've been there for about twenty years."

"Red paper flowers. Gisela sold them from door to door. She gave them to you by way of thanks."

"I let you stable your horse with us. Because two of mine had already been requisitioned that summer."

"I put my beautiful Styrian in your stables. It was the autumn of '43. We were in two caravans in the woods. And my two-wheeled carriage was put under the hay at your farm too."

"Shortly after that you took another pilot to Limburg."

"I remember. It was a Pole that time, a prisoner of war."

"You were the only one of us who could make head or tail of what that fellow was saying."

"I took him in the carriage. God, man, may all yellow-bellies get the pox, but those train rides of yours sometimes went badly wrong."

"That's true. The Zutphen-Arnhem line didn't have the best of reputations."

"It was a first-class outing. In four days we were at Chaplain Emile's. 'The greengrocer sends his regards' was the password, God knows why. We'd only traveled during the day. Toward evening, it was fire, bread and cheese, and lemon gin in the flask. That Pole was a fellow with a kind face, but he drank too fast for my taste. 'Whoa there, a sip at a time,' I said. 'Stop nagging,' he said. We slept in hay barns, it was the end of September. You always wanted me to turn back at Echt, but I liked those passageways under the Pietersberg. You find a way through by just standing still and sniffing quietly."

"Afterward it turned out that that line of yours was never wound up."

"Well, mate, may I drop dead if I'm lying, but I could have gone right on to the Pyrenees."

"Do you remember that attack near Wierden?"

"A summer afternoon. Bright sunshine. The wind from the east."

"Two thousand ration cards, Jannosch. Two thousand of those bloody cards, and a month later we were in action in Enschede."

"Fantastic! I can still see it! A nice open-air acrobatics act on the tall iron fence of the police station. The audience were wearing blue uniforms. Music from police whistles. By the light of the moon I pointed my unlicensed gun at a couple of my fellow countrymen. And if I'm not mistaken, a little later we had to run away as though all the devils in hell were chasing us."

"There was a Plymouth around the corner. The engine was already running."

"What stories! Off we raced. Shreds of red inner tube shot out of the back wheel. Oh dear. The stories I've never been able to tell my family because of lamentable circumstances!"

"Drink! Would you like another?"

"Of course. Thanks for the hospitality. What a summer it is outside. The last time I had a drink here it was the depths of winter."

"The four of us were sitting here in the same kitchen."

"Yes, two gentile louts, a fool of a Gypsy, and that woman. The arrest after half an hour, perhaps. Is it true that that cow betrayed us?"

"She helped. She helped and she helped and she helped. Mrs. Nicolien Nieboer-Ploeg. A map of the local labor exchange. Reports from the police station. She was a strapping woman, platinum blond, who seemed to be able to fix everything."

"You're telling me. Up to and including our cell in the prison. Tell me, brother, how did you manage to grow old so gracefully?"

"First a trial. Then the penitentiary in Siegburg. My papers got lost. What did you do? they asked. Not a thing. Where were you tried? Nowhere. Then the work camp where you had to dig tunnels, shafts a hundred and fifty feet deep. The hardest part was getting the drill at right angles to the face. If you didn't go straight in, the tip snapped. My wife's food parcels saved me."

"Don't sigh. Be grateful for a little luck."

"You have no idea how shitty it is to survive a disaster."

"Stop it!"

"To come back, just you. There's the linden tree, hasn't changed a bit. There are the horses, the dog, the chickens, the doves, and in the doorway there's your wife with a funny, puffy child of about five, copper curls framing her cheeks. You needn't be surprised if you get all kinds of problems at night."

"Yes, yes."

"Slides behind your eyes, all real and with real people in them. So, here you are, Jannosch, tell me. What really happened?"

"First a cigarette."

"You always smoked such a strange brand."

"What?"

"The red pack."

"Hercegovina."

"Have one! And now come on!"

"It was rotten luck, Gerard, damned rotten luck that I didn't quite make it in the end. I'll tell you what happened. To start with I wound up in Amersfoort. That was in January. I had to wait in a snowstorm in the rose garden with a couple of others for them to shave me and take away my clothes and shoes. Yeah, they called it the rose garden there, a long piece of field fenced off completely with barbed wire. I stood there so often later. After a night in the horrible cold, in the morning they'd turn the high-pressure hose on you and a couple of hundred others. Those bastards were standing there laughing when you got caught up in the wire. Then I worked in the sawmill and the brick yard, but usually there was nothing at all to do and they let a thousand of you at a time just trudge around, crawling and standing up. At the end of May I went to Vught, and from there, after a few weeks, onto the train. I'd already heard that Gisela and the children, my father and mother, my whole family had been arrested by the Dutch police in 's Hertogenbosch and The Hague.

"The journey took four days. In a wagon that you couldn't have got more than six horses into, there were a hundred of us. It's hard to understand how it's possible but, peering through the barbed wire on tiptoe at the sky, everybody knew after a while that we were on our way to Oranienburg. And we were right. One morning we were unloaded and we marched to a little town full of nice villas to Sachsenhausen camp. When we marched out of the gate the next day again in rows of ten, we saw cornfields, trees, farmhouses, and finally the fence of the Heinkel factories. There two thousand of us slept on the floor of a factory shop. At night we watched the bombing of Berlin. The sky went red. During the day we took the place of gas by dragging trucks to the railway station in squads of fifteen. You know what was so crazy? The beatings by those camp guards made some difference everywhere else except with our squad. We went on at the same snail's pace.

"Then came November, wet and cold. Because my shoes had been stolen, I was wearing clogs with no tops. Everyone lost weight and began coughing and when we were doing a rotten job with stones and sand in the forest we had two guards who kept a really close watch. One, a Pole with an amazingly low number, fourteen, was the bastard who had singled me out. 'Gypsy!' he yelled as soon as he saw me. 'Do you still not know the meaning of work?' Drop dead. Fuck you, you think as you feel the blows on your spine.

"By about Christmas we were back in Sachsenhausen. We were put in Block thirty-four. Except for the Norwegians, all the prisoners were as thin as rakes. The Dutch were worst of all because they never got any Red Cross parcels. The only time that things improved a bit as far as food was concerned was in the shed where I found myself detached to the rolling mill with two Russians. One of them was a blacksmith from Omsk. He was a huge guy, and a genius at dodging work. From where he sat, he kept an eye on the huge shop doors opposite us. Only when a supervisor arrived did he get his machine rattling and the stuff pouring out. The rest of the time he just sat sewing mittens made of thick woolen material, of which he sold a couple every day. On the third day he nudged me and gave me a hunk of dog bread. The dog bread stank like a corpse. Your mouth got full of threads, and those white dots were pieces of bone that we spat out behind the rolling mill. All in all, this was my best squad — a whole load of Russians who took it easy sitting cross-legged on the tables. Quite close to me there was a group of storytellers. From their furious or triumphant looks you could tell what strange things were being talked about.

"So midwinter arrived and the Red Army was already on the Oder. Throughout the whole camp area and in the barracks people were dying off faster and faster. Transports kept leaving, but the camp stayed packed and life went on as before. On Sundays there were soccer matches on the parade ground, except when there was an execution and you could see the steps standing ready below the noose. Sometimes there were international matches. From the gallery above the gate, the SS men watched with interest from between their machine guns that were aimed at us, and kicked stray balls politely back. At the beginning of February, the Russians were put on transport. A week later I was in a wagon that was so full you had to struggle to get on top of the bodies. With my cap over my face I was able to sleep pretty well, better than I ever did later in the Little Camp in Buchenwald.

"A couple thousand of us arrived there late in the afternoon. It was already getting dark. I was too tired to look around. I can still picture the brilliantly lit road in front of me and in the distance the gate between granite pillars topped with fat bronze eagles. The letters over the gate were in bronze too. '*Jedem das Seine*,' I can still hear a man next to me muttering. Like most of us, he died there in the last few months.

"We weren't exactly welcome. Two thousand five hundred men squeezed into a barrack that could just about cope with the five hundred that were already there. I met a Sinto from Bremen whom I knew vaguely. Among the fifty thousand prisoners there was also an uncle of mine, Uncle Mauschi from Weimar. I didn't know him at the time. The Sinto from Bremen and I walked down the central gangway.

We looked around us at the bunks, which you couldn't even see the full depth of. I didn't know what was worse, the stench of sick intestines, the human heads that gave us hostile looks from those bunks, or the skeletons on trestles and planks which we didn't realize were the lucky ones because they were able to stretch out a bit in their sleep. 'Sixteen of you to a bed!' cried a Russian from barracks squad and the Sinto from Bremen and I climbed up.

"This was the Little Camp, the worst one. The Big Camp was scared of disease and kept the newcomers apart. The Sinto and I slept with our feet in each other's armpits. That was the most comfortable. If it leaked on us, we hoped that they'd soon transfer the guy with dysentery in the bunk above us to the other side.

"One rainy winter morning, near Barrack sixty-one, I saw my uncle Mauschi. He'd been driven into the Little Camp with two others through the high barbed wire on a wagon for delivery. The other two were lying down, he was sitting bolt upright with hollow eyes. A 'Muslim,' an inmate who had given up. I saw him, but I wasn't sure if it was him. 'Are you Uncle Mauschi?' I asked. 'Are you still of this world?' Only after a while did he look at me. 'Can you say anything?' I asked. Then he said, 'I'm Mauschi from Weimar, your father's brother.'

"In mid-March my number and the Sinto's were called for work in the quarry. You threw the boulders into tip carts, and a couple of you pulled them up the hill. 'Wanna buy?' I asked one of the Dutchmen who was working there, and I showed him one of the cigarette holders that the Sinto and I made, wonderful things of glass and ebonite. The Dutchman looked, and sighed. 'How much?' he asked. It so happened that the Sinto and I sometimes went to Barrack thirty-two in the Big Camp. I can't explain the relief of being there. They had tables and stoves, and the songs by

Zarah Leander coming through the loudspeakers sounded quite different there.

"Easter came. Marvelous weather. For days nothing but air raid warnings. Gradually the discipline broke down, and instead of working everybody was talking about the Americans who were already in Thuringia. In the Big Camp people were making plans all the time, but we in the sewer went further and further downhill. I didn't even notice that I'd begun shuffling about and talking in a whine, the signs of the 'Muslim.'

"The tension mounted every day, but nothing happened, except that even then, late at night, a transport arrived from the east. Very quickly, Gerard, the atmosphere became almost unbearable. Great groups of people were herded out of the gate, but lots more people refused to go and went into hiding. On our very last day the Sinto kicked open a cupboard door in the Czech barracks, and I crawled in behind him shivering, with a fearful headache. Everything looked yellow. I already had typhus, you see. The sirens wailed, wailed again and fell silent. We went to the windows. We saw a white flag on the tower. We heard gunshots and machine-gun fire. Somehow or other I got to the parade ground. I couldn't believe my eyes. Through the gates came an American tank.

"Right then we'd been liberated. Among the Americans there were huge soldiers with gleaming white teeth. They evacuated the Little Camp in just a day, and some of them cried at the sight of us. They took me to the other side of the barbed wire, where there was a hospital. I was put to bed and given food, but not too much. The atmosphere of those last days, Gerard, I can't find words for it."

"Try."

"Well, it was a treat. But there were crows flying past the windows. A lot of us were lying there dying."

"And how were you?"

"In the evening there was singing. They put gramophone records on. Orchestras were playing."

"And how were you?"

"The windows were open. Damn it, Gerard, I died listening to a trumpet!"

"You know what I'd like?"

Gerard held up the bottle and looked. "Well? What, Jannosch?"

"For us to hitch up two of those nice horses of yours to the plow and get right out onto the land. I see you dug up a potato field next to the corn."

"Right away?"

They took the shortest route through the attached barn. There stood the old plow, its blades covered in rust. Jannosch and Gerard put the heavy Gelderland mare in the middle. She'd still know what to do, and the two young horses would follow her.

"Giddyap!"

Along a cart track between the cornfields an old-fashioned team of three horses pulled a plow on which two men sat so close together that their shoulders touched. At first their whole gait was a bit lopsided and swerved about. Once they got onto open ground, they started moving at a swift pace.

Gerard let the other man drive. He watched the hands full of gold rings on the reins. And on all sides, as far as the horizon, he saw his forefathers' fields. The sun was still high in the sky when he heard a sharp voice in his ear.

"Oh boy, before the war, this is where we came all the time, didn't we? Gelderland, Brabant, all over the country with a group of caravans and all the family. Sleeping where you wanted, eating when you wanted, playing the violin with your brothers. At night we were often on our way to the horse market, lamps on the seat, the horses for trading in a line behind the caravans. Oh boy, d'you know how great it was to be alive?"

They approached the place where a wide-branching walnut tree had once stood. Blocking the path was the long life of blossoms, birds, and sleeping animals on its trunk.

"Giddyap! Turn!"

The three horses swerved immediately to the left, then to the right, and moved back into the grove. The land was being plowed.

Each minute another piece of land appeared plowed. The autumn sun grew paler. Jannosch and Gerard had grown silent. They were smoking. They cupped their hands around the flame of the lighter and looked together at the horses' backs among the furrows.

"Oh man, d'you know how good a cigarette like this tastes?"

3

They got married. They were married under Dutch law on the thirtieth of that same month of September. I know exactly how Lucie went to the washhouse that morning, chuckling to herself, with long strides. Her mother's wedding dress was too short and too tight for her, revealing her highly polished brown shoes. With her nose close to the narrow mirror against the back wall she showed me how she painted her mouth with bright red lipstick. For a moment I caught her eye. Defenseless, with a smile that shot up into my heart like a flame. Happiness can be most unsettling.

In the village, people sniggered when the wedding procession came past. One Opel Olympia with the happy couple and the father, two Opel Olympias with farmers from the Noordoostpolder, and two low-slung American Fords with Gypsies from the camp in Enschede, where the news of the wedding had somehow wafted. The guests parked on the village green and crossed over to the town hall. Everyone says that it was windy that day, and that Lucie and the Gypsy women were walking about like flapping banners. Personally I remember a windless day, and sunlight deep into the council chamber — where Lucie and Joseph got up politely to write their names in huge letters in the register.

In the afternoon a whole lot of us were there under the

apple trees. The party had started without much planning. Joseph really hadn't notified his family, because marrying into a *gadjo* family is the last thing to be proud of. So the Gypsies who'd come over from Enschede and the farmers were drinking gin on opposite sides of the room. One of the guests must have got sufficiently in the mood to go to his car where there was a harmonica waiting in the trunk, because clapping and singing of quite legendary passion suddenly erupted. A fire flared up and Gerard allowed his free-ranging chickens to be caught and have their necks wrung with a deft movement. Dance! said the music that afternoon. Whirl around above an abyss of mutual understanding, go! In the generosity of drunkenness, show your real face for once! That's what it was like that afternoon. It was the most beautiful afternoon of the year. What I remember of that party is a row of cars on the sunny roadside and a little farther off, to the left of the house, an orchard full of gentiles and travelers. You saw them dancing and eating and drinking together in good nature. Music makes people a little childlike, more forgiving, but anyone who looked closely, as I did, saw two worlds still sadly divided from each other.

Except for that one couple. The feud didn't apply to them.

"D'you know," said Lucie to her husband, "I think I'm going to be faithful to you all my life."

"You'd better be," said Joseph.

And I can still see them wandering down the path a little way, the two of them, moving with a step that is very like an absolute insight into the world, and then I'm jealous. I observe the easy behavior of a couple of creatures who seem to know themselves and each other, their heartbeat, their circulation, like animals, and I feel excluded down to my fingertips. Not because I don't know the atmosphere around those two, the secret, it's just that I've seen the secret flowing away before my eyes, like sap from a notched tree, without thinking of cupping my hand underneath it.

Gerard saw it too. He saw that his daughter was completely crazy about that lad. She had his blessing. If anyone said to him that afternoon, "To a Gypsy!" he would nod, pour himself another drink, and reply, "That's right, friend." He felt no urge at all to discover why, but it didn't worry him in the slightest that somebody had moved into his house who drank coffee and smoked all day. Somebody who talked very loud but, in the mornings, refused to talk to a soul before he went to the water pump in the yard — despite the expensively fitted shower — and put his head and his hands under the cold jet.

If you ask me, he had long since forgotten that first time he'd taken his son-in-law for somebody else completely. That bunch are easily mixed up, aren't they? When he saw a slim Joseph opening the wide stable doors in a dark suit, he didn't think of Jannosch. When he saw the young man looking terribly worried and thinking aloud in a strange language and repairing a harness or bridles, he had no feeling of déjà vu. Although Gerard thought it was nice, since his daughter's marriage, to have a weather forecaster, a mechanic, and a horse dealer who still knew the art of making a horse walk so lopsidedly that the owner became embarrassed about its build, that still didn't mean at all that he was reminded of something that had pierced his heart like a thorn.

There are things that you simply can't face. What are you to do? Forget them? Turn on your heel? Get confused and absolve yourself of reacting logically to the indescribable illogicality of the way the world is made?

Since that one winter evening during the war, Gerard has had to wrestle with the fact that he came back from the arrest and Jannosch didn't. There was a time when he held his breath whenever he heard the dogs barking: Perhaps the door of the farmhouse would now creak open and he would see the Gypsy, in black as always, come into the kitchen. "Afternoon!" His heart leaps up. With a huge gesture, he opens his arms.

Hocus-pocus of conscience. Mists, differences in air pressure between good and evil. What should and should not have happened? Who else but you was in the thick of it? Gerard was a pawn in the resistance in Twente, a footsoldier, and he did the run-of-the-mill, deadly dangerous work. Plotting, hiding people, carrying out raids, lying by the railway at night, driving through the woods at night — there were quite a few who did that. Why? The fact that heroism for the sake of heroism exists — and treachery for the sake of treachery — isn't such an easy idea to come to grips with. As far as principles are concerned, obedience to God is a lot more plausible. Or patriotism. Or loyalty to the House of Orange. How much of that is true? That the simplest of simple things — the will not to bow to pressure — loves to seek justification in a higher motive? Gerard is a farmer, a widower who lived a fairly retiring life with his daughter. Only years later did the motif of Jannosch and his inexorable fate begin to cry out to him. Friendship, and he no longer felt innocent.

When Jannosch was arrested one January evening in 1944, it was less unusual for him than for those arrested with him. The authorities put him up against the wall, searched him, twisted his arms behind his back, and pushed him through the rain to a car with its doors already open. This was all familiar. He was well past thirty. By the time you are thirty you have got used to spending a night in a cell periodically. There was always an unpaid fine, or a residence permit that should never have been issued, or a complaint by a lady from Buss that you'd taken the washing off her line.

The three police cars drove back toward the town very fast. Within an hour Jannosch, separated from his fellow culprits, was taken to a cell past a row of gray doors in the prison. Inside, a bed, walls all around, and the iron peephole at eye level. Jannosch, already with a swollen jaw, sat down. Shortly he would get a merciless beating at the first interrogation, but for now he was still resting with his elbows on his knees. He yawned and concentrated on the thundering clatter of a gate slammed shut elsewhere. He has experienced this before. Right. This has happened before. By the light of a single bulb, he sank into the daze of solitary confinement.

That first hour in a cell he found particularly difficult. So here he was. His body had obviously been confined again. He looked at the surface of the opposite wall and in his brain there was the sense of the other times he had done that. No different from that time in Venlo or in Eisden. No different, either, from the way his father and his uncles had sat looking at that wall. *The game's up* is scratched into the plaster. Not because you parked your caravan without a permit, to tell the truth, but because you people are a big nuisance. You people speak slang. Our constitution objects to your peripatetic trading, your ingenious deals, and your Gypsylike behavior in general.

Jannosch was just a lad when he and his father and uncles had parked the caravans on a broad Brabant embankment. Beyond the poplars there was a rippling river. Ducks with their tails in the air were searching for food among the tall reeds. The line of caravans had been followed by the gendarmerie from Zundert onward. The gendarmes were aware that those types with their dark appearance often had valid papers. A nuisance, but there were always mayors who didn't see any reason to frustrate men who had enough means of existence, and women who smoked cigars but were silent when their husbands spoke. In these cases Article 41 of the Penal Code sometimes provided a solution. There was always some excuse. With a bit of effort you could throw someone in the cells for parking a caravan by the side of the road. You could create a criminal record for someone and subsequently deport him from the country with his whole family. And if you wanted, you could stop him at the border on his way back. The sun was shining. There was a slight wind. The horses had already been chased into the tall grass when the gendarmes, adjusting their coats, appeared.

There it was. Footsteps and the jingling of keys outside the door. Jannosch readily got up for the nighttime interrogation. Hard to say how many times he'd been beaten up by some hero or other of some European state, often enough in any case, but that night things were rougher than usual. Two Dutch members of the security police, Oosterlink and Plugh, wanted to know the names of everyone in the resistance group, which from their point of view was understandable. He was beckoned into a brightly lit room with a table with a Remington typewriter on it. Oosterlink and Plugh received him with smiles. Jannosch knew that he wasn't safe. Anyone would have known it. You didn't need experience for that. Don't forget that he was one of those that weren't called by their name.

Gypsy, said the police. Gypsy plague, said the paper. A thorough, international solution to the Gypsy problem was a topic of conversation in the offices of the Department of Justice in the 1930s. You could see ideas on the desks were really not so far in advance of reality. Registration by number, fingerprints, and if possible permanent supervision. In that atmosphere people like Jannosch mustn't be surprised to see an overworked policeman sometimes fly off the handle. To see him vent something with a rubber truncheon that, if you understood it properly, was nothing but a well-meant, indeed paternal, exhortation to live in a house. In that atmosphere, still in the climate of the Depression, working people who were roaming around the southern Netherlands could be chased with rakes and shovels to try their luck farther away over the border, while the police just looked on.

But on his way to the horse market in Antwerp, Jannosch was stopped at the Belgian frontier. Things happened so fast that the horse and the front wheels of the caravan were already in Belgium, while the back was still in the Netherlands. No chance of the Belgians letting the family in. No possibility that the Netherlands would take them back. After five days both the Belgians and the Gypsies got fed up with it. Just at the moment that Jannosch and his people were going to take off, the Belgians, who happened to be drunk, came up with the idea of emptying their revolvers above the horses' heads, simply to frighten them. The horses reared and fell. The Gypsies leaped forward and the gendarmes, only half knowing what to do, tried to force the whole lot back, swinging their truncheons menacingly. With the alcohol, they took their violence to extremes.

Oosterlink and Plugh went further. When Jannosch was brought back into his cell, he was no longer conscious and his head looked alarming. He'd thought, they're going to kill me anyway, so he'd hit back, and the treatment had become protracted. He hadn't given anything away. He'd just cursed, softly and coarsely in his own language, because he knew that talking with someone in a position of power was impossible. He hadn't mentioned a single name. Not even his own. On the table next to the Remington there had been a scrap of paper with a photo from his inside pocket. None of them had taken the information seriously. Gypsies — the irritating fact was well known — changed names easier than they changed hats. Forged, scrounged, or bought papers had always been a matter of life and death in their world.

Jannosch slept for hours. When he woke up he didn't know where he was. He put a heavy hand on his face, lifted an eyelid, and saw that the sun was probably shining outside a barred window high on the outside wall. Did he remember what had happened? You've been beaten up again, Jannosch, that risk is always there. God knows why, but you've been taking part in very dangerous operations, though not exactly for Queen and Country, if you ask me. He sighed. His arm dropped to his side. Off again.

Just as well, perhaps. It can't be much fun to be thinking at this moment about your heavily pregnant wife and a bunch of children who are parked illegally in the wood. Perhaps better to sleep, as unnaturally deep as you can, and at intervals just to concentrate on your broken fingers and a couple of bruises. In a few days you can get on your feet again and you'll go to Amersfoort and then to Vught. In May, well before your train leaves for the east, you'll hear they've all been arrested. All of them: your wife, your children, and a couple of brothers in 's Hertogenbosch, your parents, another brother, and your sisters on Hoefkade in The Hague, arrested by the Dutch police in the early morning of May 16 so that, after two centuries, our country will again soon be Gypsy-free.

Perhaps it's better to keep your head down for now.

Did he, I wonder, remember anything about that earlier fateful time? Would he, semiconscious on the dirty mattress, know that the circumstances of his life had their origin hundreds of years before his birth? People who can't read and write often have a warehouse full of old, hereditary memories at their disposal. I know for certain that the stories were told to him. Long, long ago, Jannosch, your family once traveled around in these parts. One of your great-great-grandmothers, for instance, was hanged in Zutphen. Her daughter of eight looked on. I happen to know a few details. You lie there, and I'll tell you.

Her name was Demeter. She called herself Maria Jansz, and people also nicknamed her Monplaisir because that distant grandmother of yours, Jannosch, was a woman with a sunny heart. The events we're concerned with here took place in about 1726. We are in the province of Gelderland. Right. Listen if you can and want to. On a beautiful morning in the last week of April a hunt for heathens was organized in the woods near Eerbeek. Heathens, I should say, meant you. That's what you were called in the days when each of the provinces insisted on putting up its own placards, but which all boiled down to exactly the same thing: Within our borders heathens are forbidden, on pain of very severe penalties.

Maria Jansz raced after her daughter at the crack of dawn. The child knew the way under the trees better than she did. Others in the group knew better too, like her husband Schoppe, her sister Laurina, her brother-in-law Cooyman, even the smallest children, because Maria Jansz had just been released from four years in prison. She had to readjust to being a free woman, albeit one who'd been banished forever. She ran after Mie Magdaleen into the burgeoning ferns and hid. That's what they all did that day and of necessity the day afterward too. Willem van Haarsholt, the sheriff of the Veluwe, was determined to arrest the group, and the law supported him. Anyone who kept company with the heathens was automatically in the wrong. You didn't need to have stolen a pair of shoes. You didn't need to have pointed your weapon at a farmer, or to have said with a dirty, filthy face, "My children and I are going to be sleeping in your barn tonight."

When Maria Jansz heard dogs at the end of the second day, she knew the game was up. Mie Magdaleen knew too. They were sitting high up in the velvety fork of an old pine tree that was still warm from the day of sun.

"Have a good look, Mie Magdaleen. Is it those rotten pox-ridden swine?"

Your two great-great-grandmothers, Jannosch, stuck their noses through the branches and saw that they were being captured by experts. Four men, chaps who had occupied the office for years, grinning, walked over to the tree which by now was a mass of clawing, barking dogs. They fired a round at random. Maria Jansz knew the red uniforms lined with yellow silk from earlier days. She rolled her eyes like a she-devil.

In the guardroom they found Laurina and her children. Cooyman too was sitting on the stinking floor, but Schoppe wasn't among them. I don't need to tell you that no one felt safe when there was the sound of footsteps and they stopped outside the cell door. To everyone's astonishment, the eight-year-old Mie Magdaleen was the first to be taken for interrogation.

"Where are your father, your uncles, your cousins? Tell me their real names. Tell me where you last slept."

The girl, who, besides her own language, understood French and German and Dutch, felt it would be a good idea to begin by telling them that she'd been baptized, which no one believed.

"In Arnhem," she said, which didn't interest anyone particularly because in those days Gelderland had bigger things on its mind. Now a century-old irritation had reached the point where there was only one way left to describe it, a *plague of heathens*. People in the Republic and outside were working on a joint solution. Sovereign passions, which went back to the Union of Utrecht, were swept aside. It was permitted to chase people far over each other's borders, to catch them, interrogate them, and lynch them. A manhunt can't be organized without good reason. A large-scale clearance needs theories or at least higher motives. What are you supposed to do in the Age of Reason with a group of paupers who refuse to be educated? The cosmopolitan Republic was a place where foreign writers and philosophers were warmly welcomed. It was possible for books that were banned in Spain, Italy, and France to appear there without any problem. The tolerant Republic of still very wealthy merchants had declared war on a group of vagabonds who, in an atmosphere of merciless persecution, had indeed become a major nuisance. What are you to do in the century of Enlightenment, with fortune-telling, animal taming, and the sacred beggar's hand from the Middle Ages?

"Names!" This was roared very loudly.

"Schoppe, Werenfridus, Abraham, Pierro . . ." whispered Mie Magdaleen.

The results were not particularly good with the child, but useful enough, the interrogators thought. They called up Maria Jansz and, after a stinging slap around the ear, got her to talk about her husband.

"Schoppe Elias," she said, and wondered silently where he was.

"He's a horseman by profession," she said, and hoped silently that he'd thought of going to the lodgings of Jan Libertijn, an ex-mercenary who didn't worry at all about the police or about the fine of three guilders that was imposed for giving heathens lodging.

Maria Jansz told them that her husband had been a cavalryman in the company of Captain Dammaerts in Holland and, when the army no longer needed his sharp eyes and his wild gallop, he became a barge haulier in Friesland. In the hope of giving the conversation a different turn, she began playing the simpleton. With bursts of laughter and grimaces, she swore by the living God that she, Maria Jansz, had never told good fortunes and, by the shed blood of the Savior, knew not a word of the language of the heathens, not a word of that devilish language. . . .

In the interrogation room, impatience grew. One of the magistrates, not the sheriff but one of the aldermen, stood up, grabbed Maria Jansz by her blouse, and pulled it to shreds with one calm claw. There. There it was. On her back, just below the shoulder, a shameful scar cried out that this heathen woman, this one here, had once been flogged in the Great Marketplace of Brussels and afterward had been banished forever from the territories of His Imperial Majesty Charles VI.

Ten days later the court could send the executioner.

Your twenty-two-year-old great-great-aunt Laurina, Jannosch, was flogged very badly, but because of the three children, she didn't go to prison. It was much cheaper to brand her on the shoulder and banish her for good. Cooyman, your great-uncle, was also flogged and branded, but he, young and strong as he was, was sent to prison and for no less than thirty years. In order to find out the hiding place of his friends, they had interrogated him under torture. They'd stretched him a bit, then winched him up and let him hang there for a while. Only when they'd strung him up for the second time did he say where in the wood between Eerbeek and Loenen there was a great oblong pit in which the remnants of what had once been an extended family had bivouacked for weeks. Schoppe was indeed picked up the following day, although not alive and nowhere near the pit. Someone in Jan Libertijn's lodgings had been unable to restrain himself. Betrayal can be quite fun in itself, and with a not insubstantial reward it's even more fun. Schoppe heard the familiar noise of the authorities approaching. He fled the bedroom, hid in a chicken run a hundred yards away, and was shot dead with a flintlock by a sullen farmer who was completely within his rights.

That left Maria Jansz with a daughter of eight.

Imagine a woman of about thirty with raven hair and sparkling eyes. Excuse me for saying so, but your great-great-grandmother was beautiful. She wore three skirts, one over the other, and a shawl, though the family capital, the golden rings in her ears, had already gone. For two or three weeks she'd been sitting with Mie Magdaleen in the cell, pending, as it's called, a sentence that she of course already knew. What a lot of trouble they were going to on her account! Heathens were heathens, rabble that camped in tents on the borders. They preferred a fight to the death to being caught. They fled from province to province. You could shoot them or punish them, I assure you a trial wasn't always needed. But for Maria Jansz, would you believe it, documents were being applied for in The Hague and Zaltbommel. I think, and you'll probably agree with me, that for once they wanted to do things properly. What was happening here was the upholding of the law.

So Maria Jansz ate for a few weeks more, and drank. The fantastic fact of her imminent violent death didn't prevent her from talking to Mie Magdaleen and herself about seas and mountains and cities and streets. Life, Mie Magdaleen, is basically happiness. Anyone who saw her sitting there, smiling a little, under a barred window which the odors of the city wafted through, was convinced that every hour, every minute, continues to exert its full rights over you, even when you're waiting for the executioner. Meanwhile the documents arrived. Zaltbommel, 1717.

Maria Jansz had been sentenced to death there once before.

When Maria Jansz had been arrested back then in the vicinity of Zaltbommel, her chances were poor. Five of the band she consorted with bore the brand of Brussels and six that of the Amstelland. Five had been banished from The Hague and ten from Kampen. One of them, IJsbrand Montagne, her father, had had his cheek slashed in Tiel. Her brothers, Willem and Nobel, still young, had been flogged in Friesland and Waterland. And her first husband, whose name was Sinte, had been punished in Utrecht *without, nonetheless, breaking arms or legs*, which was a stroke of luck. Confronted with the problem of finding anywhere to stay, they could, at least, quickly reach thickly wooded, forbidden Gelderland. There they were found later that year by the scout of the Bommelerwaard, cooking at night on fires banked up high. None of them could show that they had obtained the firewood and the food honestly. Even she, Maria Jansz, with all her talent of an outlawed twenty-year-old, was not believed when she said that she'd paid for the pig's head in her pot with a nice handkerchief.

All the men were hanged, and of the women only Laurina was spared because of her youth. But look, and it wasn't difficult to see, the heavily pregnant Maria Jansz was in precisely the kind of condition that required a reprieve. Just as no human being is ever completely good or completely bad, so a murderous government is not completely murderous. The conscience dotes on poetry. The innocent and pristine infant was born a month later, when the January sun poured into the houses everywhere and made them all light and bright. It was nice that on that day a woman in a dark dungeon, who had just given birth amid furious sobs, received good news. The deferred death sentence had been annulled.

The States granted her pardon in a truly humanist way. Go, Maria Jansz. Be off with you and never show yourself in these parts again!

Well, you know the story: Seven years later they would see her again in the Ministry of Justice. She was with a man again and, unfortunately, had again been tried and imprisoned in The Hague. Honesty doesn't pay for people who've always been persecuted. After she'd been flogged in the Groenmarkt, the house of correction on Prinsengracht had plenty of work for the sturdy young woman, but not, of course, for the child. When Maria Jansz entered the institution for hard labor, which with the three rows of windows one above the other was the largest building she would ever see, Mie Magdaleen was given a shove. There, girl, is your family. They've got forty-eight hours to leave Holland!

Today she would have to look.

Meanwhile Maria Jansz had admitted everything that was in the document and in addition had mentioned her floggings near Hamburg and in Koblenz, the latter for stealing three loaves of bread from the army.

"From poverty," she had politely explained.

What followed was a well-argued and logically constructed indictment that concluded with a cool demand for the maximum sentence.

It was a beautiful morning, May 19. Opposite the gallows on the market square in Zutphen was a row of blossoming chestnut trees under which you could hear everyday life, talk and laughter. Then you could also hear the trundling of an approaching cart. The first to get out was Mie Magdaleen. Because the civil authorities wanted to urge the young creature to mend her ways, it was included in her mother's sentence that, as an example, the child must watch the execution at close quarters. Mie Magdaleen followed the direction of a pointing finger, took an upper seat at the left corner of the gallows, and looked into the crowd with a woebegone face and astonished eyes. She knew that Laurina must be standing somewhere, the aunt whom she was to accompany after the hanging.

Then Maria Jansz climbed up with her hands on her skirts. The crowd began jeering. Ignoring the tumult, perhaps hearing none of it, she turned to the public, straightened her shoulders, and waited without moving a muscle in her face. Had her spirit already fled? Was she looking out far above everyone over the shining fields and villages bathed in the golden sunshine? While a small procession of solemnly dressed men took their seats, an intolerable tension arose in the square which centered on the body and particularly the eyes of the heathen woman. Not a soul was interested in what crime she'd committed, they were simply eager for her secret to be violated. When the sun was already warm, the executioner put the rope around her neck and the condemned woman did not resist. Don't look, Mie Magdaleen, you'll never ever learn anything from this handiwork! It went quiet. Do I need to tell you that Demeter, alias Maria Jansz, born on this side of the district of Cologne, made the ugliest face in her life?

4

*F*or years we in Benckelo saw that couple living together in a way that's familiar in the country areas. Ap-
parently he makes all the decisions. You could always see
that it was Joseph who did the business. With a fiery expression he would survey the stallion with whom Bellaheleen
was to be crossed. "Okay," he would say, already turning
around and walking away almost petulantly. "Right. I'll let
you know when she's ready."

In that first year there was an overwhelming amount to
do: the extension of the stables, the design, the wood, the
quarter-inch-thick roofing felt. Joseph gave instructions
with delighted conviction. Lucie stood a little to one side.
She followed as the negotiations were conducted in a high-
handed tone, smiled a bit, blinked, and made sure that it was
he, her husband, who paid the bills when building materials
were delivered.

You go ahead, do what you want, was Gerard's quite
sensible attitude at the time. He went on with the selling of
his land, acre after acre, which he'd decided to do for obscure
reasons. That the seriousness and imagination of Joseph
seemed to be perfectly attuned to his daughter's heartbeat
was one thing. It was quite a different matter that the little
stud became more and more profitable.

To tell the truth, I don't believe, as everyone else did, that Lucie was subservient to her husband. What he wanted was all right, that's true, and what he didn't like she thought was wrong. Once, when she was pregnant and was about to boil a great pan of mussels, he forbade her to do so with a gesture that was much like a slap. How things were between those two was hard to tell. For example, when Joseph left in the early summer, an event that always took Lucie completely by surprise but was regarded as inevitable and predictable in the village after the first few times, the horse business went on running in perfect order.

Benckelo is beautiful in summer. When Lucie took on a life of her own, the crops shot up. The farms sank into the green and yellow-brown land. They seemed to be low and flat and just as content as the cows that lay chewing their cud with their legs tucked underneath them. The soil here is diluvial sand, mixed with clay from rivulets and streams. It all sounds very peaceful, you'd say. Yet on the northwest side of the village there once was a castle with two gates. The area around Benckelo has witnessed a lot of violence. Spaniards, Prussians, and French sent their cavalry along the hedge-bordered paths to Enschede and Hengelo. There was plundering and constant feuding with the bishops of Münster, who became more amenable only in the eighteenth century when the wretched vagrancy problem was better tackled jointly. The last Gypsy to be arrested in the area at the time was a childlike old man called Doggie. His capturer was a given a reward of thirty Carolus guilders.

In the fields horses, machines, men, and women work with clutching hands the color of wheat. This land has always provided work and bread. In order to keep your business going and if possible to expand it a little, you need a partner. Yet here too people have long preferred to marry for love. There is one person, one imponderable miracle who alone fits into your world. What is more reassuring than to lead that heaven on earth into your kitchen, your stables? Isn't it by far the best thing to temper the madness of your heart, which was really unbearable, with a set of plowshares, an apron, a table for your children, a vegetable garden, a whole string of cows? And then one day love subsides and becomes so calm that you scarcely notice it anymore.

Lucie was a child who in the past often fell asleep at school during lessons. She folded her arms wide on the desk, laid down her head, and closed her eyes. I always thought that I understood everything better than she did. I left the village and started roaming. She became a farmer's wife. She got up at six in the morning and went into the kitchen to attend to the dogs. She turned on the radio and woke the children. As she made coffee she loosened her ropelike plaits. Spring after spring the morning would come when you could see her on the path next to the orchard watching her husband's car leave, a woman with sturdy knees who patiently showed that she understood it all. She was in love with a stranger. The man who slept with her, who was allowed back every autumn to snuggle up to her in bed, must be infinitely familiar to her, but preferably also infinitely strange. She had what you call curled lips. Who are you? they asked. And what adventures have you had? Then they were silent. With her elbows on the table or slumped in the old armchair, she waited for the story that was about to come. She was his sultan. For sixteen years, autumn and winter and spring, she could be quite sure that he wouldn't leave her.

She thought it strange that she wasn't allowed to give birth at home. He took her to the hospital at the last moment and there one foggy morning Katharina was born. She thought it was odd and was ashamed when after a routine house call by the GP he wanted to know which cup the doctor had drunk from.

"Was it this one?"

She nodded and looked quite curiously with him at the crockery on the worktop. The used cups, the spoons and a couple of plates looked perfectly normal as far as she was concerned. The doctor was an elderly man with gray tufts above his deep-set eyes.

"Was it this one? Do you swear?"

She hesitated and bent down to stroke the dog who was snuffling around her feet.

"Oh, Joseph," she muttered, "do stop it."

Then she had the fright of her life from the rattling and she saw him sweep all the chinaware together. Busily, but without a trace of malice, he went to and fro between the kitchen and the pantry a few times to throw everything into the trash.

The fact that he wore the same suit every day, that he made her roast hedgehogs for supper, that he didn't want to hear her peeing under any circumstances, that he cried at a film on television, that he was able to cure a horse that had something baffling wrong with it for weeks by giving it a cut in the neck with a razor-sharp knife, allowing the blood to escape in violent spurts, and then binding the skin very tightly with a piece of string . . . she thought it was all strange and wonderful. She shook her head, stroked him a little, at least when they were alone together, or said as if everything had totally passed her by: "Another week and we'll have snow. Why don't we start clearing up the sheet iron and the chains tomorrow."

And then he would obey her. He would clear the yard ready for winter while she currycombed the horses. He would help his father-in-law in the greenhouse, move pipes, and do carpentry work, while she handled the tack room. He carried the children in his arms, stroked them and kissed them and never hit them until they were nine, she did that. Everything fit in their life. She walked through the dried-up mud. He stood at the bar of The Tap. She cut cabbage, apples, potatoes and mashed the whole lot together. He smoked and watched television. The wind lashed the house, metallic skies moved in from the west, and at night a jet of water splashed from a leak in the gutter. When he suggested the plan of partially dismantling a broken-down Mercedes, fitting a speed reduction on the rear axle with a chain, lengthening the crankshaft, and so in a trice turning it into a kerosene-powered tractor, she looked at his gesticulations and thought it was a good idea. She also liked the way he dealt with horses, which obeyed him, and with dogs, which sometimes, because of the respect in which he was held by them, sank to the ground and crawled up to him on their bellies. In winter it was icy fields, ringing bells, birds. The horses sometimes in the stable for too long. It was like an intoxication to exercise those frenzied animals side by side with that man. To take that semihardened road past Smeenk's factory, to reach the edge of the wood, turn right and immediately left again, jump over a plank bridge, follow a sandy road that ended in a Y-shaped fork, and after about four hundred yards reach a stretch of heather fields that have a staggering grace particularly in winter. In the spring she sometimes accompanied him to the river. While he inspected his clumsy fishing tackle, she sat next to the bait can. She liked his bossiness and noisiness, his unusual use of words, and when he wasn't in her direct vicinity the world went slightly askew. When he came, everything was all right again. Beside her there was a faint cry. She knew that one. The lead-weighted line swung up and she knew that he had a bite, as always very quickly with bait passed through oak resin. In other words: The months went by and Lucie, constantly close to her husband, saw her love mapped out a little at a time.

Until it's time for a break, a breather. He roams across the Balkans, she schools Bellaheleen and Lucky Boy, whom she wants to take to the competition in Zwolle in September. She gives the children candy and fruit, and strips of tripe to the dogs. With her father and a few laborers she's standing by the edge of the cornfield, smoking. She hears the rustling wood behind her projecting the sound of a voice that is hoarse and loud. And then it changes into a rustle made by a tangle of birds when it suddenly flies up into the sky where an avenue of heavy white clouds glides past in its stately way. Symptoms of a delirium. A plate creeps to the edge of the table and falls. A crow sits in a tree meowing like a cat. Party tricks of an infatuation that wanders freely across the farmyard. September comes. She feels a tickling in her stomach. When she wakes up a week later, she smells a scent of iron and damp rope. He is lying with his face toward her, sound asleep.

He always asked her first about the jumpers.
"How is Bellaheleen going?"
"Like an athlete, Joseph, oh yes, you'll see."
It was morning. She walked to the stables with him with an infant on her arm.
"If you just let her loose, you don't have to teach her any movement." She burst out laughing. There was a lump of hilarity in her throat. "Stepping to the side, Joseph, she does it just like that!"

He pushed his way into the stables ahead of her. In the wash room the stableboy was grooming Lucky Boy.

"So fussy!" she explained while Joseph stroked the animal and talked to him. "Active, and nicely on the foreleg and never has his ears on his neck when you push. But he's so fussy, yes he is."

She told him about the summer. She made a gift, in words, of the past months — the work, the deals, the breaking-in, the dressage — and made it clear to him that she had been at the center of that dressage. "Damn it, Joseph, you can only do it with a horse that wants to."

"Lucky Boy, Timone, Bellaheleen," said Joseph with pleasure, strolling past the stalls. "Yes, they're all kinds of hot-blooded creatures."

"And they have to be!" she nodded vehemently. "The good-natured ones, those horses that are so malleable, oh, Joseph, in the end you simply have to kick them to get them to work!"

Later in the morning he presented his news. They were sitting inside, at the table. Joseph, with his hat still on, told her and the stable boy and Gerard that the day before he'd driven home from Magdeburg in one haul. Because of an old man who was with him, a distant relative on his grandmother's side, he'd made a detour to the caravan site in Stein.

In order to say something, she asked, "What was his name?"

"It was Lazaro Theodorović," said Joseph, and added that he was a Bosnian, from a very old family of bear trainers.

The milk came to the boil in a saucepan on the stove. She got up.

"My eyes had seen him all summer," said Joseph. "He had a sharp face that got even sharper in the dusk. He had a funereal voice."

She stared at him, the pan and the whisk in her hands. "He wore a red cloth around his head, a kind of turban."

There was a flush in her face when she poured the coffee. Smiling in bafflement, no one knew why, she pushed plates and cake forks across the cloth.

But I, of course, knew what was preoccupying her. Lazaro Theodorović, she repeated in her mind. Lazaro Theodorović. Did she see the sharp cheekbones of the face in the dusk? Could she imagine that funereal voice? What Joseph had told her in words that immediately moved her belonged to a story from which she was completely excluded, and I knew that she thought: So much the better. Why should she be in search of herself? Wasn't she the thing that she knew the taste of all her life? With her nose above the coffee with hot milk, she meditated on the red cloth, which may have been wrapped around the skull of an old man like a turban, although she didn't know precisely how.

It would be quite a while before she was to hear any more about Theodorović. Those first days were so busy. As he was painting the chicken run, Joseph told her a couple of other stories. He was frank. He was the wanderer. The fact that he went away in the summer really didn't mean that he excluded her. For example, one evening in November he said, "I'll tell you about Parasja." At the beginning Gerard and a couple of the children were there too. She was the granddaughter of a carpet dealer from Banja Luka whose half brother was unforgivably insulted by a distant blood relation of Joseph's. Lucie nodded. She listened as well as she could. She never tried to find out in what way and to what extent the mysteries that radiated toward her in evocative sentences had to do with the world. Had he never seen her again? Hadn't he looked for her everywhere? She asked when the story was finished, and she only did so to keep the voice going for a little while longer.

One afternoon in May she had an accident on her horse. It can happen to the best of us. She was riding past a rye field on a newly trained bay gelding when the animal, alarmed by some black plastic flapping in the wind, jumped to the side and slipped into the ditch beside the road. Less than five minutes later, a woman in a car who drove up behind her noticed Lucie. Pale and with a dislocated vertebra in her neck, she was walking along the shoulder. She must have lost consciousness for a moment. When she came around and saw the horse was no longer there, there was nothing to do but to walk home.

Christina Cruyse stopped. She was already reaching over to her right to open the door and drive Lucie home.

"They're all a bundle of nerves," she said a little later, half mocking, half serious, when Lucie, sitting next to her, had told her about the black plastic and the ditch. They were already turning into the farmyard. The bay gelding was waiting under the linden tree. They got out. Christina Cruyse wanted to lend a hand by unsaddling the horse and taking it to the stall.

"There's no need," said Lucie.

When Joseph came home at about three, he found it very quiet everywhere. The children were still at school and Gerard was nowhere. In the bedroom he found Lucie, not quite herself, on the embroidered blanket. Her eyes were half open and the irises were black. He squatted next to the bed and looked at the beads of sweat on her nose and upper lip. He'd never seen a woman with such white skin. When she recognized him, she smiled at him, like a lost child, he thought.

Although he'd actually been on the point of leaving, Joseph stayed at home for two of the three weeks during which Lucie wasn't allowed to turn her neck. And although he was no longer in the mood for it, there were moments when he sat orating with his back to the window as though it were winter. I've never found out what precisely he had in mind when he talked about the Vogelsberg, the tents near a mining village in Serbia, the water buffalo, the mountain roads, the money that was called dinar or florint. They were fragments of himself that he offered her. But when she asked about Theodorović, and he actually started talking about him, then it was as if *I* were the one lying there, flat on my back on the sofa with a plaster collar around my neck.

"Theodorović," said Joseph, "arrived in Kampen with a group of ten or twelve people on a boat from Lemmer. It was long before the war. They had a couple of bears and a donkey with them and they intended to go through the streets making music. But Kampen wouldn't let them come ashore."

Part Three

1

*A*nd so the next morning they sailed on. In the harbor of Harderwijk, part of the company disembarked without any problem. How those people fared in the town and the villages of the hinterland is not relevant here. Suffice it to say that the family of Lazaro Theodorović and his sister's family and a granny, along with their animals, continued the voyage. It was a cloudy day and very windy. Small birds of prey circled the ship. The light of the autumn day was already growing pale by the time they reached Huizen, a village with a thousand inhabitants most of whom would die without ever having seen anything except water, ships' masts with black sails, and fish. They moored at a quiet hour. Theodorović and his people were able to bring the animals from the hold onto the gangplank without any trouble and walk off with them along a dike lined with trees. Three girls coming toward them arm in arm stood stock-still and looked back at them for quite a while afterward."

Here Joseph was interrupted by the barking of one of the dogs in the yard. From his chair by the window he peered outside over his shoulder for a moment: an overcast evening in May. It's nothing, I thought impatiently, go on with the story. It's just a car turning. Two beams of light crossed the path, then there was silence. It was dusky and warm in the kitchen. I heard Gerard sigh sleepily in the corner next to the stove. But Lucie, stretched out almost invisible on the sofa, raised a hand to indicate: Go on, and then?

"They slept in an open barn," said Joseph. "Opposite a huge windmill with sails on gilded axles that swished around all night long like souls in torment."

"So they were given a roof for the night by the farmer?" asked Lucie.

"Bear trainers are always given a roof for the night."

"Why's that?"

"Every farmer knows that a bear takes away and drives out the plagues of the farmyard."

"Does a farmer know that?"

"Even if he's never seen a bear before, he knows."

Joseph thought for a moment, frowned and sought out Lucie's face with his eyes. "I'm telling you things just as I heard them from Ottoman, Theodorović's son," he said. "He's a blacksmith and lives in a village near Mostar. I won't forget that fellow anytime soon. Bear training is in his blood. If I tell you this evening how a girl at the market in Weesp was bitten to death by a bear, then that story comes from the area around Mostar in Bosnia, where we were sitting under the moon together one evening after the meal. If I tell you that the girl was dressed like a queen, with gold needles along her forehead and a pointed cap of gauze, then I do so in words that are the property of my cousin Ottoman. May his life be a pleasurable stroll from now on. May his enemies perish in jail!"

Joseph began coughing at length, and with a kind of satisfaction. Satisfaction that he'd settled the copyright? Afterward his voice sounded deep and soft, but perfectly intelligible even to me.

That Saturday they gave their first performance in the village. To the whine of an ancient rebec, a four-stringed fiddle from the Balkans that was played by Theodorović's brother-in-law with alarming obsession, they came very solemnly down the main street. At the front the two bears, urged on by Theodorović in the garb of a beggar and his sister in a pair of gold-embroidered Turkish trousers. Occasionally the bears would raise themselves on their hind legs and, as if searching for an audience, turn their half-blind faces toward the windows of the houses. The inhabitants of the fishing village were interested and appeared in the street. They laughed at the four children who, true to habit, extended their hands in a begging gesture. A double line of schoolboys, at a sign from their teacher, split into two and stood with their hats off, to allow the donkey with the granny on it to pass.

They arrived in the market square. It was on the dot of eleven. For a moment the rebec was drowned out by a rattling carillon. Then all that remained was the voice of Theodorović, who in order to rouse the curiosity of the public had begun a speech in the Ursari language, looking each person in turn imperiously in the eye. The girl, one of the three who had been walking along the dike the evening before, was at the front.

She was pretty, a little on the plump side. According to Ottoman, she had the moon-colored skin and the languorous look of a fourteen-year-old who would soon be betrothed to a man. As yet she wasn't wearing festive clothes. That idea wasn't to occur to her until later, shortly before the bear bit her, on that farewell afternoon in Weesp. When Theodorović, who was about to end his speech, looked into her eyes as the last person in the audience, he realized that no power on earth would be able to distract those gray depths from something awesome behind his back: one of the bears, his own, called Bruin. Without delay he leaped aside and pointed to the bear with his six-foot-long stick.

"*Hoppa, Bruin!*"

The animal trotted forward on all fours. The tambourine began its goading.

"*Hoppa, Bruin, Stara Planina. Hop, hop, hop!*"

Then facing the gaze of the girl, the honey-brown animal rose wildly, its front paws outstretched with claws that reminded her of something for which there were neither words nor concepts. The face with its snout was set in an amiable grin, and seeing its narrow eyes she understood that there are two sides to everything.

Bruin danced. He stepped forward and to the side. He shook his bottom. He had a luxuriant coat. The other bear, called Martin, was now introduced into the spectacle by the woman. "*Ole, Martine!*" she cried and everyone could see that it meant: Dance, Martin, and be quick about it! The bears, Joseph told her, amused the people of Huizen and commanded their respect, not only because of their tricks but because of the heathen patience with which they'd been rehearsed in a camp in the Balkan Mountains. And, in a deeper sense, because of that camp and the mountains themselves.

"Christ, Lucie, just catching those animals at the end of winter!"

In order to do it they'd gone to the Bulgarian Balkans, through the pass near Tárnovo, in the western section called the Old Mountains. At the time when the Cossacks fought here, a branch of Theodorović's family had settled in the area. Like Lazaro and his relatives, they belonged to the tribe of the Ursari. They observed Ramadan, but at the same time also celebrated the festival of St. Petja. All of them were very skilled with bears. After weeks of piercing cold, father Aasap Theodorović arrived with his wife, children, and baggage donkeys at the high spot where the family camped in tents made from the skin of the black goat.

Hard, mysteriously indifferent, these people endured the torments of winter. They said that they knew of a couple of good bears, two years old, for Lazaro the son of Aasap Theodorović and for Thuli the daughter, that they'd seen just before the onset of winter. They said they would catch them as soon as the mother came out to sniff the spring air. And so it happened. On the evening of one of the first spring days, there were in the camp of the Ursari two animals that, if the omens did not lie, would bring pleasure and money and health.

After their initial disconsolate behavior they soon settled down, with the whole tribe spoiling them and whispering sweet things into their ears. None of the Ursari were stupid enough to believe that the period of apprenticeship, which was now beginning, would affect the soul of the bears. Just as they themselves were enriched by the wildness of those two, the bears would learn to enjoy and understand the human signals that made them roll, turn, and raise their paws.

In the ground by the river where the earth is clay Lazaro and Thuli built a smoldering fire. They covered it with an iron sheet and made the bears walk in turn over the sheet toward them. When the animal, surprised by the mysterious heat, raised its leg in a reflex, they rattled the tambourine. Soon Bruin and Martin knew the irrevocable link between the tambourine and their muscles.

"Bruin!" said Lucie suddenly, and I was glad she brought it up. "How could that bear be called Bruin?"

Joseph turned toward the countertop. As his father-in-law had fallen asleep in the armchair, he poured coffee only for Lucie and himself. Lucie half sat up with a cautious movement, her face empty, completely smoothed out by the story that she may have found especially beautiful because of the time of year. Tomorrow the whole orchard would be in blossom, but as far as Joseph and she were concerned, it was winter.

"Certainly," said Joseph. "Brown. Ottoman could pronounce *bruin* properly, you know. He said that they had always known that name as a bear name, ever since the time of the Turkish war, when one of his great-great-grandfathers had gone through the Netherlands, yes, to that plain where so many cows moo, but where it didn't go so well for his ancestor when his group was chased onto a ferryboat by the border police and hounded out of the province of Limburg with rifle shots along the river Maas. The bear that was hit was called Bruin."

Joseph walked back and forth, a couple of steps toward the dividing door and a couple toward the windows through which rain was pouring. Lucie seemed to be watching and following her husband with her eyes, but I know that what affected her really was his talking with a soft, God-given intonation — heartbreaking — that seemed inconceivable in their everyday lives. Was he really letting her hear in all sincerity what she was so in love with? There are people who prefer to transpose what they have to say — and I'm now talking about the very personal things — to an area that is much clearer, much more revealing than their own psychology. What I mean is, when Joseph said, "Later that day, when they gave a second performance in Naarden, the girl was there again," it made Lucie shudder for a second.

She had followed the troupe through a wood of birches and ferns. She had forgotten that it was Saturday. While her mother was plucking and roasting the chicken for Sunday, she had crossed Huizerstraatweg and, passing a couple of prosperous farmsteads, had arrived in Naarden. The town was like a star-shaped cell with its only view the church, the largest in the Netherlands, that stands smack in the middle and takes up the whole sky.

When she sat on the ground at the front of the audience in the square, which was no more than a widening of the path around the church, she again felt the terrible charm of the bears.

"Careful," said a boy sitting next to her. "Those creatures are capable of anything."

She looked at him with a pitying smile.

Let me once again tell you what Bruin did for her, because the training, the conspiracy of Bruin and the Ursari, was part of the obsession that was to determine her fate.

He waved one paw and got Theodorović to fetch him a comb. He waved again and was given a scarf. He danced for a few minutes and then lay down on his side right in front of the first row of spectators, put a paw against his cheek and held his head cocked seductively to one side, much to the amusement of the audience. She wanted so much to touch him. The girl, who Ottoman knew worked in her father's fish-salting factory, put out a hand, and nothing would have prevented her from grabbing one of the monstrous claws if the tambourine had not jingled and made Bruin scramble up as quick as lightning.

"He wasn't used to strange hands, anyway."

It wasn't Bruin but Martin who could be touched. Ottoman said that the show acquired a different, deeper character when Martin took part. Because he, trained through the power of a woman, had learned how to bring healing. This bear could cure gout and tumors by laying on one of its paws, which had been declawed, and without any discomfort to the person concerned could banish migraines, epilepsy, ruptured blood vessels, and pains in the groin and sometimes, under certain circumstances, could cure male impotence.

That afternoon, in the square in front of the Grote Kerk in Naarden, Thuli Theodorović was able to create a special moment by persuading a fisherman's wife from the audience to come forward and lie on top of the bear stretched out on the ground. The rebec played a lingering Transylvanian dance, the bear lay there calmly, and the fisherman's wife closed her eyes and everyone who had ever begged for a miracle to happen understood that she was praying with complete faith for the cure of something.

"Thank you, boy," she muttered as she scrambled to her feet in disarray. "Thank you, my dear."

The girl had watched with curiosity, unmoved. With a stubbornness bordering on incipient madness, she kept her thoughts focused on Bruin.

In the days that followed, things began to assume an air of abnormality, and it's difficult to decide whether they carried the germ of it with them, or whether this was all ignited prematurely by the tragedy that was about to happen. Ottoman said that the bear trainers remained in the area for two weeks, that they were welcome everywhere in the villages that were walking distance away from each other, and that the girl was always present.

"Rich villages," said Joseph, "on the coast of a small stretch of sea, no more than an inlet of the North Sea, really, but fabled for its dangers."

Savoring the moment, he lowered his voice even further. He shifted his chair to the middle of the room, close to Lucie who, in her plaster cast, literally didn't move a muscle when she heard that in Dutch villages the houses are all made of beechwood, with tiles painted bright red, and that through the windowpanes you can see coffeepots, smoker's sets, birdcages, and mirrors. The windows in the back reveal small gardens with dovecotes and chicken runs and lines full of washing that is whiter and stiffer than a granny's bones.

Joseph smiled in the dusk. I understood him better than anyone.

"Brass bellpulls on the doors, brass lamps, brass flaps with springs on the mail slots . . ."

Here, in the kitchen, his restlessness has completely gone. Suddenly he has no need to go anywhere, because he can see everything perfectly well as it is. Details come to the fore. Ready-made stories slide from the murky past into the shining future. Friends! His eyes glide magnanimously along the paneling, the statuettes of the Virgin, the rubber plant, and the bookshelf. He doubtless knows how right it is to give people who are used to traveling and hoping for the best an idea of what they will encounter. Towers and windmills, funnel-shaped harbors far into the center of the country. Chilling rains that, even before you've seen them, appear in your dreams and provoke homesickness. Because the wind is always from the west, the houses are built leaning forward. All the trees are at an angle. The rivers are diked in. The roads bricked. From every tower there is music every quarter hour all day and all night and every child can read and write as well as the monks of the monastery of Sam Trapista near Zvigezda. Remember that the farmers' wives, like all farmers' wives, want children, health, and happiness in love, but there, in that country, books as well. There are prophecies that they will have bookcases full of them, leather bindings, gold spines. And as far as generosity is concerned, the people are tough, they amass their riches step by step, but sometimes, all of a sudden, they are seized with a fit of generosity, no one knows why, and they give strong black horses in the north. Flower plantations on the sea. They say that in the northeast they still keep slaves. Stay away from Limburg, and make sure you stay away from the southern borders.

"Good God, yes!" stammered Lucie after a silence.

And then, "Give me a cigarette, darling." He obeyed, but first took a deep drag on it himself.

"After three days, Theodorović began to imagine how much money he could make in those villages."

"How much, then?" Her tone was just as cozy as when she looked up from her account books.

Joseph actually answered. "At least the price of a horse."

They went from Naarden to Muiden, and then along a blue river with a cement bridge to Weesp, a big town, where they gave three performances, after which, at the turnoff to 's Graveland, they had to promise everyone they met that they'd be back within a week. Lazaro Theodorović and his people will always remember that this ill-fated journey was bathed in an autumn sun and the festive sound of church bells.

When they entered one of the larger localities, their first port of call was always the town hall. The mayors who received Theodorović in their chambers were, without exception, impressed by the distinction of the stranger dressed in rags and by the sum in cash he carried on him. Moreover, they knew about the cures, the popular entertainment, and the teachers who had invited Theodorović and his sister to bring the bears into their classrooms for a fee. There wasn't the slightest reason to refuse them a work permit.

The journey proceeded in this way in a peaceful atmosphere. The citizens of the area, hereditary farmers who were really not the most temperamental of people, were genuinely enchanted by the bears. They watched in amazement at the begging children of rich fathers. They showed their hands to the brazen wife of Theodorović to have the lines of their illusions explained and have the craziest things promised to them. You can't help but conclude that they sensed something in the whole exotic troupe, something, it's hard to tell what, that linked with their own nature.

"If those poxy dogs hadn't stuck their noses in, nothing would have happened," said Joseph.

The most loyal of the spectators was always the girl. She followed the group through the villages. Ginger, pale, her hair washed with honey soap, she stood without fail in the front row. It hadn't been difficult for her to induce her favorite, Bruin, to make closer contact. He twisted his head when she called him, and padded over to her. The bystanders waxed lyrical about it. Oh, the things the girl, proud of her good fortune, dares to do, and look at that huge bear taking that white loaf of bread from her! She talked to him, and the fact that he understood her, that something obscure, something essentially and eternally different, was nevertheless becoming part of her, was clear to her from the beating of her heart. One evening in bed she conjured up the image of the bear so powerfully that she couldn't get to sleep. Thinking of the ears and the paws, she had the feeling that she must console him at once. She slipped out of the silent house to the bicycle shed. When fifteen minutes later she arrived at a farmhouse on the coast near Valkeveen, she saw the Ursari sitting and eating in the curling smoke of the fire, and she found the barn she was looking for. She wasn't able to peer into the sweltering darkness for more than a few seconds before the Ursari gave her a slug of raki and a cigarette and sent her back to her father.

Joseph rubbed his face.

"What comes next, I'm reluctant to tell you."

He got up to pour himself some of the coffee that had gone cold. I looked at his back and knew that he meant the arrival of the gendarmes. I could feel that his mood was darkening. Damn it, the gendarmes arrived! And a rage seeped into his words, black as gall, that pervaded me too. The damn police. This was the confirmation of a premonition. Right from the start the wanderings had been accompanied by something evil in which the people of the Gooi, who had found the bears so delightful, so refined and wild, had absolutely no part. The Ursari hadn't really expected problems either. A pity for both of them that the gendarmes came to check up on them. Why, why on earth? Theodorović again showed his money. And his brother-in-law came up with the bottle of liquor. They pointed to the granny, who was really ancient, they smiled, everything about her was old, her bones, her tar-colored skin, and her eyes that still shone coal-black with the full measure of what she'd seen and forgotten again in her life. So why? Then came the eternal answer.

"Papers!"

It was two inspectors of the gendarmerie who disturbed that afternoon in Eemnes. Imagine the scene. There were a number of farm cottages, low and white. A square with a pump. A throng of people and animals in the still pleasant September sun. Then two men came forward who'd been standing at the back for a while. They were wearing long coats, kepis, and truncheons on their belts.

Theodorović showed his papers. His courtesies weren't reciprocated in any way. He then showed the papers on which he himself, his brother-in-law, and all the people and animals in his group were listed. They were completely in order.

On with the show, you'd think, no trouble at all, and indeed the performance was resumed. The bears danced, but Bruin especially was upset, and while the rebec spouted fire he just shuffled a bit. Some people decided they might as well go home.

A day later the police came from the neighboring town

of Laren to interrogate the wanderers about the legality of their nocturnal camp. It happened during a heavily attended performance. And in the center of Blaricum the following Tuesday, two policemen declared the ground at the foot of a magnificent chestnut tree a forbidden area for shows, and referred the strangers to a site that was suitable, but ugly — the ugliest site imaginable. Fewer and fewer spectators felt comfortable in the increasingly criminal atmosphere. That same week Theodorović decided to leave the area. And the girl, with a cold and the beginning of a fever, realized that that Sunday afternoon in Weesp would be the last.

I'll say goodbye, she must have thought on Sunday morning. What shall I wear? My party dress with a striped pattern? My earrings? My starched cap with gold pins? She opened a window of her bedroom and looked with a light-hearted feeling, not heavy at all, at the courtyard of her parents' home where the dogs were lying asleep. All of this will soon look colder and emptier. I'm going to wear my red corals.

I should mention that she had a temperature, and had slept badly that night. Toward one o'clock she gets her bike, I'm going to say goodbye, and pedals down an endless road lined with already yellowing poplars to what awaits her. Weesp. Again police. And Theodorović is standing shouting at a couple of pedestrians who find that this is really unsuitable for the Sabbath. What's happening here? she thinks, and puts her bike away as quickly as possible when she sees Bruin there, tethered to a post with a chain, waiting for her, supernaturally serene. I see that she immediately puts her arm around his neck, prods him gently. I don't even know the name of this girl who's about to die. What's wrong? she thinks. I don't know what's wrong with you, why are you growling, you're in a bad mood, but can't you see it's *me?*

She leans far forward, oh, what can I say, he's just

standing there on all fours. She pushes her head against his head, she strokes the ears, smells the breath, and then by the Immaculate Virgin, by all the blistering powers of hell, the image of the world blurs. The bear bites her, in a reflex, when she accidentally pushes one of her gold pins into his eye and a maddening moment from his early youth returns. He bites. Her astonishment changes to terror, her terror into concentration, her concentration into an awesome moment of assent. I'm appalled. A throat is bitten through with a short, hard crunch of the jaw.

There was a police investigation. It was established that Theodorović bore no responsibility for the drama in terms of the criminal law. After six days he was released, promising that he would take the bears to the zoo in Amsterdam. In reality he and his group left in a wide arc for the southeast, where together with the French animal tamer Charl Ismael Dollé they performed in Arnhem and later in the year crossed the border near Babberich.

2

I'll tell you about Parasja was what flashed through her mind one August morning. She'd heard about it from him years ago, when it was winter, but of course the story had never completely disappeared. Wheat and corn were high as she walked to the straw barn, there were poppies growing along the bank. Stories are like rivers. They draw water and air toward them, and they are constantly changing, but through everything they still remain themselves. She slid open the barn door with both hands. The cat shot out. The sunlight on the bales of straw was inviting. She sat down obediently, her eyes darkened.

Words can describe things that are in fact alien to you. Yet something can radiate from them that your heart already knew. I'll tell you about Parasja.

Her grandmother on her father's side saved her life. She was still small, about three, but she told me that she could remember everything and what she didn't remember was told her later. It was after the April War of 1941, when the whole kingdom had surrendered after only ten days and the Ustashi in the north began wiping out the Gypsies. Parasja's grandmother, Nenat Glan — imagine an imposing woman who smokes a stone pipe — was an experienced leader. We call them *puri dai*. She immediately prodded the family into action. She already knew in those first April days that it would be better if they left the campsite north of Zagreb. At a trot, with four caravans, the family took flight, Nenat and her blond husband Simon, their daughter, their two sons, all married and with children, and the family of Simon's half brother Lajos, of whom you'll hear more later. If I'm honest, I've got to say that he was an imbecile — well, a semi-imbecile and terribly proud into the bargain.

For a year they made grueling journeys through the areas in the provinces that they knew from long ago. They traveled through Turopolje, Cazin, Banja Luka; nowhere did they find anyone they knew. But even in the smallest hamlets, they did find traces of rape and murder. Sometimes, when they stopped in a place where the people were on their side, they were told where the Ustashi were hanging out and how they could keep out of reach of those evil people. And then they went on.

One day they were descending from the heights of the Prosara and after a considerable distance found themselves near the river Sava, where it is very wide. Downstream there were gigantic waterwheels that turn slowly with the power of the water and generate electricity. Can you picture it? Well, there what had to happen happened. I think that Nenat Glan must have badgered the family for at least an hour, she wanted to go on that same night, and she did, with Simon, with the family of Lajos, as well as Parasja who happened to be sleeping in her grandmother's caravan. The others were too tired. Six adults and more than fifteen children said they would catch up the next day and that evening camped on the water meadow. Seven mornings later Parasja stood with her grandmother in the same spot. She always said that every second of her life she could still see the skirts of her mother, her aunts, and her cousins turning with the waterwheel in the river.

Oh, you think that's been told too quickly? Must I do it better?

Well then, this is the story that Nenat Glan heard after seven days, when she appeared in the courtyard of a farmer who lived close to the site of the drama. The man took off his hat and crossed himself. It happened that very first night, he said. The family was camping on the grass on the bank. There was clover for the horses and good water. It had rained the whole day, but now it was dry and they lit a fire.

Two men had come to the farm to buy milk and meat. They were skinny, friendly men. They offered him a Bukhara carpet for sale.

Rada, thought Nenat Glan, Golubo! Her sons.

Well then, they lit their fires, they ate, and they went to bed. What time was it then? Ten o'clock? Eleven? Everything went quiet and you heard nothing except the water of the river being scooped up by the paddle wheel, falling and flowing on as always. The Ustashi came just before dawn. They were in a good mood. They'd been patrolling in the area around Sisak for days and before they went back to Zagreb intended to catch another group of Gypsies they'd heard were traveling around in the vicinity. Who passes on that kind of information? How can one know? Betrayal is simply with us all the days of our life. Someone went into the café where the Ustashi were drinking, cheerfully, with their tunics open, and told them exactly where the vagrants were camped and how to find the place.

Oh, and then everything took its rotten course. The Ustashi arrived in two trucks and stopped under the willows. And the Gypsies rushed in all directions and released the horses. They didn't have the ghost of a chance. The men in army coats, cheerful, yes, but also impatient because of the sight of the women, threw a grenade among the horses. Two or three of them gave orders. The Gypsy men had to be arrested. Why? Did they want justification for their operation? A tangible reason? Close by was the camp of Jasenovac, a somber, dreadful place behind barbed wire. But with a gate open for everyone who didn't belong to their own people. Serbs, Jews with their medallions on their chests, from the station they ran to the gate, driven on by the gunfire of the soldiers of the Ustasha state. There was an ironworks there, an embankment had to be built. A certain hangar, 3B, had no roof, no running water, and no food was ever brought there. It was the end of the line for the Gypsies.

There were two of them left. Golubo had been killed. The eldest boys had also been killed.

Dusan, thought Nenat Glan, Wansjo, Remi!

Meanwhile it had begun to rain. The wind picked up. Rada, Parasja's father, was tied to the shaft of a caravan. Around him on the wet meadow the children were hurriedly cut down and the women were pressed to the ground by two or three men at once. Not that much later, perhaps twenty minutes, the chore began of dragging the bodies to the river by their arms and legs. At this spot the bed of the river Sava is deeply hollowed out. On the bank there was a variety of plant that hangs forward, close together, with stalks full of leaves that bend and spring back above the water's surface. The bodies floated to the surface after a few days. Parasja must have seen how a couple of them, with their skirts spread wide, were carried along in the dripping arc of the wheel.

* * *

As I've already said, her father was called Rada, Rada Georgević. If I don't tell you about him and what happened to him after the horror, I'm not telling you enough about Parasja. Right then, he and her uncle Janko were carted off that morning, wedged between Ustashi in a truck. Janko had been completely disoriented by what had happened, but Rada felt colder than a frozen stone covered in ice. As he endured the pressure of the shoulders and thighs of the men next to him, he knew that in less than an hour his life had changed into something hard and dirty. For starters, the members of his family were lying dead in the meadow.

The route followed the bends in the river in a southerly direction and then turned off. Through the open back of the truck he could see burnt-out houses of Serbs in the landscape — black trees — it was strange to see a fat pig just wandering around.

Near Gradina the road again came out by the river. There, in the shallows, was a wretched boat. They stopped. This is where they were heading for. This was the miserable ferry that linked the bank with the camp of Jasenovac on the other side. The Ustashi, tired and out of sorts by this time, fired a salvo to call the ferryman. From a hovel a man with oars appeared. Perhaps a minute after the ramp was raised, a yard or so from the bank, Rada and Janko dived into the water. Janko was lost immediately, a hail of bullets right through him. But Rada made it in the gray, overcast weather, floating beneath the surface, swimming, resting in the mist among the driftwood against the bank. It lasted for two days. Then he was noticed by a man with an axe in his hand. Who said nothing, but smiled earnestly at him in the reeds because he could guess what it was like to be on the run. Rada followed the woodcutter to a hut at the edge of a field of young corn. A woman pointed him to a sheepskin behind the stove. He slept in the warmth, in the smell of wood, and those who sleep feel a soft arm around their waist. Yet it made no difference at all to his fate.

Now a man appeared, Josip Broz, remember that name. In fact, all his life everyone called him by his nickname, Broz, but Josip Broz was his real name and the woodcutter who took Rada to the mountains knew it. "Right! You want to fight? Well, what are we waiting for?" And then the name was mentioned that would remain of central importance to Rada. A day later he was with the partisans.

Oh, and he liked it, that life where thought was action. Always on the move, sometimes on horseback, ten or a hundred men at once. The partisans captured village after village. The losses were enormous. They set up their bases in Muslim and Serb regions, and liberated the country around. All of this happened under the command of a distant voice, Josip Broz, who maintained lengthy, friendly radio contact with his *plukovniks* from the front in the south. They were cruel times. For every German killed, fifty to a hundred Communists were put up against the wall. Both evil and good assumed abnormal forms. Those men of Josip Broz. Rada felt comfortable with the extreme violence they used, but was amazed by their well-washed and shaven faces. They also cursed little and didn't rape very much. A soldier who had stolen two potatoes from a comrade had the barrel of a carbine placed against his head and: bang!

Listen to the rest. In the summer Rada hears that Broz's army has broken through a heavy encirclement, by Germans, or by the Italians, because don't forget that the Italians are still involved, and that he is on his way to the north with his wounded and all. At that point Rada's group gets moving too. They travel along roads of murder and destruction through massacred villages into Croatia. Every Ustasha they catch is killed — no one worries about that. But no civilian, good or bad, has anything to fear, because that's the code of Broz's troops. Northward, beyond Jajce, Rada is given a horse and sent on ahead as a scout for a munitions transport. By then he has long been regarded as a hardened soldier, brave and wild. Next morning he meets the already legendary Josip Broz at his headquarters, a man in a light uniform, tanned, steel gray hair, and with those blue eyes, perhaps you know them, that can stay cool in the worst fury. As for him, he too is expertly shaven.

From that day on he and Comrade Stari — the Old Man, as the leader was sometimes called — went on quite a few expeditions together. Through Kula, Prozo, Bosanski Petrovac, they came to the small Bosnian town of Bihać. A meeting was held, proud, large, at least five times as large as the population of the town itself, since by the end of that year Broz's army numbered eight divisions, each with three complete brigades. That's what you call power. Rada looked at the red flags, shouted the *Smrt Fašizmu!*, death to Fascism! and drank raki from crates full of bottles requisitioned from the best distilleries. But peace was not the order of the day for him. Happiness, that is, the portents of joy, is something he experienced only when he felt the heartbeat of war again.

They captured Jablonica. In February they cut through the lines of the Chetniks on Prenj Mountain and retreated into the heart of Montenegro. There, at the end of the winter, the most violent battles of the war were fought between partisans and Chetniks. A battle between brothers, oh, is there anything more furious and magnificent than a battle for one's own land? I know that Rada didn't give a damn. Our kind doesn't fight for this or that area. Nevertheless here we have Rada, one of Broz's *plukovniks*, a man with a ragged mustache and terrifying courage, cruelty, low cunning, everything necessary to sharpen the knife in his heart. A man of utter fury. Do you understand when I say that the loyalty to Broz, the affection for that soldier, emanated from his former life?

Let me tell you the rest of the story. Rada was there when whole divisions of Italians deserted and the Germans, very strong, with elite troops, were forced to give up area after area. The winter was severe. The sky ideal for bombardment. At night the snowfields spit flames and earth. Rada moved from firefight to firefight with his battalion, to areas where everything exploded. When they sang at a serene hour and hot coffee was made and they said, "Soon, after the war, everything will be better," he strolled off with a look of indifference and stretched out on the ground to sleep.

Oh, and then one fine day he was with them when they entered the capital. The White Palace was requisitioned by Broz. The Royal Palace and a beautiful villa went for the partisan marshal, who among his people had a Gypsy taking beautiful care of the horses in the stables in the back garden. Things were to turn out differently. Fact is, things would go to the dogs. Damn it, just imagine. In that jubilant city, in the footsteps of the famous Broz, Rada could not know that ten or eleven years later he would be hunted by the police, a criminal, who in peacetime had a nostalgia and predilection for weapons.

In May 1955 in the prison grounds of Mitrovica an execution was called off at the last moment. When Rada was let out of the gate, he realized that the marshal, the man whose bust you find in even the smallest village, had heard about his case. You see. And had remembered a comrade from the struggle.

Is this the end? The story of a life? Let me say that someone saw him sitting in a café in Zagreb not long afterward. A rascally Gypsy, with a mustache out to his ears, playing tunes on an accordion.

But you're right. I must get back to Parasja. Are the children asleep? Leave the dividing door open and sit down again. That's enough about Rada. Did she ever see him again? No, never. Not that I'm aware of. That said, one last thing: Wasn't he her father? Oh. Let me talk. I like a good sprinkling of digressions. Because the story about Parasja, here in my head, is a plain that I can travel through for days without crossing. That I can't see the end of. Where's the road? There isn't one. Really not. Parasja is my blindfold.

At the time when her father escaped the executioner by the skin of his teeth, she was seventeen. A girl with blacker than black hair that, divided in two, flowed down her Tartar's face. Her lips laughed of their own accord, I've never seen that since. Even later when I lived with her sadness, her face kept the expression of a woman with a radiant humor. She had been brought up in the tradition. Nenat Glan and her husband Simon, the latter recently dead at the time when this takes place, had instilled the old Gypsy law in her. The Romani Krissi flowed through her head and her heart. So it was nothing less than a disaster when, in the summer of 1956, I think, she chose the wrong man. The wrong one: Imagine a twenty-year-old Rom, a Dutchman, but with a Lowara pedigree, which like hers went back via the Balkans to prerevolutionary Russia and from there to God knows where. And with a grandmother on her father's side whose Ursari family came from the area of Karnobad, near Burgas in eastern Bulgaria. They were bear trainers and horse dealers. Well, this is how it went: In the summer in question the twenty-year-old Rom, touring Europe incessantly in his car, bumped into his Ursari family in Bosnia. He saw immediately that these were people who knew how to live. Uncles, aunts, children who delighted in dancing feet. What he also saw at once was the black tent of half-rotted goatskin in which Dragica, the old woman of the family, chose to live. It was the ancient kind of shelter of the former mountain dwellers. He felt at ease with those people. He felt like traveling with them for the rest of the summer.

On we go, then! At the end of August, getting on for the feast of Santa Maria, he alighted with his family on the site of an abandoned monastery near Maricka, which is north of Banja Luka. The sun had already set. He was helping out with pitching the tent and with the caravans. He saw the vague outlines of other caravans. They told him that they belonged to such and such a family. Almost immediately he realized, with his eye and his heart, that there was something wrong between the two families, but no one told him anything that evening. The next day, he met her. It was a look, nothing more, exchanged in a field among the horses, but Dragica had seen the truth straight through the ragged goatskins. "Hey! Gypsy! Did you speak to that woman?" she cried as he walked past.

"Yes," he lied. "Aren't I allowed to, then?"

"You mustn't tempt the evil God."

Then she explained to him why there must be no intermarriage between the two families.

"Take off your shoes and come and sit next to me. By the ancient Virgin of my mother, by the white scorched God, how on earth can I avert the disaster!"

It had begun with a matter of offended honor, she told him. Her eldest son, Bajka, had called Parasja's imbecile uncle an asshole. Yes, Lajos the madman who two years ago at the entry into the horse market at Sitnica was determined to ride at the front at all costs. His argument was that he was the eldest of three sons who were already married men.

Now Bajka, according to everyone, had a level-headed nature, created for friendship and honor. Although most of the horses they were going to sell had been groomed and bridled by his people, he was intending to let Lajos, that knucklehead, have his way. Near Sitnica the group of horsemen reached a small bridge. It was no more than a plank across a pool. At the edge of the mud there were pigs. Lajos pushed forward so abruptly on his stallion that Bajka had no choice but to go through the pigsty. Yes, and pandemonium followed. Men roared, rage bared its claws. Simon, old but still in the saddle, tried to persuade his half brother with his whip to make a timely excuse. But then that word, in all its ugliness, came from Bajka's mouth. Asshole — it was heard by everyone.

Dragica took a drag of her cigarette and shook her head. She hugged herself. "From then on the worst thing was the fermenting of rancor. The two began spying on each other. I saw the drama catching fire long before things came to a head one evening toward dusk. The crunching of bone, their fists could easily have settled it. But at a fateful moment Lajos fell and hit his head on the rusty reinforcement of a concrete edge. His eyes stayed open. A light-colored liquid ran from his hair. Then he lay in a coma for at least twenty days in the hospital of Jajce. There are still screws at the side of his head."

Ah, that's murder! There's no doubt about it. And murder calls forth murder. Two families are at the beginning of a vendetta that cries out for victims. Not exactly a pleasant prospect. For cases of this kind we have the *krissi*, the very secret judiciary of the Sinti and the Roma. A sentence, severe, by impersonal judges, is the only thing that can cure what cannot be remedied. The trial of Uncle Bajka was held two months after the crime. A café in Trieste filled with men who had traveled, sometimes from very distant countries, because of the gravity of the matter. There were hundreds of them. The parties directly involved had been able to put their case, but had to remain silent during the session. The verdict came in the middle of the night. Bajka had to pay his victim a fine of thirty thousand German marks. In order not to offend the latter, he must stay out of his immediate vicinity for five years. In the meantime no man from his family would be able to marry a woman from the victim's family.

Only now did Dragica look me straight in the eye. She said, "Listen, lad, that blood money turned out to be the easiest bit. It was paid a year later, and was burnt by Lajos the very same day."

And then she said nothing more. She no doubt thought that the whole matter, and the rules that went with it, must be clear enough. And you too may well say: Of course, where's the problem? A man has been warned and he knows he must watch his manners. But look, that's easily said, because the following day I met Parasja again and she looked at me, straight at me, and let me pass along a path leading to a stream that was sparkling in the first sunlight. Birdsong. Smell of young tobacco. Parasja was a girl with deep black eyes that, ah . . . what more must I say about them? A beautiful song, perhaps, might make them glow again.

In the campsite both parties became immediately aware of the infatuation. No one saw them together, no one even heard them say a thing to each other, but everyone was losing his or her head over it. Quick-tempered and terribly jealous of their own honor. One of the girls had only to be careless and throw washing water in the wrong place in the stream for things to go awry. And the horses would be stamping their hooves, restless.

On the third day things turned bad between Nenat Glan and Dragica. When they met each other, by chance under the trees, Nenat Glan suddenly remembered that one of her great-grandchildren had been sick all night and crying. She walked straight past. Of course, she walked on and so did the other woman, but they'd looked at each other. When they were back on their home ground, Nenat Glan in her sheet-metal caravan, Dragica in her tent, those looks came to life. "May the rotting flesh fall off your bones!" cries a loud woman's voice suddenly through the camp, and soon Dragica is accused of sorcery. "Nenat Glan is descended from the dogs and everyone on this black earth knows it" is her immediate response.

"*Pustistu!*" Drop dead! It can't get any worse and what happens then? Exactly. Two ancient furies, each with a full head of steam, come tottering out of their holes. Both of them mad as hell and all the families in the campsite flocking to watch.

Do they enjoy the fists, the clenched lips? When Nenat Glan and Dragica, cursing without restraint, turn carefully and without the slightest haste head straight for each other, the audience makes room between the tents and the caravans. "Comb seller!" "Half-breed!" Isn't there anyone to stop these two? Now they are thirty paces from each other. Does the public really want to calmly watch the gory spectacle of our two grandmothers scratching each other's eyes out?

Well, that's a shame, because other things happen. At ten arm's lengths from each other they stand stock-still. They don't budge another inch. Oh, those two still know how to curse, with singsong voices they go on heaping imprecations on each other's heads. "May the Goat's Foot roast the souls of your ancestors to the end of time!" "May the scurvy Satan . . ."

Summer afternoon. A site where bone-dry washing is left hanging in the sun. Silence after a great quarrel. You can imagine it, I assume. You can imagine the caravans on the stinging nettles flattened by wheels, the children, the horses, the wretched horseflies. You may think that the rage has burnt itself out, but that isn't the case. It's simply located in other spheres. In sadness, for instance. After her retreat Nenat Glan sits down in her caravan. Her lips are muttering, first silently, then moaning. Suddenly she howls like a she-wolf on the plain for her dead husband Simon and blames his death on her enemy. Dragica. I assume you can imagine how she pounds the ground with her fist. "Your fault, Nenat, that my son was sentenced!" That night Parasja and the Dutch Gypsy elope together.

They take a pair of Lajos's horses and quickly cross the cornfield. They follow a path upward. The ground becomes stony, they see a valley with dark yellow farms, the moon is half full. He calls to the girl, who still hasn't said a word, to ask if she's tired yet. "There's a haystack farther on," she shouts back. "There's a river too!"

They keep going in the direction of Busnovi, plum trees, on their left a wooden mosque.

"Just a bit farther!" she cries.

It's approaching Santa Maria, the time when the summer's warmth stays hanging in the air for twenty-four hours a day. It's he who sees the excellent spot first.

"Enough. Stop!" He reins in, jumps to the ground. "So here we are!"

When she slides from the saddle, he takes her by the waist. There isn't a moment, on that hasty journey, when he has *not* felt the movement and the shape of that waist. And the glow. And you surely know what it's like when everything around you is simply bursting with those things? The haystack, a tobacco field, within hearing distance a stream where for three nights the toads sit singing. Can you imagine that all this flows at the same rhythm as your blood? He and Parasja, and that's the world. Or should I now say, now that everything has been accomplished, simply: Parasja, for three nights so terribly beautiful under those blue-tinted skies. They fish in the river. They catch hedgehogs. He doesn't know what's happened, but he knows that this girl is his soul. By the fourth day they are so sure of each other that they saddle the horses again. What they want are cheerful faces and the blessing. They imagine that everyone in the camp will regard them as a couple from this moment on. They have no doubt about it. Unhurriedly, but eager to return, they retrace their route. They think that over there, they're already lighting fires, and they've bought wine. The feud has taken its toll on everyone, but now there's an overwhelming need for a few good songs.

The caravans are there. But all is silence. And empty. Dragica's *kumpania* has already upped stakes and left. Later Parasja explains that she saw the curse of Nenat Glan sitting like a crow in the trees.

Six years go by. Parasja and he travel through the countries of Europe and they do so in the company of his family. Nikolaus Andrias, also a Dutchman by birth, has received Parasja as pleasantly as possible. His first wife and two sons were driven into the gas chambers during the war. Now Kata, a Hungarian Gypsy woman from a family of coppersmiths, who gave him his new eldest son and two daughters, immediately embraces Parasja. She keeps a hopeful eye on her monthly wash.

But the seasons go by and nothing happens that points to the greatest family reward. Nevertheless Parasja and he are happy. I maintain that. He buys, sells, and trains horses, she provides food and thinks of the children that they are simply bound to have one day. He argues with his cousins Branco and Sanyi about the profitability of the motor trade. She attracts the attention of gentile ladies in villages and towns and seizes their reluctant hands. I maintain that in that first stage of their lives together, there wasn't a cloud in the sky. At night, against his cheek, her heart beat like a young bird's. I'm telling you as well as I am able what it was like. Before she crawled under the quilt with him, she appealed to the ancient Virgin of Kiev in the glow of a prayer lamp. Mumbling and crossing herself again and again, she made a whole series of curtsies before the icon.

Then as time passes she loses heart. He doesn't realize immediately, even today he can't exactly remember when that happened, but she stops her fertility measures. What were they again? Things like making him suck a raw egg and getting him to spit it into her mouth. One fine day she stops believing in all that. But she goes on cooking fantastically well. And she maintains a friendly expression on her face. She's too close. He doesn't see that she has had enough of her body that stays as firm and smooth as a girl's. The curse of Nenat Glan? It weighs heavier and heavier.

One day they're standing in a meadow near the Ammersee in southern Germany. It's still early in the morning. Parasja has gotten up at about six o'clock. She wants to be at a neighboring farmhouse for milking time. She takes a milk can with her. When she comes back she gives the full can to her sister-in-law, walks on without a word, and climbs the steps to her kitchen. Her husband is standing in front of a mirror clipping his mustache.

"Oh, damn!" she says. "They're there!"

He knows immediately who she means.

"They're camped behind the reeds a little farther on. I saw the caravan tracks when I went to fetch milk."

He says, with the scissors still close to his lips, "Do you mind telling me what you mean?"

He looks at her seriously in the cracked mirror. She wants to leave him. He realizes it instantly and with retroactive force. The need to leave him has been nagging in her ears for a long time, she hasn't been able to listen to anything else.

"Lajos has no horses anymore. There's a big Mercedes next to his caravan."

"Well, well," he says, and turns to face her. He knows what she's been working at all those weeks, with her senses primed. She has been piloting her family toward the reeds near the Ammersee.

"Have you said hello yet?"

She lowers her eyes. "Not yet."

In the evening he and Parasja are strolling along the banks of the lake. In the skimming light of a low-lying sun that turns the water a copper color, kaugi ducks are swimming about. When they return there is the irresistible smell of a roast in the camp. Parasja is given a golden-brown leg. He sees her gnawing at it with joy. The bottle of raki goes around. Cigarettes, pipes. The Andrias family smokes and is rather silent. At night he hears her snoring against his shoulder. That's how it was. Do you know what makes you lower your head? What you can't understand. In the early morning she again took the milk can and went down the steps of the caravan.

A sigh. That was Lucie. Who realized that it was over and done with, completely. She saw her father sitting at the table reading the newspaper. On the other side of the corridor Hanzi, Katharina, and Jojo were asleep. She'd put them to bed an hour ago.

Joseph had got up from his chair. He'd like to take a quick look at the horses. It was getting on toward nine.

"But did he never see her again?" she asked.

He took something off the sideboard and put it back again. He gave no sign of having understood her.

"Didn't he look for her everywhere then?"

One of the dogs stood stretching next to the stove with its back arched, with much wagging of the tail. Full of happiness the animal looked at Joseph. Who now went to the hall and put on his coat and boots. She watched them through the dark window in which the furniture was reflected. She saw the other dog running toward him across the yard. There was a hard-edged moon in the sky. Still full of the mood of the story, Lucie looked from the shreds of cloud to the privet hedge that she had pruned that afternoon. The branches were still lying on the ground. When Joseph came back after about half an hour, he brought in with him a draft of air from outside. His face had a contented expression. He went over to the television. At the moment that he pushed the button, she asked again, "Did he never see her again, then?"

3

Not her."
The television was on a table in the corner next to the window. Joseph pulled up a chair so that he could reach the buttons without much trouble. Images of a western appeared — horses, cattle, a woman with nice breasts. Gerard also turned his chair around. He watched along with them with one elbow still on the table. His large shadow fell on the wall between the windows.

"Who did he see, then?" she asked.

"Lajos!" Joseph leaned back. The sound of the television was loud. "Lajos and Bajka," he yelled.

Lucie turned and went over to the cupboard to get ham, mustard, and bread. As she presented the plate, she said, "Those two!"

Gerard and Joseph watched television. Gerard had poured a glass of gin for himself and his son-in-law. "I might as well have one too," said Lucie. She pushed her glass toward him. While Gerard carefully managed the bottle, he thought: I wish they'd be quiet for a while.

"Those two!" his daughter repeated at that moment.

Joseph replied without taking his eyes off the film. "Yes, goddammit. It was three — no, four summers back in Vienna!"

Lucie served another helping and then, with her face turned toward Gerard and Joseph, sat down by the side of the television, blocking the sun-drenched pictures of horses in full gallop a little, unintentionally, by paying absolutely no attention to them. This Gypsy, her thoughts went on nagging, and those two who've actually brought him bad luck. They saw each other in Vienna.

"Look," said Joseph to Gerard. "Look at that wild calf!" And to Lucie, "Do you want to know the details?"

She nodded. "Oh yes. I'd really like to."

"He had bumped into Bajka, his uncle, Dragica's eldest son, in Lechfeld, when he was going to Vienna. Bajka maintained that Lajos had spoken to him that night in his sleep. That he had said, 'All right, I'm going to die. Let's grant each other forgiveness before I'm forever lying low in my grave.' Because of the great distance his voice had been very faint!"

Now Joseph also muted his shouting. Gerard had turned the sound of the television down. Struck by he knew not what, he was now listening too.

"He went along with him. He drove behind Bajka and his wife to Vienna where Lajos, having grown rich — God only knows how — was living in a house. 'Comb your hair,' said Bajka's wife when they arrived in the middle of the night. He too was impressed by the house on the edge of the city. So much light came from the windows that the cars and caravans of the families on the hill sparkled in the rain. The weather was awful. In the courtyard he saw people around fires under lean-tos made of canvas. The wind played with the flames. 'Come, friend.' Past rooms full of people and children playing on the stairs, he followed Bajka, the cousin of his dead father, to the deathbed where he came to settle the issue of forgiveness while it was still possible."

Gerard glanced to the side, very briefly. Then he brought his eyes back into line with those of Joseph, who, with a sunny landscape at eye level, said, "There he lay. In bed, with his hands folded under his head as if he were simply listening to the rain against the windows. His eyes were trained on the door. He grinned cheerfully when Bajka walked toward the bed, and seemed not to have noticed at all that somebody else had come in, a younger man who sat down shyly in the corner next to a cupboard. Lajos didn't look at all as if he was to be mourned within the next twenty-four hours. His hair lay over the pillow and his hand with the golden rings squeezed Bajka's hand powerfully. Nothing indicated that the women would soon start screaming and tearing their hair in this yard, and that an Orthodox priest would be required to sing his texts at the edge of an open grave, above a passionate wailing, while nearby there would be a tussle to prevent an inconsolable old woman from plunging into the grave.

"'It's me, Bajka.'

"'I knew, brother, that it was you.'

"And his voice sounded deeper, and with more sense in it than it had all his life.

"'How do you feel?'

"'I'm done for.'

"'You look pretty well, though.'

"'Well, then, have another look, I'd say.'

"'You've become a rich man, Lajos. You've got a house.'

"'Yes, a house. You can hear the stairs creaking. You can feel the strength of the walls. When the wind blows you can hear the trees in the street. Still, a house wears you out in the long run.'

"They started talking as people everywhere talk when night comes. At night you've all the time in the world. He, in the corner next to the cupboard, had given his thoughts free rein. They could do what they wanted. Meanwhile, he sat and looked at the shadows moving over the ceiling and listened to the night. A gust of wind made the closed windows shake. A tile slipped down with a sharp swish. He looked at Lajos, among the pillows on his bed, and remembered the screws that he had once had in his head through Bajka's doing. It seemed to him that those screws, of which there was no sign, had maybe not done any harm to the brains in that head.

"'I was an idiot.'

"He could hear that the two men were magnanimously forgiving each other.

"'No, damn it! It was because there was a devilish fire in me. Do you remember how hot it was that summer? The marrow in your bones melted.'"

Gerard had got up, for no good reason really. He walked into the middle of the kitchen in his socks. Hands in his pockets, head bent, he stood there for a while and didn't know what thoughts were guiding him. Did he want to go to bed? Then he saw the half-smoked cigar lying in the ashtray. He took a long time relighting it. Without surprise he noticed that Joseph had meanwhile stopped talking about the house in Vienna with the dying man.

"Sit down, Dad," said Joseph.

He sat down again as he'd been sitting, with his face toward the television screen, and then was told what he'd missed in the film.

"They escaped," Joseph explained earnestly. "Those cowboys jumped into the saddle, in one swift movement, one leap. It was unbelievable, and they escaped, shooting like maniacs."

For a moment they both sat intently watching the

soundless images. Out of the corner of his eye Joseph must have seen Lucie put her arm out to him, because he hunted through his pockets and handed her his lighter without looking away. "As I was saying," he went on, "there was nothing to indicate that within a few hours Lajos would be dragged into the courtyard on his death mattress. It was a rotten night to die, a rotten night. The wind sometimes seemed to be coming out of the clouds, and then in huge gusts out of the ground. Eight men were leaping around with oilskin sheets, and had the greatest difficulty in making sure that Lajos, lying in front of the stable door, didn't get wet in the rain. From one moment to the next he started to look really terrible, with hollow cheeks and hair that was already falling out. Suddenly it seemed to be a miracle that his soul hadn't started on its journey days before.

"Which was not the case. Earlier that night, still a prince in his own bedroom, he had even knocked back a last glass with Bajka.

"'Listen, Bajka,' he'd said. 'There's the bottle. Come on, man.'

"And then he had rolled his eyes, looked around, and finally seen that in the corner next to the cupboard there was a completely unknown person.

"'There you are, Lajos.'

"'Thanks a lot, *phral*.' He brought the glass to his mouth, took a good swig, and hiccuped. His eyelids trembled. With great effort, but without a spark of fire, he then looked from the shadows on the ceiling to the figure in the corner, who had the vague impassive appearance that outsiders simply always have.

"At that moment Nenat Glan had come in."

"What!" cried Lucie, really surprised. "Was she still alive then?"

"Oh yes," said Joseph. "Why not? She must have been in her eighties by then." He made a resigned gesture. "She'll live to be a hundred."

And he bent forward to put the sound of the film back on, orchestral music, nasal American, and rifle shots. Lucie now pulled her chair up too. Together they followed the chain of events that after approximately ten minutes resulted with perfect logic in a happy ending.

All peace and light, finally? Lucie smiled in the blue light of a last muslin dress. Probably she thought nothing else except, how nice, how sweet! Gerard yawned and pushed his chair back a little. His mind was still on the forgiveness, on the deathbed, which, with the wind and the rain at the windows, had somehow appealed to him. Did he see two men in front of him, just those two, because the third one was too vague for him? It really beats everything that's happened between them all those years. A swearword — *asshole*, now, I *ask* you — a head with screws in it, and a ban on marriage. Gerard hooked his thumbs into his vest pockets. As an elderly man and a farmer he probably knew that this was a well-known chain: insult, crime, punishment. With the basically quite sensible idea of deathbed forgiveness. There's always something nice about a happy ending.

Yet there had been someone else sitting in the corner next to the cupboard. With a blind spot on one side of his heart. Gerard stood up. His face had resumed its surly expression. As an elderly livestock farmer and market gardener he might have little time for abstractions, but there are a few experiences that go on lingering in his head. Evil has produced a debt. Some things, in creation, go into the red. Then there is the settling of accounts. The debt is gone, evil is left by itself. As what? As a natural phenomenon? As a dark thing? The Devil only knows. At the dividing door he stopped as if he were hesitating about going to his bedroom across the hall. Then his eye caught sight of the clock. Let me say goodnight. Why should I stay up late tonight? Let me just take off my suit and crawl into bed. But as an embittered Twente farmer I should like to point out that there are some things that can't be forgiven.

Part Four

1

*M*ust one forgive deliberate acts of baseness? But that's the last thing those acts of baseness need! Mrs. Nicolien Nieboer-Ploeg didn't have an unhappy childhood. For a start. You could present magnificent excuses for her: Little Nicolien was savagely beaten as a child, humiliated and neglected, and here you have the consequences. But that just isn't the case. The case is treachery. And the traitor is a young woman who at the age of twenty-seven has no need at all to be ashamed of her life story. A pity for psychology. A pity for science too, but informing on those who attacked distribution offices, from the summer of 1943 to the spring of 1944, can't be traced back through rational examination. Resolute, vital evil is simply part of the system of the world. The woman who is prepared to name names does so with all her heart. There's scarcely any question of self-interest. Can you call a glass of cognac at a party with foreign officers an interest? That same week, of her own free will and completely in her right mind, she tips them off about a house where a couple of residents, father and a son of scarcely twenty, will be put on the shooting range near the Twente airport. With blindfolds on. Look. Two life stories end at a stroke and a third, hers, continues for the time being. Imagine that she was still alive at this moment. How would she accommodate half a dozen dead people in her autobiography? It doesn't clarify anything to ask yourself that.

Until the summer of 1979 Gerard had never told his daughter how and by whom he had been betrayed. That summer he was to break his silence, but because he was not a talker, it's doubtful whether Lucie, a receptive creature but also quite a simple soul, could deduce enough from his words. She listened to him while she sat at the stone table in front of the house filling jars approximately a quarter full with well-washed blueberries. Gerard sat watching. She would later pour as much sugar as berries through a bone-dry funnel. He was puffing at a cigar butt and for some unknown reason suddenly started in about the war. And she listened with half an ear. Well enough to understand who and what Jannosch Franz was? Anyone who tells his life story is bound to touch on that of others. Familiar passages from one autobiography are sometimes heartrendingly absent in the other. What a pair. Gerard tells the facts. They are enough for me at any rate to form a pretty good picture of what happened.

Nicolien Nieboer-Ploeg was a woman with beautiful blond hair and a voice that on the telephone had a sharp edge to it. Men were attracted by her youth and her hospitality: She had been left alone with two small children when her husband had been transported to Aschersleben as a prisoner of war in May 1943. Now she gave amusing parties in the family holiday home at Benckelo. Gramophone music, *Liebling, wir müssen uns wiederseh'n* . . . on the edge of the woods. Thanks to the military people stationed nearby, she was never short of guests. There were plenty of devotees. Like the security police from the Dienststelle in Almelo, like those of the Prinsenstraat in Enschede. Kriminal-Assistent Jürgen L. also stood with her in her drawing room on more than one occasion downing strong drinks that made him cough. She liked it when he asked her where she'd learned to speak foreign languages so well. When a little while later he asked her, "Can't you tell me anything interesting about the resistance here, Nicolien?" she liked that too, though she couldn't have said why.

One Saturday she noticed that the conversation in the Matenweg Bakery stopped when she entered the shop. Someone from the underground had been arrested, a fuel dealer against whom the Kriminal-Assistent had no proof, however — she knew about it. She broke the silence. "God," she said. "Damn it. Esmeyer. What rotten luck. I heard about it." She put exactly the right degree of understanding into her look and her voice, and in the afternoon the primary school teacher dropped by to see her. Could she possibly do anything to help? She glowed with willingness as she poured tea from her Rosenthal pot. A day later Esmeyer was released.

Without doubt she had relished this, this feat, I mean, but what she really relished were the eyes. Those of a couple of farmers, a shopkeeper, civil servants at the town hall: a random assortment of people in the area began looking at her seriously, and sometimes, when she returned their looks, it gave her an exuberant feeling of success.

Kriminal-Assistent Jürgen L. meanwhile kept visiting her. He brought her stockings and soap, played with the children before they went to bed, stayed for dinner, accompanied her to her bedroom for an hour or two, and one autumn night just before leaving asked her for a small favor he was sure she would do for him, infiltrating the Twente resistance.

Since the end of July 1943 serious combat teams had entered into operations. Students, ex-soldiers, and workers wanting to avoid the forced-labor Einsatz in Germany had gone underground in large numbers and needed ration cards. Nicolien Nieboer pulled a sympathetic face that evening when L. told her about the security police's concerns in Almelo and Enschede — there had been a sabotage incident on the railway, attacks on town halls and distribution offices, the annoying theft of cars and weapons, and the escape of prisoners from police stations. He couldn't trust the municipal police in Enschede, he complained.

She accompanied him quietly to the hall. As he took his cap off the hat rack, he casually suggested the method of friendly infiltration. "All that is needed from you is a bit of effort, and they'll trust you," he said. It wasn't the small fry he was after, he made clear to her, but the leaders, of course.

She opened the door for him. With a mocking laugh she said, "What if I started by having someone in hiding come live with me?"

She took someone in, a difficult case, a Jew, already elderly, with an appearance that spoke for itself. She negotiated the ransoming of two post office employees who had connected a clandestine telephone line. These were fast-moving times. The arbitrary system of death and terror was working without a break and anybody who wanted to fight it needed a quick intuition. Mrs. Nicolien Nieboer-Ploeg was trusted. She was soon able to report to the Dienststelle in what houses in the surrounding area meetings were held.

That is what brought her close to Gerard. No small fry, she'd been told. I don't know if Gerard and Jannosch were small fry, they broke in and stole distribution documents, that was one thing. Then, the other thing was that the airplane crews shot down sometimes had a way of disappearing without a trace in Twente. L. found it hard to accept that those airmen should return to their units in England and Canada as if nothing had happened. So when she told him one fine day that the leader of the escape route was a greengrocer from Hengelo, he laughed. Laughing too, she said,

"He's called Jules. He talks with a French accent." She then added that Jules had organized a meeting for that Saturday in a given farmhouse.

It turned out to be her first failure, what a pity. The leading figure they were looking for didn't show up, sick, she heard later. And so, Gerard's farm had been surrounded for nothing. A week of planning, then a second failure, something to do with prisoners who were to be freed by the underground around Nijverdal, a nice ambush had already been laid, but who showed up? Not a soul. The situation was becoming intolerable. L. was no longer prepared to wait. Attacks were now being carried out on a weekly basis in Twente and Salland. At the end of January he decided to attack the few hitherto undisturbed addresses in Borne, Wierden, Markelo, Goor, and Enter about which he had been tipped off by Nicolien Nieboer. When he told her, she nodded. She'd like nothing better. She too felt impatience and, deep in her heart, an unreal kind of adrenaline. She had this desire to see things for herself. Leaning forward, she placed her warm, dry hands on L.'s desk.

"My dear, I'd like to see things close up for once."

That is how one evening in January she became part of the difficulties at Gerard's home. Cars had stopped in the front yard. Doors had been pushed open and dogs leaped in. In the farmhouse kitchen three men and a woman had jumped up from behind the table. In a fraction of a second they realized what the pandemonium outside meant. A fraction of a second — no more.

But still long enough for the men and the woman to look at each other for a moment in the smoky room.

Gerard was the first to run out. Ignoring the clear eyes of Nicolien Nieboer, he grabbed the weapon under his coat. But they were already inside. Before Netty, Gerard's wife, had even drawn the front door bolt, five or six men with machine pistols had forced their way through the rear of the house. The suspects were disarmed and hit from all sides. One of them, a dark rogue, leaned forward and gave such a swipe with his elbow that a youngish sergeant of the Home Guard began gasping heavily. Only the woman was treated with some respect, although she also had to put her hands behind her head and had fast-moving fingers frisking her whole body.

Then outside. Wind. In the darkness were the cars. The four who had been arrested were pushed to the right. One of them felt a tingling in her breast. With her eyes wide open she walked past the black, wide-branched linden trees. We don't know what her thoughts were at that moment, she probably couldn't understand them herself. That same evening she would be back home, and that was that. Nicolien Nieboer-Ploeg, one of those cases that occur in every war, and not only there. But what about the others?

Gerard was the kind of man whose only ambition was to keep his business and his family on track. At the time he was thirty-three years old, and married to a woman from Friesland, a woman with a clear head, proud, good-natured, who supported him fully in his dangerous activities. They had a daughter of two who slept a great deal and couldn't yet speak. He was thrown into the car under a shower of blows, his nose broken, his mouth cut to pieces. He felt no regret. Until recently, he had never allowed his life to be dominated by any ideology whatsoever. His decisions were those of a congenitally conservative farmer. He didn't want to go to any extremes, certainly not to be a hero, and so one may wonder where he got his courage from. The backseat of the car was soft. He crashed on the velvet. Licking the blood from his mouth he certainly feared the immediate future but didn't think of death. And indeed he was to eventually return to his family.

The number two man was also to see his loved ones again. The police sergeant, who had been living underground for a few months, was a practicing member of the Calvinist Church. At the beginning, like many of his colleagues, he'd always "seen nothing" when they had to hunt for people in hiding. His religious conviction told him that terror wasn't his department. One day a remarkable young leading member of a resistance group from Meppel landed in the guardroom of his station. The sergeant found him sitting writing a letter of farewell at an iron table — one of those tables that are screwed to the floor. A moment later a police pistol was placed on top of the letter to his mother. That evening the doors were unbolted, the resistance man escaped, and the police sergeant's cover was of course completely blown. Can one assume that that winter, in the name of his strict faith, he had used illegal force, subject to severe penalties? Handcuffed to Gerard and also badly beaten, he too fell into the car.

Then the last one. Jannosch lived in a caravan in the woods between Benckelo and Driene. It was six feet wide and twelve feet long and accommodated himself, his wife, and their three small children. Besides this room on wheels there was another, in which his brother lived with his family. It was illegal. The head of the German police in the Netherlands had decreed that summer that absolutely no one could travel around anymore. All caravans had to go to one of a number of large camps that could be easily guarded. To think that this was exactly in accordance with the ideas of the senior Dutch civil servants! Much to the liking of the Director of Social Services who in May 1940 had found the new circumstances useful in at least one respect — *The caravans must go* — and had written as much in a government brochure.

But quite a few remained, certainly in the initial period.

Next to garbage dumps, by cemeteries, and at the edges of fallow fields you could see the caravans, complete with their wild, strange occupants who, according to the Welfare Department, belonged to the antisocial type.

Jannosch too refused to be interned. Why should he? He was a headstrong man, and in a certain sense innocent, he'd been used to police ordinances all his life. So he continued to travel with his family and the families of his brother and cousin from Gaasterland to the Hondsrug, and then on to Twente, the Achterhoek, and back to Salland, because all his life he'd been used to roads and horses and the rattle of wheels. Accustomed to the contours of villages toward which you drove in the early morning. The markets, the addresses of your regular customers for grinding and blacksmithing work. The blue sky full of starlings above the cherry orchards in the Betuwe, when the ladders have been placed against the trees. The picking season, the harvest, the fires on the emptied potato fields when everyone feels like telling a story. The pubs where a farmer taps you on the shoulder because the following morning he needs you to go out in the fields with the deep plow with eight or ten horses in front of it. The spring rains. The trade in umbrellas. The summer nights when your feet stick out of the back doors. The horse dealing. The brown November sky with the stars out very early between the branches of the trees. Peddling yarn and ribbon. The snowed-in villages and the women shivering in the doorways inspecting your baskets and mats. All that work, that gap in the market that demands not order but flexibility. But the policymakers can't stand you. Your nomadic behavior is a personal challenge to them. The Dutch government regards the tendencies of your kind as a mental defect. You give them the shivers and they talk about antisocial behavior.

He was thrown onto the floor of a truck with his arms

tied behind him. Troops on either side of him. They lit up cigarettes and carried on cursing a little, still intoxicated by their triumph. The cars bumped their way out of the farm-yard. Jannosch recognized the road with its potholes and bends, but didn't feel that he was in fact heading steeply downhill. There was the village, the shop, the pub where no one would ever see him again. He lay with his ear against the wooden floor. Past the crossroads a right-angled turn. He recognized the road to Hengelo and far away in the woods felt the warmth of Gisela and the children, but not the awfulness of farewell.

How can a man who is so crazy about his family and his relatives, a show-off who has the knack of avoiding conflicts with authority, have got himself into such a mess? Perhaps out of loyalty with Internal Affairs, which wanted to segregate the annoying vagrant population from the rest of the nation behind a huge iron fence or else an earthwork barrier? It's not easy to find an answer.

It had all got very difficult by 1943. Jannosch had asked the police no less than three times to waive the ban on traveling, using the argument of the pursuit of his occupation, and three times the answer was no. He and his brother went underground with their families in the woods near Benckelo, their cousin and his family sneaked into a hovel in Zutphen. Their entrepreneurial flair was no longer any use. People had become scared, and often hostile. In Wierden complaints were made. In Benckelo they said, "They're still in the woods, beyond the path to 't Stroof," but went no further than that. A few people helped. "Listen, Jannosch," said Gerard in the early autumn. "Better put that nice horse of yours in my stable. Then he'll keep dry and we can feed him."

They were standing behind Jannosch's caravan and looking at the stallion, which was already getting thin.

"How do we know those bastards won't come and get him?" asked Jannosch.

"They'll stay away for the time being," said Gerard, thinking of his two best Gelderland horses that had been requisitioned in August. "They've already been around to mine."

It was the time when the Wellingtons and the B26s flew over the northern Netherlands to the German cities. Planes were regularly shot down and the crews had to be picked up and taken across the border to the south. The trains were patrolled by Dutch and also German police with a list of missing persons who ordered travelers to show their papers at random. When Gerard had asked Jannosch one day whether he would help one of them, one of those pilots, escape through the woods, the Gypsy — purely according to the code of friendship — hadn't hesitated for a moment, he had just nodded.

She didn't discover the address immediately. Gerard and Netty's farmhouse was outside the village. The fact that an occasional farmhand who never had a shovel in his hand was suddenly digging with boundless energy in the vegetable garden was not noticeable, nor was the lodger with the bleached hair who was afraid of the dog. People came and went. Sometimes there was suddenly a sociable guest, some Tom or John with a heart of gold who didn't understand a word of Dutch but had learned to cycle on the path past the orchard. That kind of customer usually wound up with Jannosch Franz. I imagine how the Gypsy and the Allied foreigner have settled themselves in the trap in the pitch black of night, with blankets and headgear made of sheep-skins and mole fur. A bag at their feet. "Are you sitting okay?" asks Gerard. "Yes, we're sitting okay, just open the gate." Jannosch gives his horse a quiet command.

Now back to the evening in January, a date that can't have been any more ominous than the rest of the calendar in those days. The weather has been gray all day, with rain clouds that toward six o'clock merge imperceptibly with the darkness. At seven o'clock the farm lies there cold and still, with just a bicycle by the door and a dog sprawled longingly under a lean-to. No sign of the horse that will shortly be fitted with saddlebags by the farmer's wife.

There's an operation on this evening. It will be a well-prepared raid in which three men and a woman will take part. When I think of that evening I think first of all of the moments before the woman comes in along the tiled hall and, half amused and half contemptuous because of the inner knowledge she has, pops up in the kitchen doorway with a "Here we are, then!" It is the moment when Gerard, Jannosch, and the policeman are sitting waiting for her impatiently, because she is the one who has been able to borrow Controller De Krol's car for one or at most two hours.

In front of them on the table there is a map. They are looking at it, but do not discuss much because their attention is focused on the cold and silence outside. Within the hour the town hall in Delden will be broken into. The woman will keep watch by the car and the three of them will ring the bell, give the password, and then tie up or knock unconscious the civilian custodian, from the Dutch Nazi Party. Then they must remember to turn off the alarm. The ration cards, inserts, and control stamps are in fireproof safes behind the distribution rooms. They'll get those first, and then, if the whole business goes as easily as they anticipate, they'll mess up the system of personal registration of the municipality by taking the population files and the pedigree books and breeding licences, which, except for the blank passes — Ausweise — will later be burnt in Gerard's backyard. The Zwolle district of the Dutch underground is in desperate need of distribution documents. The ration cards will be transported that very same night by Jannosch in his saddlebags.

There is the sound of the car. Gerard walks to the window, pulls the blackout curtain aside and sees the round yellow headlights turning onto the path. A dog rushes outside, hair on end, but the animal will only leap around the visitor a little: She is an habitué.

Fine, everything's going according to plan, the only question is, whose plan is it? Gerard stands by the table again and the other two are busy exchanging cigarettes and lights when the woman, almost on time, appears in the doorway and turns the whole scene — conspirators, kitchen stove, chairs and table, coffee cups, ashtray, and hanging lamp — into something desperately absurd.

"Here we are, then!"

She unbuttons her coat, her face set in an expression of greeting, and smiles at Gerard and the policeman, both of whom she's gotten to know very well. When she turns to Jannosch, at her ease and still standing, she clarifies her smile by extending a hand. She makes eye contact and offers her name.

"Here," says Gerard, when she has sat down between him and Jannosch. He places his outspread fingers on the plan of the municipal office. She cranes her neck. "Here's the situation."

Lively but unconvinced, she joins in the conversation about the details of doors, corridors, rooms, and the alarm. The policeman is now leaning over the table, all useless attention, but the other man, the one with the coal-black eyes, restricts himself to the occasional nod. She glances in curiosity at the dark hand resting on the table, very thin, a cigarette between the fingers. He takes deep drags on it and keeps the smoke in his lungs.

She — I note — has no idea who he is. Nor where he comes from or with whom he's connected. For a few weeks she and her friend the Kriminal-Assistent have been looking for an opening in an illegal escape route. The man whom the lady now has next to her is someone used to going his own way. Yet, almost without knowing it himself, he is a member of the organization of Jules Haeck, a wholesaler in vegetables and fruit in Hengelo, a Frenchman by birth, who helps prisoners of war and shot-down airmen across the border. Recently a trap was set for the man from Hengelo. Reliable information obtained by Mrs. Nieboer came to nothing because of the illness of this leading figure. Only in October, when everything in the farmhouse is long over and done with and Netty is living there alone with her silent daughter, will the man from Hengelo be caught through the agency of other people and shot after a few days. Even then, however, it won't have become clear exactly how many fugitives from Twente and Salland found their way to Limburg and from there through untraceable channels to Nancy, then on to the south of France.

"So we'll go via Beckum," she says now.

And Gerard nods. They're talking about the shortest route and how and where they can attract as little attention as possible.

"Yes," he says. "Just after the crossroads you can take the back roads across the heath."

"I've got it." She brings her face close to the army map in front of them. She scratches her chin. "Fine," she says softly. "And then?"

Gerard looks from her to the two others. "We'll keep to the sandy road, then the canal." He thinks for a moment, drums with his fingers on the map. "I think it's best if we take the Wiekbrug."

"Seems good to me." The policeman coughs, he can feel a dryness in his throat. Reaching for the packet of cigarettes on the table, he says, "It comes out onto the Hengelo road. It's a minute from there."

He opens the packet with a deft movement and offers it to the others. Gerard is still smoking, Jannosch accepts, and Nicolien Nieboer, who ordinarily is someone who prefers to stay healthy, reckons that this evening she mustn't refuse. "Thanks."

Does she feel that ashtrays and cigarette butts are part of the props of danger? That the sharp taste in the nose and throat combine excellently with the sharpness of disobedience and that the smell and the smoke, which drifts blindly in all directions, are perfectly compatible with the craziness, the silent triumph of going your own way in the face of all the regulations? She sits in the smoke-filled den of the kitchen. Can you picture it? We can assume that, inhaling treacherously, she can in her mind's eye picture what battle-handed combat troops can expect as recompense for the mortal danger they endure; the reward coupons in each pack of cigarettes — sometimes five or six per man.

The light in the kitchen is pretty hazy. The smoke is so thick that the black blind in front of the windows has taken on a look that, if not celestial, is at least bluish and transparent. A silence falls. There's a short moment of complete peace in which none of the three men can imagine himself standing one day like a begging dog watching a smoke ring curling clandestinely from under a table. Nevertheless, this will happen. Nevertheless, within the foreseeable future, they will see tobacco no longer as a compensation but as a gift from the gods. A cigarette stub, a few puffs on a pipe as a safe-conduct that allows you to have your thoughts transported from the avenue through the camp to the beautiful moonlight above the parade ground. Another world, unimaginable as yet, and Jannosch will tug a Polish fellow prisoner by the arm and lure him with gestures into a corner in Block 34. A quick look around. Then he opens his hand and shows the Pole a block of margarine. *"Drei,"* says the Pole. Jannosch knows the black market prices too. Impudently he says, *"Fünf."* A block of fat has a new owner, a dim Pole who doesn't realize that for five cigarettes he could have got a good hunk of bread too.

"Oh, thank you," she says again, emphatically, as the ashtray is pushed toward her.

A little longer. Gerard looks at his watch. From the farmhouse just outside Benckelo to the municipal offices in Delden it's about twenty minutes by car.

Those twenty minutes haven't started yet.

"Shall we have a quick one?"

He and Jannosch are used to having a stiff drink of something shortly before a job. This evening is no exception.

Weapons, gloves, sacks to put the loot in, rope. The coming hour is gone over once again in three heads. But what's relevant is what's going on in the fourth one: They must have left the Dienststelle in Enschede half an hour ago, she thinks to herself.

Then there's the fraction of a second that has already been mentioned, is already known about and could be passed over now. No, listen. All of them have shot up from the table. As Gerard turns away with a furious leap, he meets the eyes of Nicolien Nieboer. Is one ever aware of what is happening in one's life? In a single look there's occasionally a sharp knife with which you can cut something loose from the world. His heart contracts. Not now, but many months later he will observe with revealing clarity how those eyes darted from the windows back to the table and went around, from one to the other. When they crossed his he caught something of a speechless, very strange pleasure.

I'd like to know if she listened that time. Nothing could be read from her face except the instructions to fill Kilner jars a quarter full with berries and sugar. Then I saw her feel in her apron pocket again and, sure enough, bring out black French cigarettes and a lighter. At the stone table under the linden trees, under the August sky, Lucie was busy with the first phase of preparing blueberry gin. As she did so she cast the occasional glance at her father, who'd sat down near her. The not very talkative Gerard obviously felt a need to express himself that afternoon. His words had flowed on for quite a while. I think that his daughter was listening, but I'm not sure to whom exactly she was listening. With a Gitane in the corner of her mouth, she poured sugar through a funnel and the only thing she felt was an inexpressible longing.

She'd been talking a lot that summer about an Appaloosa.

Gerard had of course noticed something of his daughter's autumnal mood. For months she'd been getting up at five o'clock to exercise the top horses Linda, Walton Beauty, and Viking in turn over the ripe and tall fields. She also looked after the broodmares together with the stable boy, and the one- and two-year-olds and her husband's favorite, Bellaheleen, the prize winner. So why did she need a tiger horse as well? More than once, when they were sitting having coffee at around nine-thirty in the morning, Gerard heard her holding forth in a kind of intoxicated rhapsody about the light undercoat of an American purebred, with a pattern of yellow or brown patches on its head and body.

At other moments, he found her very silent. She would be feeding the geese, and when he asked her something, she didn't necessarily give him an answer that made sense. How was he to know that in this heat, with a glazed look, as if she'd been switched off, under the brim of a sun hat, she had already tuned her ears completely to the winter season? In the garden the tomatoes rotted on the vines. Insects buzzed among the trees. The moments became more and more numerous when nothing existed for her except that one compelling voice. The voice that on winter evenings told her things she couldn't always fully understand. Gerard had sat down opposite her at the terrace table. I can imagine that the slight air of madness hanging around his daughter infected not only me but him too. The atmosphere of messages from afar. The concerns, mythological in scope, of a very present absent person. The scope of the story is that it attracts related stories to it. Gerard looked at the busy woman's hands and began talking about the past.

More than thirty-five years ago. January 1944. Himself and an ex-policeman and a Gypsy. The awareness of having fallen into a trap in his own house. The traitor was Mrs. Nicolien Nieboer-Ploeg, who seemed helpful and had once sent her little son to him on his bike with the message that they would be looking for somebody in hiding here or there. He still remembered the attraction of resistance operations, the sense that you'd actually been made for them. The Gypsy called himself Jannosch Franz. You never know the real names of those people. Jannosch Franz was a crafty man who knew every area, every country road from here to the Belgium-France border. At the age of thirty-one he already had a family of three children and a fourth on the way. Gerard had occasionally been inside that caravan. Dark faces. An icon cabinet with saints behind glass. Of the three of them he was the only one not to return after the liberation.

With an imperturbable expression Lucie was cutting out squares of cellophane. What was she thinking about as she put them over the Kilner jars and pulled them taut with a red rubber band? Something precious? Shall we say an Appaloosa? A mystery about which her heart wanted to know everything, now that another mystery was still wandering through Central Europe and for the time being was giving no sign of life? Gerard put his cigar on the edge of the table and talked about a missing resistance fighter. A strange guy with an unmistakable accent, illiterate. Who did she think of when Gerard told her that only after the fight on that last evening had he seen him without his black moleskin hat? God knows, but it may be that this daughter's heart is shrewder than her head.

The jars were done. Lucie got up to put them away in a warm place indoors; after about ten days, when the sugar had melted, she would fill them to the brim with young gin. Gerard took one in each hand too.

"That son of his," he said, "he sometimes brought him here. A lad of six or seven."

2

I was born at night during a snowstorm. My mother was lying under a caravan in the Dutch part of the woods between Nijmegen and Cleves. Those caravans have high wheels. My mother had crawled underneath with an aunt and a sister-in-law after the side where the wind was howling had been covered with branches and rags. I wasn't long in coming. "A son!" cried the aunt and the sister-in-law. As the snowflakes swirled past, my mother held me tight. She whispered a name in my ear that she would never repeat to a living soul. Not long afterward she straightened her back, with me tucked in the warmth of her woolen cardigan. She smoothed her three or four skirts and clambered back inside, to her warm goose-down quilt. And how she slept!

That's how it went, when the southeast corner below Nijmegen had been turned into a winter tundra. My family wanted to lie very low for a while, do a bit of trading with the farmers, just enough to buy food and fodder. It was too cold for anything else. When it's cold you don't want too many strange faces around, you prefer a little peace. The rotten thing is that that day at the crack of dawn, at about half past seven, ten gendarmes cut through the pristine white wood on bikes. They found three snowed-in caravans and horses under a stretched piece of oilskin.

May those bloodhounds be thoroughly cursed by their offspring! May they catch the raging scabies!

My father hurriedly slipped his shoes on, cursing all the while, but assumed a polite expression when he told them as he handed over his papers that a son had been born that night, whom he wanted to register according to the rules at the town hall and have entered under his lawful name in the records. There is a kind of inconvenience that barks — checks, swearing, we don't make a fuss about that — and there is inconvenience that bites. My family had to leave there and then. Under the strict supervision of ten cyclists my family went back to the border post where it had been let through a few days before.

How old was I then? Ten hours, perhaps.

And less than a week later I was back in the land of my birth, because what's a border? Moonlight, and a cart track. Shadows past a shadow. With the aid of a passport carefully selected by my father, I have since then been known as Joseph Plato, son of Jan Andrias Plato and Gisela Nanna Demestre.

My parents: impossible to know the course of their lives. And yet I feel a longing that looks and listens, quite separate from the ordinary things that happen. You can't explain it.

From my father I know that he had five brothers, four sisters, fourteen male and sixteen female cousins. They'd been born in Russia, Transylvania, Croatia, Germany, Scandinavia, or Holland. Some of them were in possession of a very precious local passport. My father was a skinny, muscular chap who could swear fantastically without any malice, I loved to listen to him. He, his brothers, and his cousins were blacksmiths and horse dealers, and when they were asked on Saturday to come to the pub in the evening with their violins, or to a farmer's barn, they would negotiate a price and then give a whole spectacle including the number with a dagger tucked in their boots. I heard and saw that musical rumpus on my mother's lap. You don't forget things like that.

In the first years of the war my father simply went on with his horses, he had customers in the east of the Netherlands and they knew they could trust him. In Twente he drove off one January evening and never returned to the campsite. And that's a mystery. The ultimate facts are missing from the truth about my father, which after all is my truth too. They exist, and they're powerful enough, I assume, but they're totally invisible. There's no voice left that can tell what trap my father was on his way to that evening. Silence. And what happened then, up to the end. Again, not a sound.

The long dry summers with the sunlight till late in the evening among the caravans were reassuring. My father was a versatile man, so they said. He could mow, sheave, fish, and carve wood. In the container under his caravan, beside a bellows, there was a stock of well-maintained tongs and hammers for shoeing horses. His greatest talent was trade. If I go back far enough, I can find something of his calm superiority in my spirit. It must have been in the penultimate autumn that one day people checking the license plates of the caravan or men from the census or something like that came. I am about six and in a little jacket buttoned up tight, with a scarf on, I'm stroking a blond pony with droopy ears as I look at the group in front of our caravan. With their backs to me: three men in homburg hats and someone from the border police wearing a flat metal helmet. Opposite them is my father, shorter in stature than they are. He has pushed the brim of his hat so far down that only his nose and the chin catch a bit of light. Hands in pockets. He doesn't say a word. Dressed in a rumpled suit and a pullover he waits with a barely perceptible smile until the delegation has got to the point. An audience between the shafts. Amenability. A few yards away a washing line full of clothes.

Then I remember that my father didn't defy the bunch of them all by himself. Half turned away from him, facing me, stands a solidly built, beautiful woman, with her hair hidden under a scarf. She holds her hands entwined under her breasts, her elbows wide, and is carrying a child on her left arm. Her whole face is bathed in light. Frowning forehead, broad jaws, she has opened her mouth as though she wants to tell me to do something, something trivial, something about the pony, that must be done despite the invasion of the authorities. This is Gisela, my mother, who I think is carrying the two-year-old Umay.

I know more about them.

A few mornings after the disappearance in 1944 my father's Styrian stallion came trotting up to the caravan in the wood by itself. It was on that horse that my mother rode to the police station in Benckelo, and my uncle went with her. They were told absolutely nothing there. Nothing. No one knew anything, so they said. All that happened was that my mother and my uncle immediately had to leave the municipality, leave their illegal site and clear off to one of the big assembly camps, they suggested the one near Westerbork. My mother was pregnant. She wanted to go to 's Hertogenbosch, where her Sinti family was camped. There, after the passage of some months, we experienced May 16, the evil spring day. We had to take the train. By sending me off the train along with my cousin Paulko, my mother ensured that my life would go on normally. I heard later about her end, and that of Wielja and Umay and Leitschie, who was less than two months old.

When that news came, everyone was talking about liberation and I too was in the mood to feel that the worst was over. A mistake. Oh, the cold had been terrible that winter,

I won't deny it, and no one can imagine the way I was chilled to the bone at the time. The news came in November. We'd spent the summer with the farmers in Brabant, without problems, because Paulko was a good thresher, oats and barley with the flail, and I cleaned out the pigsties. September had ended very bleakly and you only had to look at the sky to know what was coming — cold and misery. Paulko wanted to go to the family in Rotterdam. There we lost touch with each other. How and where?

We arrived at the beginning of November and discovered that only a sister of my mother's, Guta, was still living in Katendrecht with two small children. A week after our arrival the whole city filled up with soldiers and Paulko was caught during a roundup. Auntie Guta and I saw him coming along Hoofdweg with the men selected for transportation. It was early in the afternoon, rain, a terrible throng of women and children. Paulko wasn't wearing an overcoat, just a jacket, and open shoes. He'd been picked up in the street just like that. Guta put a hand in her bag — Paulko! — and threw him a loaf. All the women did that. They threw packets, ran forward with blankets, and cried, "The House of Orange forever!" until the soldiers had had enough and started shooting. We saw the thousands of men jogging in the direction of the windmills. Paulko had to dig fortifications in the Achterhoek. He survived. A sergeant-major had smashed his nose, he told us when he came back, but apart from that the German army hadn't been so bad.

As I said, the cold came at the end of November. Rotterdam had started to starve. There was no fuel left. After we'd burned all the wood from the inside of Auntie Guta's house, we left one morning in the direction of Holland's southern islands. We planned to hide in the straw barns, we wanted to have immediate salvation — begging from the farmer — in sight.

Under clouds scudding from the west, a woman and a boy pushed a cart with a couple of children shrouded in blankets through an area of plowed fields and water. The weather was harsh that year, colder than usual. In December the freeze set in. Guta was a very strong woman with calming eyes. We walked and walked and sometimes we got something to eat and sometimes we didn't. We sometimes slept under a roof, among animal noises, sometimes in the snow. One thing's for certain: The farmers saved us.

There was a severe freeze in January and an icy northeast wind. We were in the vicinity of Rhenen. When it's very cold you soon get a headache, and afterward, because everything has changed, you feel a drowsy weariness. Water has become ice, and metal feels burning hot. There are moments, when the sun goes down and the sky has become pale red, when you don't give a damn anymore where you are. Under the roof of a frozen and destroyed shunting yard Guta and we children reached a state of peaceful apathy. We crawled away into a corner, felt that our lives were no longer worth anything, and no longer thought of it.

Then? Then the moaning of the wind like a ghost. Yes, and on one of those mornings when it was still almost dark, a sound that pierced the wailing and suddenly drowned it out with an exuberant quacking that our sleepy souls couldn't possibly remain deaf to: wild ducks. A whole flight of fat brown teal had landed between the rails in front of our eyes.

By God and his almighty miraculous power, said Guta. What shall we do? She crawled forward on her hands and knees.

So, we caught one and ate it after we had boiled it in a large tin can. How did we get hold of hot water? Well, for weeks and weeks we'd been trading with the houses in the area using coal dust and the cinders hidden in the ground of the shunting yard, like gold. I dug it out with my fingers on the morning of the duck. One day a woman burst into tears when she saw my crooked hands as black as birds' talons.

Don't just stand there in the doorway!

We were allowed to stay and eat for a whole week and sit by the stove. When we went off again I was wearing knitted sheep's wool mittens.

We experienced the liberation in Colmschate at the beginning of April. Guta had already buried her baby by then. There were three of us. We ran across the meadows through fire and a pounding bombardment and dived into a cellar with a couple of families and a German soldier who was also frightened. Ah, and then I saw the war directly through a barred window. For one or two days it went on! If only we could crawl deeper into the ground, said Guta. I looked at the cannon in the farmyard. They barked every minute. Soldiers ran around bent double. If they were hit they simply lay where they were. While grenades flew over the stables and everything shook, the farmer's wife left the cellar to cook porridge upstairs. Big fire over Deventer way, she said when she came back with the pot in her hands. I saw it through the kitchen door. A day of silence dawned. Then a couple of tanks turned into the yard with a frenzied roar, greenish monsters with antennae on top like a crab's. In them sat soldiers wearing olive drab uniforms, helmets and headphones, throwing cigarettes at people. The sun appeared. A flag was already hanging out of the house on the other side of the road.

Oh yes, liberation, and everyone could reemerge and get on with their lives. Back home, back to their life story. May was magnificent that year. In the countryside the orchards were in blossom and the rivers rippled in the wind. In the course of the summer, people who had been deported started to come back. There were very few of the Jews and Gypsies. It turned out later that of the Dutch Gypsies, almost all Sinti who'd been arrested, only sixteen women and fourteen men returned, no children. Paulko and I were reunited in August with the help of the Red Cross. After that we could not believe that nowhere, not in The Hague, not in 's Hertogenbosch or IJsselstein or Oldenzaal, were there any of our people camped.

One day we went to one of the Philips buildings in Eindhoven. Uncle Nikolaus was lying in an emergency hospital there with detached kidneys. He didn't say a word. Only afterward did I get to hear through him the last facts about my mother, my sisters, and my little brother. And that marked everything that happened subsequently in my life. The train from Eindhoven had arrived in Assen that afternoon. Those who had been arrested, guarded by the Dutch police, were transferred to the train to Westerbork. Arrival in Westerbork at four o'clock. Uncle Nikolaus and his family arrived after eight on a train from The Hague. All the Gypsies had their heads shorn and were robbed of their baggage, jewelry, and violins. The shame of men and women having to undress together in one place is terrible for a Gypsy. After three days the train to Auschwitz. When they arrived there was music played by a nice orchestra. There they were left alive until the end of the month of July. Then the last parade of the last six thousand remaining Gypsies. The Dutch Gypsies were among them. They were selected by doctors. Nikolaus Andrias was young and he belonged with the workers who were directed to the right. To work. He saw Gisela and her children together with his wife and sons in the other group, on the left, destined for the trucks into the forest.

No story is ever told for the sake of its denouement. No one's life coincides with its end.

Oh, so I've noticed, but supposing that end is so heavy, so black and huge that it gets in the way of all kinds of other things? The ordinary things, let's say, that the child wants to inherit from its parents? When Paulko got married there was a party with a young bull on the spit. When two years after his survival Nikolaus married the daughter of a Kalderascha from Hungary, Kata, the *verbunkos* was danced at the wedding. The *verbunkos* is a dance in two-four time with a rhythm that carries one away and enchants. I may have been ten years old, ten, and for the rest of my life I wouldn't take a step, not even a dance step, without taking with me what had happened to my father and my mother and the whole procession of members of my family. That's why I say: The worst part came after the liberation — the reports, the unmistakable last facts.

Can you ever come to terms with those?

They lived on in everything that came afterward. In the homes in which I was placed by child care authorities. In my escapes from them. In the police collecting me from the caravan site and taking me back, under guard and with a stick in my trouser leg, to the institutions where they wanted to teach me to read and write. Education, certainly, with some of the higher things that human beings are capable of. But those last facts lived on in the hours of the night when I lay awake and those when I slept. I was difficult, furious at the smallest provocation. The things that were handed down to me, in me and my daily doings, did not appear so exalted.

Were the measures of the occupation withdrawn? Or of the years before?

When I was thirteen I traveled around with a few members of my family who'd appeared from the border region.

We weren't allowed to camp anywhere. There were always police who drove us away like riffraff! We had to go on, travel on within twenty-four hours, or go back to the place we'd come from. Away from Tilburg. From Enschede. Arnhem! In Arnhem we were camped in two caravans, respectable households, and the police raided us with a squad of thirty men. We were allowed to stay for one night, and the following morning all the roads were cordoned off by policemen with riot shields, dogs with them. The government made trouble for us just as before. You must realize that they were already preparing the law that later came, designed to make us all into citizens and lump us together with the rest of the caravan dwellers. Can you imagine it? The dismembering of our souls? Large educational camps where there was everything: welfare workers, a clubhouse, a soccer field. Oh yes, they came, complete with barriers and a police post. We were told through loudspeakers when it was time to take a shower. Grown men, men of name and reputation who knew their way all over Europe, were rationed to two beers an evening. Because by the wounds of Jesus there were fights! There was no work, of course, after all the scissor sharpeners and car wreckers had been dumped together in one area!

Anyone who thinks up camps also thinks up the good and bad use of those camps. In those sites where there was no place for families to drop by and no one could leave without a permit, there were no bloodhounds. But apart from that, everything was in place to let loose all hell on you again.

I'll jump ahead a bit, and that brings me to Guta. I'm talking about the time when Guta, in a camp near Rotterdam, told me her dream. I came home last night, she said. It was summer. The trees were in leaf. I walked toward a fire that had been built in front of our caravan. All my brothers and sisters were sitting there talking. When I arrived they looked up and said nothing more. I recognized them all. I saw that my eldest brother needed to shave his beard and wanted me to get the mirror from the caravan for him. But they kept looking, with those wide-open eyes, until I realized that I had to go, because I was alive and they were not.

That's what Guta told me that time. And another time she said she hated seeing the pipe of the Pernis refinery from her caravan, she meant the tall pipe with flames coming out of it. She hated the railway line too. And the wire around the camp.

I've been through quite a lot on the borders and on the side of the road with the men in matching uniforms who, like God's own villains, are forever strolling toward you with Article 61 on their stupid faces! God grant I may keep the lid on my rage, but it gets to you, believe me, those eternal gendarme escorts! Even though your papers are more or less in order, even though you've got money, ordinary people no longer trust you.

From Belgium we arrived in Best. We wanted to do some shopping. The Best police kept us out of the village with reinforcements from all over the area. By about two o'clock we'd had enough and issued an ultimatum: If we haven't eaten by four o'clock we're going to break right through the cordon with our cars. By the time the riot squad arrived from Eindhoven, we were already rolling barrels out of the road. Curse all those bastards and let their ugly mugs be smashed, the police wanted to keep us in Germany at any price! After a while the mayor came. A well-mannered man wearing his chain of office. Oh, and then he and Nikolaus Andrias simply talked, in a civilized way. We'll head in the direction of Venlo and the border, Nikolaus decreed after an hour.

In those days he'd been living with Kata for quite a

while and his son Sanyi was seven. He was friendly to me, but remained timid and didn't laugh much. When we were sitting together in the evening, he sometimes got a bit drunk and I would see him crying, silently as a decent man, a man whose family doesn't understand the twists and turns of fate.

This brings me to the summer of my wedding. That was when I met my Ursari family in Bosnia and spent time with people who were brimful of life. The most exuberant of them was Dragica, an old woman from a tribe that went far back in time. She wanted to go on a pilgrimage to the mountains near Suha Gora, because that was where, so she said, the Virgin had appeared. Look, those Ursari weren't Christians, were not Catholic or Orthodox in the first instance, but followed the Muslim creed. Yet they missed no opportunity to worship the Virgin passionately because She, they believed, had the loveliest form, the sweetest smile, the most understanding heart, the most beautiful clothes.

Lad, said Dragica, no trouble is too great to calm your soul. Just to be on the safe side, I observe Ramadan. Pray. Sing with an imploring voice to appease our ancestors, it's far from safe in this life. We went into the mountains in the burning sun. Among the rocks and bushes the vision was indeed beheld by some of us. And without a trace of madness. I did not want to force my eyes. I simply say that I know very well what it's worth to have someone with you, on the road, someone to think of and sometimes, when it so happens, to address in words. Someone who can get very exalted.

About three days later I met Parasja. And Dragica saw my look and got angry. By the cheating Devil himself, she screamed, why this one Gypsy woman of all people?

I maintain that we were happy! Imagine us in a caravan built of sheet metal, eighteen feet long. With glass in the doors through which you can see St. George and the

Dragon shining. After a year I got rid of the horses and bought an Opel, then a dark green Wolseley with air conditioning and side mirrors that you could adjust from inside. Parasja went into the villages with a fine assortment of combs, elastics, shoe and stove polish in front of her on a tray. She sang, screamed in her Gypsy way, and got along well with my Dutch family, but after six years her fertility still hadn't been blessed. That was it. I don't need to say any more about it. When she left, I assumed that that woman would go her own way in my heart, that she would continue making her trail of laughter, walking and singing without ever appearing again.

And that's what happened, for many years?

By all the saints of my mother, I don't say that this isn't possible. I went on wandering, although I'd been with you for a long time, Lucie. I'm not denying that for a long time I'd been a happy man, a wife, children — a man wants to have his dignity. But I traveled around in the summer and crossed that path now and again. Without being set on it, that's true, without imagining anything about it at all, I sometimes heard where she was hanging out and that she had remarried and had children, good for her! Longings? Particular memories? No, not at all. I lived the varied life of little towns, camps teeming with children, family, and I liked that. Nothing more. I was cheerful. Really at ease. What? No. If I was aware of the nice horse business in the east of the Netherlands I didn't think about it. How do you explain that? Sea air, country air, and nocturnal smells of sun-scorched fields, flowers, always different. I never thought of you amid all this, Lucie.

Go traveling, then! Drizzle has already accompanied the spring for quite a while. The orchard has finished blossoming.

For a couple of weeks urges — going far back into European history to the lifestyle of caravan and tent dwellers — have begun to take over your thoughts. Off you go! A huge sense of relief came over you today. It isn't that you're not delighted with your house, your animals, your father-in-law, your wife and your children, because on this May morning of all mornings everything is shining with enchantment, but you're on the point of leaving. Look, there's Lucie. She walks with you to the door of the car and then she sees you off calmly. If you hadn't decided to leave, she would have fried eggs for you at noon and at about two she would have exercised one of the competition horses beside you in the young corn. You know her seat. Her feet in the stirrups. Her firm heels. You have been familiar with the plait dangling down her back for all eternity.

All right, then, you really are not thinking of her anymore, that's right. On the expressway the signposts glide past you. You watch for the turnoff. You quite simply forget that by now you're intertwined from top to toe with the country girl who's long since gone back inside to devote herself to the eternal recurrence of things, starting with washing the dishes. June, July, August, it's the nicest time of year. After sunshine comes rain and then the sun shines again. Anyway, you are happy. You are fulfilling the tradition that calls for to you to move around in clans with lots of hullabaloo. Do I need to say that in all that fuss about freedom you know you remain touched by that house behind the apple orchard? You seek out the familiar campsites. In your heart that stud in Benckelo has quite a big say.

The stable had been expanded over the years. It wasn't long before Joseph decided to buy two beautiful star mares in addition to the geldings that still worked on the land and have them covered by thoroughbreds. He made snap decisions. Because Lucie thought her husband was wonderful and because her view of breeding was scarcely any different from his, she usually smiled in agreement. Her father appreciated his son-in-law too. Fifteen hundred guilders for a foal was a lot at the beginning. Concrete was laid on the stable floor. Almost immediately it struck Joseph as a good idea to breed from the Gelderland broodmare, Nelaleen. This turned out to be fortunate. From a natural coupling with the thoroughbred Furioso his darling Bellaheleen was born. The offspring of opposed breeds like this is called an F1 product. There is an excellent chance of good qualities. Bellaheleen was a jumper with strength from her mother's line and a paternal infusion of courage. After crossing with a couple of Prussian Trakehners which had a very good pedigree, she produced daughters with a rare bent for jumping.

Days are long in a stud. From six in the morning Joseph trains his horses by putting them in front of a cart and riding them at a gallop along the country roads. Sun, rain, pheasants flying up. He doesn't maintain that the lunge is useless, but it's better for their condition if you make animals work hard and use their backs. He shouts, whistles, his method sends shivers down their spine. He doesn't mind hitting them — he is held in high esteem by them. For sixteen years Joseph has been dropping in at the stables on winter evenings to talk to the horses and to explain a few things to them.

In 1964 when he comes home he is handed his son Hanzi. In 1967, deeply moved, he counts the ten perfectly formed toes of Katharina. Two years later there is Koos, who is given the Gypsy name of Jojo. Joseph loves his children. He cherishes them, lifts them up, rocks them. He puts one of them on his lap at the end of the day: The stove is burning, the little one starts nodding off, Joseph looks from the bare linden trees behind the window to the little head slumped against his chest. His eyes grow moist. These are the moments, aren't they? These are the moments when paternal love takes such hold in you that you can leave, you can go where you like while your mind remains alert to all that is essential. Yes, you're lucky. You can laugh to your heart's content because here are the three children. They urge you on. On you go. Have you ever felt so cheerful?

And it's just the same with Lucie. Your most carefree destination is this woman, and your everyday love life never becomes drudgery because it starts again every autumn. She cooks. You repair the tractor. She makes coffee. You make a window in the stable door to provide fresh air and put some netting in it to stop birds flying in. In the alder wood behind the orchard she sees a footprint in the snow. You sink to your haunches, you grab her hand, they are the pads of a fox, your fingers slip along the inside of her wrist. Every month there are days when she looks a little paler than usual. You look past her out the window. The cycle of the woman's body is something you don't want to hear about, you turn your back on her in bed. Returning from the village, she has a wrinkle of annoyance between her eyes. There's a good chance that she has met a fellow villager whom for some unknown reason she doesn't like one bit. That's why, to cheer Lucie up, you always call the owner of Second Eden "that cow," "that bitch," or "that prickly cunt."

On the kitchen table there are onions and carrots from the garden. She has poured tea and looks at you with her usual smile. Her eyes stare at you unmovingly: Only with her, Joseph, only with her can you talk! Having somehow drifted imperceptibly into your stories, for God's sake, she's the only one who knows what you're talking about. And it's been like that from the very beginning. From the first time you arrived here, she realized who you were, and subsequently she's realized it another fifteen times. It was only this summer that a few things went wrong.

*   *   *

Of course, I bumped into her after all. It was in Italy, in the eastern area of the hills near Tolmezzo. I'd been feeling tired. I felt an inappropriate and malicious pleasure in drowsing and sleeping, and that had never been my way. That evening in the campsite near Tolmezzo I was sitting by my car when someone said to me: "Look out, the *kumpania* of Parasja and her family has parked by the water this afternoon. Past the western side of the site there is a branch of the Tagliamento that cuts through a luscious plain with blue skies and green fields."

"Very good, friend," I said. "Thanks for the news." I even hesitated to look up.

I was quite simply too drowsy that evening. Later too, when the fires were lit, I kept my distance from the world of real emotions. I saw her a little way off, dealing with her children, an energetic, majestically blossoming woman. Once I'd seen heaven in her eyes. Now all she made me think to do was to bend over and poke the embers with a eucalyptus branch.

The night only got going when some of them began singing. After supper. With all the stars in the sky. Two men tried out their voices, softly at first, in the usual way, but soon they rose to piercing heights. And then, God yes, then pain came out of the far distance of my soul. A sense of drama, things like this can happen when they start singing in these tones. The hands clapping, these eyes closed. And then a deathly silence. What did this night mean? The voices set me thinking, far beyond thought itself. They brought with them a certain understanding. But what that night had to tell me was not about this or that woman. To be honest, even in those couplets there was something that kept me from remembering them. Then, great seriousness and fate being decided, more or less. If I started my car the following morning and drove away from the camp on the banks of the Tagliamento, it was because the music the night before had sung to me so convincingly. The emptiness. To seize life wholeheartedly even as it is changing, therefore the emptiness. What the night had decided would henceforth be the order of the day.

I couldn't care less.

The way back went smoothly, but I remained listless and uninterested. Beyond Verona I camped for a day by the lake. At a campsite in the Val d'Aosta I spent three days taking apart and putting back together a diesel engine for a chap from Albania. He was a drunkard. I didn't like him. I didn't know why I helped him. When he pushed the bottle toward me, I refused with a growl. Around Mulhouse I headed directly north.

In Holland it was still full summer. Green doors, gardens, linden trees with crowns spread out in front of the houses. When I drove through Benckelo I noticed that I'd run out of cigarettes. I stopped opposite the supermarket. When I got out, a woman I knew stopped on the other side of the road. "Hey! Joseph!" she shouted. It was Christina Cruyse of Second Eden. A truck came between us. I waited. When I crossed the street she was still standing there. What was that woman looking at? What did she want? Was she trying to give me the evil eye?

3

*D*amn, there he is! Yes, it's him. He's back. Summer's more or less over and his lordship is going home. If you ask me, he's quite early this year. What date is it today? September 2, the sun is still warm. Look, he's stopping. He parks his filthy car by the curb opposite the Konmar. His windshield is covered in flies — he's come a long way. Isn't he in a hurry? No particular kind of impatience now he's so close to *her?* I can just see her reaction when she hears that typical eight-cylinder whoosh in her yard: a smile, quick, disbelieving. That's all. And happiness, of course. Well, I've got a nice surprise for her in my field, too, a very nice one, I'm sure of that, which will make something flare up in her face — that innocent face that is equally pale in winter and summer — a longing. And she'll come to me whether she wants to or not. She detests me. She distrusts me. I'm going · to supply the Appaloosa to her. I'm really dying to offer the mare calmly for sale to her, at quite a good price. But now her husband's suddenly on the other side of the street!

I call him. I think he looks in my direction but I can't see properly because a truck drives past. Why do I call him? What do I want with him?

God knows.

"Hello," I say when he's crossed the street.

He greets me with a nod, his black hat on his head, and is about to go into the Konmar. It's six on the dot.

"Listen, Joseph, can I ask your advice about one of my horses?"

"Got to buy some cigarettes first."

"Have one of mine. Here."

I don't let him go. I present my packet to him. "It's about a mare that does nothing but sweat and sweat."

When he's lit up, he looks at me dubiously. His skin is dark with the sun. I can see silver hairs in his mustache. I realize that I'm impressed by his proud patience. To my original desire another begins to attach itself.

"A brilliant mare too," I go on lamenting. "Really, a super jumper and I don't know what's wrong with her."

The Appaloosa and the Gypsy start to merge, to become one, I can feel that. I deliberately breathe in the smell of his cigarette. Could I get him to come with me?

"How long has she had that?" he now asks.

"Since yesterday, Joseph. The day before she was perfectly fit."

"What did you make her do? Has she been near strange horses, by any chance?"

"That's just it. A week ago she was still with the dealer."

He frowns. Does it interest him? Or does he want to be on his way? It's very likely that he's tired.

"A quality horse," he says. "That shivers and sweats."

I nod. "Yes. A mare with stunningly beautiful lines. You won't believe your eyes, really not. But she's shivering."

He looks past me into Brinkstraat. I go on talking.

"I don't know if it means anything to you, but she's a daughter of the Bavarian champion Cesare."

Again I seek out, asking openly now, the already more interested look of Lucie's husband. Just back from abroad.

Still full of God knows what impressions, but definitely intending to turn left at the end of Brinkstraat and under the tunnel. Has she been looking forward to this moment for the whole summer? He pushes his hat back a little. Has she already imagined how he'll come slinking back?

"Listen," I say, "you know about these things. Got any ideas?"

Soon he'll be given a roof over his head as if it were the most natural thing in the world, a floor under his feet and a wide bed with a freckly white woman who spreads her hair out over her pillow like a fan at night, I imagine.

"It might be glanders," he says, "or heaves. You haven't said if she has a temperature."

Red hair, which he may like, but which long ago I saw as something intolerable, something completely unacceptable that in some way she would have to pay for.

Pulling it loose was the last thing you thought of, in those days, when it was wound around her head in long braids. Snapping at her and making fun of her was also obvious — the whole group of you turning your backs on her when she came into the playground. And then putting your heads together and bursting out laughing. Or making faces as if you were dying of the stench. She kept seeking our company and particularly mine! Didn't she realize that we couldn't stand the sight of her? Her idiotic bolt-upright way of walking, her watery eyes, her bright yellow eyelashes, very long too, her impudent habit of standing near us in gym lessons as if she were one of us and came to visit us on Saturday afternoons. She was stupid. She slept with her mouth open during lessons. When we played tag-with-a-ball no one wanted to pick her. Didn't she realize that her breasts, which were beginning to ripen, were just begging for her to be tripped, or to have her heels stepped on? One time another girl and I laughed at her sweetly and took her with us to Meulink's stable. Come on, the three of us will go up the ladder, we said, we've got candy in the hay. We climbed up a bit and then I stood with my back against the rung and looked into the sty where the pigs were. Filthy as hell. Look, we said, and pushed her over the wall into the pen. Yes, then it's indescribable — your mood, your happy mood which swells up to the farthest corners of the stable. She's lying in the black shit and gasping for breath. There are threads of spittle coming out of her mouth. It's impossible to describe how it feels to be standing watching, blond and clean, high up on the ladder.

Patiently, almost lovingly, determined to put one over on her, I say, "Temperature? I don't know, Joseph. I haven't taken it, but I don't think so."

Now a narrow smile. His face takes on a mocking expression, and I quite like that.

"So the wonderful pedigree mare is letting her head drop," he says.

I laugh too. "What?"

"So she's letting her head hang?" he repeats. "I bet she puts her hind legs far apart and walks with short steps."

Now I must nod seriously in agreement. To get full value out of this summer day, and to get the very special surprise from it that at the end is clearly in it, I have to put a faithful "yes" in my eyes, with a dash of respect.

"Exactly," I nod. "It really is just as you say." I gesture toward his car. Mine is right in front of it. Go on, another prod, it's going well, isn't it?

"Hey, Joseph!" I sweep my hair back. "Drive behind me if you've got time. Have a look at the horse and give me some advice, please!"

His reply sounds flat.

"Okay."

* * *

We go into the field. Cesare's daughter is standing right over on the left by the wooded bank.

"That's her."

Of course I know perfectly well what's wrong with the mare.

"You can see what a beauty she is."

He strolls one step ahead of me with his shoulders hunched and says nothing.

Yes, I believe he's tired. I see these things. His lordship is rather weak. Bet he's driven a long stretch in one go and he's now just as light in the head as a trained jumper after a round. As a horsewoman I know that, as a true show jumper. What do you think, Joseph? What do you want? Look at me!

He looks at the high-legged horse. He could of course say, Put her in the stable and be sure not to give her anything to eat, but it's as though he has seen through the pretext. Absentmindedly he pats the pied nose of the horse. In the distance a dog barks, the evening air is still warm, and a certain idea begins to entice him, to convince him, but he's not completely sure yet.

"What do you plan to do with her?" he asks.

"Sell her on." I now gaze at him openly.

"Have you got anyone in mind?"

"Oh yes!" I nod with an enthusiasm that fits effortlessly with the simply precious atmosphere of the moment. "It's all fixed."

He still doesn't come a step closer, but his eyes are certainly not dull anymore. Sensing that I want him, his smile goes from me to the horse, he touches the light red, too-dry nostrils. Feel like an unexpected treat?

"I know someone who's been thinking of nothing else but an Appaloosa all summer," I say.

I squirm inwardly with pleasure and turn around. Having agreed in principle, let's say, we walk side by side in the direction of the two high rows of trees in front of my house.

Here we are in the kitchen. The open upper windows and the stone floors with the dog in the middle.

Into this big room a low band of sun falls against the wall like a spotlight on a marquee: Here you are free, go on, completely without any plans. Here you can leave what you were planning to the moment itself, and that moment, darling, will devour it. Will twist things that are obvious and turn them on their heads a little, did you mean this? Okay, let's do that. Look, he's standing next to my sideboard, the collar of his shirt is open, the sunlight shifts and starts shining even lower and harsher. I put out my arms.

"Listen, Joseph, aren't you thirsty?"

My dress already a little unbuttoned, showing him a little of myself because, oh, this party's going to last a bit, I play the hostess.

"Try it," I say. "Taste!"

My first-class Beerenburger. I'm crazy about the stuff myself. He leans with his shoulder against the sideboard, smoking, yes, okay, yes you go ahead and make free with my cigarettes!

"Very nice," he admits.

"Isn't it? Personally, I don't know anything nicer before a meal."

He's put his hat on the mantelpiece. His dark face is taut. I interrupted his impulsiveness by turning around, bending down, and muttering a few endearments as if I were talking to the dog. Wham, bam, thank you, ma'am: Will I be satisfied with that on this exceptional occasion?

So let's eat, my friend. Don't pull such a suspicious face! I'll come and sit so close to you that our legs touch. There's going to be action this evening. A plan with a good chance of success. I note that he's tired, but on the other hand not at all. He is alert, looks, endures, with a smell of fire and cooking oil around him now. I put heavy silver cutlery on the table, he takes a knife and weighs it in his hand.

"Solid," he says. "Old."

I must be crazy, but it amuses me, it amuses me enormously to fill an old Delft blue dish, a family heirloom, with beef and beans. He stubs out his cigarette. I thrust the wine at him.

"Here, you open it."

Brightly and flickering, the evening sun falls into the glasses and colors our hands red. Do you think all gentile women are sluts? Except for her, Lucie, that is? When I look for his eyes, I see nothing except defenses lulled to sleep.

He pushes his chair back with a jerk. The dog growls.

"Put it down."

I assume a subservient expression and put my glass down. All right, I'm ready too. Now we might as well head for the bed, which as far as you're concerned could be any woman's, but tonight happens to be mine. I push the door open with the tip of my shoe.

"Mind the hook."

In the side room it's serious work. Why should a kiss, ice-cold and fiery at the same time, not be able to say: Make yourself at home? On the bedspread, on a pattern of black and blue flowers, an alliance is forged. The simplest one there is. And the shortest, of course. And wouldn't *I* find it funny if, in a little while, she can't get it out of her mind for the rest of her life?

A white shirt on the floor, dark arms that know exactly what the intention is, under the circumstances. Fantastic, really, Mr. . . . . Mr. Plato? Your deep-set eyes don't look at me for a second. I praise my fellow villager for having fallen for your typical stern behavior back then.

Fifteen or sixteen years ago, if memory serves. When she'd long been accepted by virtually everyone. A creature that quietly, almost half-wittedly, but somehow determinedly, went her own way. And she was good with horses. I saw in astonishment the completely coincidental talent with which she set about rearing jumpers at a time that, in hindsight, was just right for it. You saw her in every market and in every stable: upright and sturdy, and often dressed in the silly wide skirt, with which she also sometimes got into the stirrups and, leaning back like an English hunting amazon, her legs forward, raced over her father's land. A village gets used to someone like that. To someone who always says hello only at the last moment, who says very little and replies with a smile as if not she but the person who's asked something isn't quite right in the head. In those days, like most of us, she went into The Tap when the market was over at the end of a Wednesday morning. Then I'd see her standing smoking at the bar with that face with those thinly arched eyebrows and that line around her mouth that had a way of infuriating me. She seemed pleased with herself. She pressed her beer glass against her lip and stirred the froth with her tongue. And one rainy July day the Gypsy went over to her, this one here, yes, her great love whom she'll find in the bed here tomorrow morning, with his arms outstretched, dead to the world after an exhausting journey followed by the kind of adventure that happens to men quite often. A stroke of fate.

The room is permeated with pleasure and satisfaction. His head has sunk down a little way from mine. Through tousled black hair a shining cheekbone is visible. She can do whatever she likes, but from tomorrow onward Lucie will know that I've experienced a few things. And when we look at each in the future or get into conversation, then

I can, if I want, allude to it very delicately, a look, a word, and whatever happens she'll have to show me that she's understood.

He turns sleepily away from me.

"What's that pounding noise I can hear?" he murmurs.

I raise myself on my elbows, my interest still completely intact.

"That's my neighbor," I say. "He's profiting from the full moon and is dredging the ditch with his digger."

I myself don't feel at all like sleeping. I get up, take his shirt off the floor, and go to the pantry where there's the tub for hand washing.

Five hours of sleep is enough for me. It's scarcely daybreak before I get up and go into the field to get the Appaloosa. The mare gives me a lively look and her skin shines. As I walk down the path with her, I breathe the delightful morning air deeply. The poplars rustle, the sky is already turning blue, blue and with that calm feeling of September for which there are simply no words. I tether the horse in the yard and glance at the dusty car that has been parked there since yesterday. Well, and inside a man is sleeping so wonderfully that he won't want to be woken for the time being. Let me go and make some coffee. The real fun won't start for a little while. How often can you lure one stupidity toward the other so that together they make an accident?

On the kitchen table are yesterday's plates, mine still half full. While the smell of coffee spreads through the house, I unfold the ironing board to iron a shirt. Then I pick up the phone.

" . . . Come before nine, please."

I call the dog and put a dish of tripe by the hedge. The

old, lethargic cat creeps in after me as though he knows that there is a plate with gristly meat for him on the floor.

Let him gulp it down.

I sit at the table with a cup of coffee in front of me. The light has meanwhile become even brighter, even more cheerful. A fly buzzes from the window to the sideboard and then to the table, where it lands. What will she say about the Appaloosa? With my eyes I follow the bluebottle as it crawls across the table. Now I can hear a car coming down the road, slowing down and then turning into the yard of Second Eden.

Right.

Part Five

1

*T*he red December sun is still low behind the apple trees as they drive down the path. Joseph is at the wheel, Lucie next to him. For the last week or two you can see them leaving home regularly at this time, because Joseph has to go the hospital for tests. They usually appear about nine and get into the car without a word. When they turn onto the road they always give the impression that the only thing on their minds is to take that drive together as warmly and as comfortably as possible. They put the radio on, adjust the heater, and pull the ashtray out of the dashboard. The roads are usually quiet at this time. Today they have luggage with them for the first time, it has struck me, but Lucie puts the weekend case containing her husband's pyjamas by her feet as if it were nothing and leans back in her seat. He's got to stay, they're keeping him over there, the operation will be tomorrow.

"Stupid, isn't it?" she says when they've driven through the wintry landscape for fifteen minutes. Even she has finally noticed that his right hand keeps straying from his knee to the steering wheel and back.

"Christ, yes! Have you got some candy or something?"

She hunts in her coat pockets, then in the side compartments of her handbag. He mustn't smoke. He hasn't been supposed to smoke all these months, but only today, with the obscure tour de force that the doctor must perform on him in prospect, does he obey.

"Here."

She has found a couple of liquorice sticks. When she puts her hand to his mouth, her fingers brush the mustache that's just been trimmed this morning. His lips are warm, she knows that, they always have been. I look at her as she stares at the road again. Her face expresses nothing except the calm agreement not to light up either. She and Joseph are now driving along the canal. Then there is a drawbridge. The barriers are down, and on one of them, would you believe it, sits a cockerel.

"Look at that cockerel," says Joseph.

"It's a Harreveen cockerel," says Lucie. "They can fly as well as a pheasant."

As they drive on, she turns to watch the creature take off. What does it matter to her? Today Joseph has to report to Department B on the fourth floor of the Wilhelmina Hospital and she gives her attention to a piece of poultry that's showing off. I've been worried, for over a year. And for over a year I've been wondering why she isn't, or if she *is*, why she doesn't act more anxious and sad. She's noticed that he likes to stay in bed for a bit longer in the mornings and then needs some fresh air. But when she sees him strolling past the fence by the chicken run she doesn't see, if you ask me, what I see in his eyes: so much emptiness that absolutely nothing else could find a natural place in it. Where is her grief for him? There was always something lighthearted in her blood. Since last summer there's been no sign of it anymore. Has the affair with that creature, with that Christina Cruyse, wrapped itself around her heart like a collar?

I don't know, but I do feel that she could consider a few

things now and then. When she makes coffee at about ten in the morning, she has already finished the necessary work in the stable and in the house. She stands at the countertop and pours milk into a saucepan. Plump hands, a round face that shows nothing except peace of mind. Where is her grief, for God's sake? At the table by the window sits a waiting Gerard. Joseph usually comes a bit later. No stable boy. Now that a lot of horses have been gotten rid of, it's no longer necessary. My glance wanders from Lucie at the stove to Lucie in the geometrical square of light of the window putting cups on the table and then calmly sitting down by them. And then words arise in me, sentences that try to connect with the impossible musings behind that face opposite me. But when she looks up, she looks right through me with ghostly eyes.

He's ill, Lucie, and you know that. You were standing there when a couple of transparent photos were placed on light boxes and a doctor showed you the patches that were dark, darker than they ought to be. He's going to leave you. Don't pretend it's something you've known for years: You stood and looked down with him at a series of scans of his lungs split into thin vertical sections and when you looked up you had to sit down and were given the result: malignant, Lucie, and malignant has something evil in it. Their faces had remained unmoved. They shook hands with the doctor.

Now they're driving down the almost deserted road along the Twente Canal. The fields are empty, the contours of trees, banks, and ditches blurred in the winter sunshine. He drums his fingers on the steering wheel. She leans forward and turns the dial of the radio. A dusky woman's voice comes on singing a song that was very popular back in the 1940s. *Merci, mon ami, es war wunderschön. Tausend Dinge möcht' ich dir noch sagen. Liebling, wir müssen uns wiederseh'n.* . . . She can't understand the words. He would be able to, but he's not following them. They're both silent, caught up in the throb of the engine, the song on top of it, and the mist along the last stretch of the Twente Canal where the road forks and after about a mile and a half the sheds of the Dykel industrial zone appear.

They park behind the new building of the Wilhelmina Hospital.

"Brrr!" she says once they've got out.

They walk up the granite steps and go through the revolving door. On the left is the counter, neon lit. They take the elevator to the department and are shown into a waiting room by a nurse where together with some other patients and their families they can look out through tall windows. There Lucie bursts into sobs. Her face goes red. Because of the other people she tries to control herself, but that has the opposite effect. Under Joseph's sympathetic gaze she raises her face to the view behind the windows and with her eyes squeezed shut, bolt upright in her chair, tries to smother her sobbing.

I'm afraid she won't be able to do it as long as she lives.

Coffee is put down for them. What is there to say, anyhow? Without a word being spoken they're given the opportunity to look at the ailing young plants in the enclosed garden below. It's a cloudless day, and yet no shaft of light falls on the rhododendrons. A small pond has dried up.

Then: "Would you come this way?"

The floors are marbled linoleum and the sinks gleam. Of the six beds of white-painted metal, the one by the door is still free. Soon the doctor comes by to say something about the operation the following day, and Joseph's and Lucie's eyes look stunned. A kitchen worker has just asked them an enormous number of questions. "One savory, two sweet," they decided when they were discussing the morning sandwiches. Now the doctor tells them that he will be starting at eight o'clock tomorrow. As soon as he's finished, he will phone Lucie. She doesn't understand.

"Phone me?"

"It'll take hours . . ." she hears. "Sometimes there are unexpected complications. It would be better if you waited at home."

Shortly after the doctor has gone, she realizes or thinks that she has to say goodbye to Joseph. She grabs his hand with a startled smile. Then she buttons up her brown over-coat.

"Give the children a hug! Kiss them!" he orders her with a seriousness surrounded by thick snow-white pillows.

When the elevator doors slide open on the landing, she peers inside for a moment but she has, I suspect, long since realized that she can't make herself leave Department B. Without asking anyone's permission Lucie has gone back and sat down in the waiting room, and when I see her sitting there again the following morning just after eight, there's every indication that she's simply stayed there passively and stubbornly next to an ashtray full of cigarette butts, looking straight ahead with the confidence of someone who knows how to wait.

Outside?

On the bed of the dried-up pond a couple of pigeons are now hopping about. The leaves of the rhododendrons are shaking, there's a wind today. From the harsh blue sky around the buildings a multicolored bird sweeps past and lands fluttering on the place where the pigeons are, it's a jay and the pigeons quickly take flight. From behind the windows my eyes follow the jay and I see its beak tapering im-perceptibly into a wafer-thin scalpel making an incision. An invisible line breaks into loose ends of blood from the neck to the navel. While fingers in surgical gloves place clamps on the tissue, Lucie moves her feet apart. She looks into the courtyard garden where the wind and the cold are exactly the same as between the stables at home, with the hoof-prints of Linda, Walton Beauty, and Viking, who were sold off quite a while ago, still in the mud of the outside trough.

No one asks. When Joseph does the rounds of the stable in the evening, one of the children always goes with him, teenagers, two of them are at high school in Enschede. They too think there's something nice about the animals and their whole fragrant accompaniment of fodder and straw and dung between whitewashed walls.

The three of them have enough knowledge of horses, but the size of the business doesn't interest them much because one wants to become a ship's captain and the other probably a film star, and Jojo is only eleven. The indoor ring is closed. The trotting mill has been shut down. Joseph and Lucie are content to look after their remaining horses and no longer deign to talk about things like the Groningen horse trials, which they missed for the first time this year with their star mares. Sometimes, when the sun shines on the stable wall on nice days, they still trot to Rutbeek Heath. Nothing needs to be added to that. When they get back, they see Gerard come shuffling gray as a spider out of the chicory house and their animation disappears because they're worried about Gerard. Gerard — and I started talking about this ages ago — is angry. They have no idea why. They don't waste any thought on this either, but the furious way Gerard looks at them makes Lucie sad and upsets Joseph. Personally I think the old man has almost lost his marbles.

Last year Joseph bought a dwarf billygoat for him, a tiny one. Joseph had thought of certain horses, lonely thoroughbred horses that cheer up when they have a cat or a donkey near them. It's well known. The Normandy top

trotter Jeanne wouldn't put a foot into a train compartment
if her friend, a white rabbit, didn't go with her. And for a
time it really worked. Gerard enjoyed the beautifully
marked creature and followed it everywhere. Lucie saw out
of the side room of the courtyard how he pushed his fist
against the ribbed horns to make the billygoat charge.
"Look," she said when Joseph went past, "Daddy's clamber-
ing up that slope along the ditch with him."

The recovery room is a large area with a fairly chaotic atmosphere. Three nurses are still wheeling a bedside cupboard closer, fixing a needle to the hand with adhesive,
checking a catheter. One of them looks up and says the operation has been successful. White light. Dripping and bubbling of various liquids, clear in a flask hanging at the head
of the bed, tea-colored and soft red in the narrow flat packs
at the side of the bed. So soon after the operation they often
continue to give oxygen. She moves her face over his and
sees that his eyes are focused at the ceiling, completely lost.
"Joseph?"

On the cupboard are the three gold rings and the wrist-
watch.

She's allowed to sit down and stay for as long as she
likes. He's not allowed a sip of water, but she can run a thick,
soaking-wet cotton swab around his parched mouth. Aside
from the constant interruptions of the care-givers coming in
to give injections, measuring this and that, and taking notes
of the same, the two of them are alone.

She is dreaming. He is dozing. An echo of that one
story that was always theirs.

Once, on a winter evening when there was a layer of
snow over the countryside, Joseph and Lucie were driving
home towing an empty trailer from Westdorp in Drente.

Just after the crossing at the forestry station at Odoorn, the car, which was traveling fast, began to lose speed of its own accord. Joseph shifted down a gear but realized that the engine was losing power whether he accelerated or not. He stopped the car on the frozen shoulder and got out with the headlights still lit. For a moment Lucie saw his face illuminated from below, then the hood went up. A moment later she was standing next to him with the flashlight, shining it on his hands, which were already covered in motor oil. First he undid a couple of screws and then lifted up a heavy square part and half stripped it and then put it back together again with unbelievably delicate, patient movements. She had no idea how much time it took. It was cold. While she stood there in the wind, beneath a small crescent of moon and icy stars, Lucie looked with a calm that became increasingly serene at a couple of dirty hands that were assembling a dirty engine, because in them she saw the order of her life. Start her up! She went back behind the steering wheel and obeyed. Then a gesture of his hand, enough! His narrow face was still set in a surly expression. Without the slightest hint of the kind of courtesy — so hard to describe — that exists between married couples, the chore had been done and he slammed the hood shut.

Lucie scrambled out of the driver's seat. He went to the trunk. She picked the wrenches and pliers up off the ground. He twisted a cleaning rag around his fingers.

Having lost more than an hour, they were able to leave the roadside and take the route through the forestry area. Lucie said she thought the road, with trees with creamy white trunks and intertwined crowns of ice, was just like a fairy tale. Joseph smiled, he thought so too. Without any problem the car raced through the wood, across the bridge over the Oranje Canal, and onto the expressway to Coevorden. Joseph pushed the engine hard, as though nothing had happened. They were home before midnight. Joseph got out, opened the gate, and got in again. I look at the car driving past with two shadows in the darkness. Their consciousness surrounds me like light, like wind, and sets mine working too. As they drive toward the lighted windows of the house — Gerard is still up, the children are asleep — they both have the feeling of regaining something, just like that, a lost happiness at the end of the day.

Just under a week later Joseph is lying in the six-person ward and is allowed visitors. The children have already been, and now Gerard is sitting on a stool in front of the washbasin looking disapprovingly at the floor. He's completely thrown and doesn't say a word. Only after about five minutes does he get to the point of speaking.

"How's the greenhouse doing, Dad?" Joseph has asked. And he added, "I'm very comfortable here."

But Gerard doesn't react. He is troubled by the murmur of the visitors at the other beds. The smell of flowers and disinfectant is foul, serving only to remind him of something that presses on his soul with a formidable weight. Once he knew what he loved, what troubled him, and what he could best leave alone. Now his understanding has been disrupted. His consciousness makes connections that no one can follow except him. In a room bathed in the light of the sun and a couple of diabolical ceiling lamps, Gerard thrusts his neck out, furious he looks at Joseph, and opens his mouth.

A linear pattern of wrinkles. Suspicious eyes, certainly, but still with something principled about them, although he has forgotten exactly what principles for the moment. When someone says hello to him, he doesn't return the greeting for perfectly good reasons. When someone sits down next to him, daughter or son-in-law, he quite rightly looks angrily to the side. If he goes into the potato field, he sits down on an upturned crate, pondering a question he can't ignore that draws his eyes down to the unplowed ground for hours on end. What can you do against evil, against injustice? The afternoons go by and the umpteenth sun turns to a bloodshot eye. Not bending is the least of his worries. When he pushes against a rickety gate with his shoulder, he starts cursing as soon as it springs open. Once he used to look around his land and have contact with a logical world. Now there's something wrong with the climbing rose, the trotting mill, the horses, the chickens that spend the night on the rusty perches, the bench outside the house, and the ringing of the church bells after supper. Now incomprehensible statements are being made by his daughter and by his son-in-law, the Gypsy he had to find today, for Christ's sake, in Department B on the fourth floor of the Wilhelmina Hospital. What is he supposed to do? Nod in agreement?

"Fools! Bunch of idiots!"

People in and around the other beds look up in interest.

The following Friday, January 9, Lucie is able to collect her husband. Joseph is sitting fully dressed at the table by the window waiting when she appears in the room jingling her keys at about ten in the morning.

She takes the bag. He goes around shaking hands.

In the elevator they watch without a word the changing numbers of the floors. It's busy in the hall, with a smell of coffee. He heads for the revolving door, she follows him outside. She stops when he stops and looks at what he looks at, huddled in his coat. Along the wide street opposite the new building, a streetcar consisting of three compartments full of schoolchildren passes. What will she remember of this moment later? He pushes his hat down over his eyebrows.

"It looks as if it's been freezing," he says.

His face is extremely pale, but in the eyes you can see a hint of good humor. The real Joseph is still there. Handsome, and a little disheveled. Happy at the simple fact of having regained the freedom to go outside. Despite the fact that, within this wall, he keeps for himself something that belongs to someone else, that will never see the light of day. He's wearing a heavy blue-black overcoat with epaulettes, which has been buttoned up under the collar. A scarf up to his side-whiskers. Beautiful, deft hands. And fancy semibrogue shoes, buckles, by which you can recognize his kind immediately, if you know. His portrait of January 9.

Would it have been any better if she'd realized that at this moment his last journey home was in fact beginning?

"It certainly has," she says. "It was at least four below last night."

She has parked in front of the yew hedge by the exit of the site. In the porter's hut sits an old man with a cap and heavy spectacles, through which he examines every car that comes or leaves with great authority. The barriers are up. The Chevrolet stops by the shark's teeth painted on the road to yield to a cyclist and then turns left. Past the traffic circle is A35 toward Enschede.

She drives. He lights up a cigarette.

2

*T*hat feeling of surrender almost always comes. I think it's something to do with the drugs. The one who is about to leave looks in a detached way at the curtains, the drinking glass, and a few flowers from the garden. It was great while it lasted, but I won't mind in the least ceasing to exist shortly . . . won't mind?

This must be a fraud! Deliberate deceit by the enduring world. Worried about her guests of honor, nature provides a serum at the difficult moments — arrival, departure — to make us forget or be calm. How many would be born if birth were not the most ethereal torture that exists, a dream pain, forgotten at the baby's very first cry? How many would go without regret if they had their senses? Surrender? No. Never. Forget it. They would refuse. No one would die if that superintoxication hadn't blotted out that desperate consciousness.

Leave the windows open, he would have said, I'm sure of it. I'm sure he would have said: Leave my shoes where they are. Wash my shirts. Just leave my toothbrush and razor on the shelf under the mirror, from where I want to make faces at you as I stretch the skin of my face while I'm shaving. I'm staying, you see. Why should I disappear into nothingness? I've always liked breathing. On spring mornings the wind came in through the windows and pushed up the leaves of the calendar. I'm staying, staying to go on holding my possessions, you and the children tight in my hands. You remember when we took them on adventures? The children in the sand drifts, the children by the windmill, the children at the seaside, tanned, with red swimsuits and the wildest eyes in the world, those children of mine, when they outran themselves from the top of the dunes and we saw them rolling like tops, like red things you can wind up, down the slope toward the sun. So don't get rid of my clothes. At the small offices of the Salvation Army you have to push your loved one's clothes through a slot, where, untouched by human hands, they then land on other unwanted clothes. You have to tie up shoes in pairs by their shoelaces. Don't do that. For that matter, don't get rid of my passport, my driver's license, and the wallet with the photos in it either, because whoever has those things has a right to exist. Who's trying to get me to surrender? Why should I be so keen on the ultimate dream? Who can guarantee me that there in the world of the pure spirits they won't do something terrible to me? Hold my hand. Hold me tight with your eyes. Listen. Buy oil for the outside lamp, buy a crate of lager. We sat talking outside on warm days thinking that it would stay like this forever. Memories, expectations. Between them the facts. What can I expect at this point from the eternal dimensions? When it's a matter of our words? Sometimes we talked sense, sometimes we just babbled. The fire on which we'd cooked smoldered under the holly tree. A good storyteller takes the things that happen and fuels the wildest ideas with them. So I'm refusing. I'll do without the hereafter. I'm staying. Even if it's only to believe in God for a little while longer.

Can't we agree on something? That, let's say, I'll come and sit with you when you're alone? And walk with you

when you go out? And look with you under the light of the
lamp, into the dark of the stairwell, under the blue of the
sky, and that then I will see earthenware, letters, silver,
carpet patterns, blue-painted wood, leaded glass, leaves of
trees, light, colors? We ate those golden-brown plaited
rolls on Saturday mornings. On Sundays the children crept
into bed with us like young kittens. Can't we arrange that
when you're sitting alone outside on the veranda I come
and smoke a cigarette with you — keep my lighter, buy cigarettes — and then we can discuss the necessary repairs to
the house? You know how handy I always was with that kind
of job. I liked a quick, spectacular result. Have the outside of
the house painted every three years at least. Get them to
coat the cracks in the wood with epoxy resin and then fill
them with a preparation against rot. Every winter I remembered to turn off the outside tap. Sometimes there was frost
as early as November. And then we'd come outside and immediately smell that typical crisp air that sometimes brought
exotic birds on big, powerful legs onto our grass that same
day. So remember to turn off the well in the garden and
open the valve at the end of October. Remember there may
be huge spiders at the bottom. Don't be frightened by the
toads that can suddenly leap up. Don't be surprised if you
can lift up the heavy stone lid of the well easily, without the
slightest twinge of pain.

He dies in the second week of April. In the village there are
quite a few who say that they have been expecting it. They
say that they've noticed his absence for quite a while and
agree that when he did occasionally turn up, in a shop or in
the street, he looked bad and didn't feel like talking.

    "He just looked," says the landlord of The Tap to me
and tells me that one evening Joseph sat down at the corner

table. "He scarcely moved a muscle. After maybe half an hour he left without drinking anything."

There are quite a few people who come up with a last image of him.

"He was with his daughter," remembers the cashier of the supermarket and describes to me how Katharina lifted the light shopping bag and he the heavy one off the conveyor belt. To my astonishment she adds, "I thought he looked as if he hadn't slept a wink that night." To my astonishment, I say, because I had thought I was the only one who'd not only looked at him but also seen him.

In the countryside. In his car. Occasionally still on a horse. Digging his heels in. In the winter weather. In the rising cold and the wind that shook the copses where a few birds fly off and return. His medication had long been affecting his sense of time. In the evenings, lying on the sofa, he followed Lucie's bustling about: He and she were ultimately not inseparable.

"He was driving over there," the former stable boy says to me, pointing. "In his Chevrolet in the square. And when he saw me he waved, but he didn't brake."

Personally I believe that he wanted to live for as long as he could and then stop. Come and sit next to me, he would sometimes say to one of the children, and they would watch television together. Once he said to Lucie that in a while it would be best if she started breeding carriage horses as well. Buy a handsome-looking team, he recommended to her, for example from Plaisier's stable in Adorp.

Joseph often walked along the side of the ditch huddled in his winter coat. During the day he didn't stay in bed for long. He preferred looking out at the silvery spring sky or hanging around in the stable. A couple of nicely trotting stallions, Lucie, he repeated with conviction. Horses that look really stylish in front of a carriage. He didn't seem to worry that she didn't interrupt her work and didn't answer. Once or twice he'd left home for a day in this period. Quite likely he visited one of the camps in Best, IJsselstein, Nieuwegein, or Oldenzaal, still his natural environment, or the camp behind the railway line in Rotterdam where Guta, his maternal aunt, had lived in her caravan.

On the day of his death Lucie felt he was different from usual in the morning and rang the GP. He came and together with her sat and looked at Joseph muttering restlessly in his bed for a while. After half an hour the doctor gave him an injection and left without having the idea, or having said, that things had reached crisis point. So Lucie left her children at school and her father somewhere in the barns or on the land. Not aware of the heaviness in her arms and legs that had been increasing for months, she hung around in the bedroom looking from Joseph to the windows and the furniture. For a while she kept her eyes fixed on the reproduction of a painting on the sloping ceiling above the bed, an interior, with a vase of yellow and red flaming tulips in front of a window. Then she lay down fully dressed beside him on top of the blanket. And allowed his now soundless sleep to overcome her.

Why shouldn't those two give in to their exhaustion for a moment?

Around them, above the farmland and for miles around, hangs the April light, the most active light there is, falling fully on the grass and on the germinating plants and forcing its way into the earth. But it is very subdued as it brushes the walls of the room where they are lying asleep. Joseph with his hips twisted, to the left of her, motionless. It's she who moves in her sleep, produces a couple of groans as one does, and at a certain moment wakes up. She sits up. She puts her hand on his chest, which moves a few times and then no more. She looks from him to the window behind which there is exactly the same light as in the reproduction with the yellow and red flaming tulips. When she looks back at his face, she sees immediately that he's no longer there.

Gone. Miles and miles away. And not a sign.

Can she actually believe such a thing?

A funeral chapel is not usual for our village. The dead are laid out at home, in a north-facing room with the curtains closed and the mirrors covered. In amazement we obey the summons to take our leave of him in a building in a neighboring municipality from such and such a time to such and such a time. Even on the threshold we can smell the carnations and heliotropes that have been brought in great abundance. The family that we know from the village has been extended by a score of outlandish strangers who are all in distress and give the impression of absolutely refusing to accept the disgraceful facts. It strikes me that Lucie doesn't look at all out of place among women in skirts with flowered layers and not completely buttoned blouses.

The day after, there is a harsh wind. The clocks have just chimed half past eleven when the gate of the cemetery has to be opened wide for the mourners who follow the coffin onto the central path. We people from Benckelo are confused and surprised by the presence of death. By the supernatural gusts of wind and the swishing of the spruces. By the quantity of Gypsies who have attended the Catholic mass for the Orthodox Joseph and drowned out the *requiem aeternam* with their din.

"They make lots of noise, but they mean well," you could hear people say afterward on the steps of the church.

The sky is a motionless, splendid blue.

Lucie follows the signposts along the path upward with her children and her father. The coffin is wheeled ahead of her quite fast by a couple of hired mourners, but the disorderly flock around her dawdles and seems to want to slow down the speed of the dead person. From where I stand the distance gradually becomes greater and greater. Having reached a high spot, near a pile of sand, in the unstoppable wind, one half of those present become very quiet. At a certain moment there are various people among them who more or less out of self-defense start thinking of the raising of Lazarus from the grave. The other half in contrast get to the point of throwing coins quickly followed by handfuls of sand into the hole with a great deal of fuss. And *they* are thinking on the contrary: Stay. Make sure you stay where you are. I observe that they fill in the grave with their bare hands and then turn their backs on it without so much as a backward glance.

Only Lucie stays and looks as she takes a couple of hesitant steps back.

The asphalt is dark as anthracite. The wind is coming from the west. Behind the bars of the fence, on either side of the entrance, are the outlines of a couple of big American and German jalopies. Their owners know distance, but also know what closeness is. Farewell, poor brother, they think at this moment, much luck in your irrevocable circumstances. We shall honor your soul until it's old and it closes its eyes and ears with the last of us. But do us a favor and please keep your *mulo* under the floral tributes and wreaths. For Heaven's sake don't let your desperate double emerge to pursue us from under the mud here. We're giving you over to the Eternal One, that's all right, isn't it? When we've dried our tears, we'll discuss among ourselves what you most liked looking at and what you could sit and chatter about like no one else. What was your favorite food again? If you like, we'll rediscover you in a leg of lamb covered with molasses and coriander and, if you like, with the help of a nice bottle we'll penetrate as far as we can into you, but let it stop at that!

She's wearing a dark dress and dark stockings. Clutching her hair with both hands, she crosses the cemetery with that typical bolt-upright walk of hers. From time to time she turns around and stops. When you consider how often she let him go without batting an eyelid, it's striking the amount of looking she does now. Close to the exit there is a stone shed for vases and small garden tools. I see that someone has turned the outside tap on.

But she doesn't see it. She's oblivious to the fact that the dark, foreign-looking funeral guests are all, without exception, holding their hands under the powerful jet of water. Farewell! May what has happened be over and stay that way! What makes you more restless than unfinished business? What keeps you awake more than a debt or a claim on you? The truth is that some things weigh more heavily than fifteen or twenty feet of earth. Let's not ruin your death with regret and remorse! Don't let us give you an overpowering need to come and console us a little!

She extends her arm to Jojo and walks in the wake of Katharina, Johan, and Gerard toward an imposing Cadillac. The right rear door is already open.

3

She regarded her house and her land as the whole earth. For three seasons its rotation brought her to a pitch of intoxicated clarity in which everything fit and the disturbing things weren't so disturbing at all. For she who is left at home: There is snow on the branches of the trees, a half-rotten roof gutter collapses, one of the horses stands there black, asleep, still in the field, the dusk becomes icy . . . good, luckily, there's Joseph, he's walking from the path to the back of the house and kicks at the dogs that leap up around him. Autumn, winter, and spring she had the feeling that when Joseph wasn't at home, he'd just stepped out for a while. Then the summer came and things were different. Then time stretched, then hours gone by freewheeled in the sun and in the work. People were harvesting everywhere. She got lots of work done. Sweating in cotton overalls she daydreamed in passing about a vagabond with a good line. Until an end came to the beautiful system. For whatever reason and in whatever way. Once there was that excruciating scene in the kitchen of Second Eden. To give yourself completely to someone and to nestle in a pair of arms with princely naïveté requires a certain sense of your own worth. The temptation of the Appaloosa. The dirty, dusty Buick. It's certain she never understood that combination. She and

Joseph drove home in convoy. And it's certain that Joseph's subsequent account, the main thrust of which was a horse that was sweating and wouldn't eat, hadn't explained a thing to either her head or her heart.

If only something absurd, something completely insignificant hadn't forced you to wake up! And taught you things that were absolutely no good to you in this transient life!

After the funeral Lucie is nowhere to be found for a few days, not at home and not in the outbuildings or in the fields in the lashing rain. The wind is still blowing. It is Katharina and her brothers who look after the horses, and more than once the former stable boy can also be seen strolling along the muddy path to the paddock. But on Thursday she's back. Then she walks past the side of the barn to the vegetable garden to push aside the wet branches of some bush or other and look at the ground. There is twittering in the tree above her. When she lifts up her head to see what kinds of birds are there, the light falls in her eyes.

"Tinko!" she says when the dwarf billygoat comes up to her as she closes the garden gate. "Have you been drinking out of the ditch, by any chance?" She presses her hand against the swollen side of his stomach. Then she crosses the backyard and walks past the lopsided graying fence to the stable. Two in the afternoon. "For God's sake let that fucking rain stop," she says crudely. The stable is empty, the six horses are grazing in the meadow. Under the sloping side of the roof on the left next to the sink there are a number of iron tubs, tubs or troughs. She lifts one off the ground by its handles, gets a steel brush and begins scraping the bottom with small circular movements. There's a draft. The wind is pounding against the skylight above her head. "Now, now," she says. "It's as though you're trying to get in." Instead of fixing it more firmly, she opens the whole window outward and pushes the lever up to the last hole. With her loose hair now as if it were possessed by something tempestuous, she continues her maintenance work. When she looks up, once, and laughs rather anxiously in her usual way, I think that she's acting as if somebody has come and squatted down by her to see what she's doing. Don't ask me what.

Indefatigability, calm despite the blowing of the wind, and a chalk-white skin against the backdrop of the dark stable: her true face, which she shows to me freely now. It almost gives me the shivers. Something very personal, something that a human being instinctively hides, appears via the busy hands on the face above and makes something clear to me.

In the weeks before his death Joseph was sometimes very active again. Lying on the sofa which had been made so soft and springy with a piece of goatskin that the tumors under his ribs exerted scarcely any pressure, he could grab the telephone to buy a batch of jumps and stands and immediately sell them at a profit somewhere else. He also found a buyer for the eleven-year-old Zeta. Flashbacks of his fieriness, considerateness, pride. It's over, all right, but still nice to get eight thousand for that lazy Zeta. On those occasions his voice sounded just as powerful as before. Later in the day he said a lot more softly to Lucie, "Carriage horses, Luce, don't dither around for a little while. Now take that son of Highness, that Romanus. If I talk about a profit of twenty thousand, I'm still on the low side."

"Well, I quite like the idea, you know."
    "Begin with two."
    "Must they be a pair?"
    "Better if they are."
    "And train them separately."
    "Of course. With double shoes."

"Double shoes? In competitions too?"

"Not then. Do you remember us going to the Northern Area Competition a couple of years ago? It was in Friesland. I remember that there must have been twenty newcomers that came trotting up onto the great green carpet of grass. They were nervous as hell. A brilliant blue sky, not a breath of wind, men with bowler hats and striped trousers were driving the single horses. I remember that I had no quarrel with the winner, a grandchild of Oregon. But you turned to me as you leaned against the fence and half closed your eyes in the sun. You said to me that you thought it was a bit coarse and had a bit of a ram's head. A little later we watched the competition for the carriage and pair, which was won by two unregistered red grays from Beilen. Above us, in the sky a row of birds kept flying in the same circle."

"Are you comfortable?"

"Fine. I can't feel a thing."

"Shall I make some coffee?"

"I don't like the taste anymore."

Some people say that you have to *be* the other person really to understand what that other person is like, or: Another person is unknowable. As if you understand *yourself!* You observe yourself all day long, that's undeniable, you irrefutably feel yourself, hear your heart beating, and taste yourself the livelong day. But how on earth can you know somebody when you've never looked into their eyes? Except if you catch them looking at themselves in the mirror. I look at Lucie who in turn is looking at the fine circles her hands are making as she cleans the dark yellow rings of a metal sink. She doesn't know it, but her face betrays that this is a simple but precise way of observing yourself. Work is the counterpart of the mirror. The complicity between eyes and hands is the opposite of the silly piece of glass we call a mirror.

I'd really like to ask her in an intimate tone a couple of

questions that cut to the core. How would she feel if I gave her certain insights? But she's not someone to have a smoothly flowing conversation with. She, my sister, goes her own way. I really can't follow her. I can only observe her and carefully note her movements. I. My hands are brimful of life. Sometimes I feel life leaping up from under my hands.

Then she's had enough of it. She springs up as though she is being told to hurry and hoists the iron tub on top of the pile of others. As she does so her nylon jacket catches and reveals the line of her hips, sturdy. In front of the entrance to the stables she looks for a moment to see what the rain is like. The sky is already a lot paler against the barns and woods. She's not sure if the old man is in the chicory house but nevertheless goes in the direction of the outbuilding. As she climbs the three steps, both dogs come charging toward her. They force their way ahead of her through the heavy rubber curtain with which the door is shielded to keep out all daylight when necessary: Chicory grows in the dark. Gerard is sitting chewing on his pipe among his racks with the neon light on.

"I think that I'm going to pop over and see Plaisier tomorrow," she begins.

He looks deafly at the dogs snuffling his boots.

"I said I'm going to Adorp."

She has sat down on a stool and looks calmly, longingly at the half-bald skull of the old man with the impression of the cap remaining on his forehead and in the back. Now she sees the corners of his mouth trembling.

"To do *what?*"

She is shocked. He's yelled at her. She is alarmed for a moment, because involuntarily she still relies on Daddy, not the old man on whom some dark force is at work, abusing the memories in his head so badly that they start biting and clawing.

"I'm going to get a couple of young stallions that I can train myself on the wagon every morning," she says.

She looks in rapture at the face with the heavy eye-brows and the pipe pointing at her which flicks up and down.

"I'll get a couple with soft mouths because you can do more with them than with the ones with leathery mouths."

She is silent for a moment, listens absentmindedly to the wind in the distance.

"They must be green and completely unbroken," she says next, "and they must be" — Gerard gets up to button his coat — "four-square on their legs."

Her arms imitate a trotting movement.

When he goes to the fuse box to get his soaking-wet cap from the hook, she says, "I've heard that at the Plaisier Stable they breed for carriage-worthiness."

"That's nice!" He stations himself in front of her with his head tucked in, bent down, almost hunchbacked, but still taller than she is. "A pair. So we're going back to before the war. Two identical blazes, brown with white feet. God, what a job it was finding them!"

His mouth has closed as tight as possible.

"I object!"

She sees the pupils contract to the size of a pinhead.

"Come and have supper, Daddy."

The dogs, stirred up by the wind, leap toward her when she walks past the garbage shed and the chicken run. She's already stopped thinking about Gerard. He'll come in a moment and feed his bad temper, don't you worry. She goes past the creaking roof beams of the barn into the house where everything speaks of Joseph and will go on speaking to her for as long as she doesn't think of taking his hat and coat off the hat peg. On the workbench lie his tools, which in the course of time fit better and better in your hand.

She goes on Monday. And it's Monday that I hear his voice again for the first time. Lucie has driven to Adorp after explaining on the telephone what she's coming for. The foreman, wearing a service cap, shows her around the place. It's eleven in the morning, sunny, windless.

She asks something.

The man in the service cap nods. "Young horses," he says. "Scarcely used to the bit yet."

Now they are standing near a paddock behind the far left building of the complex. Lucie hangs over the fence and with her eyes judges the youth and exuberance of the one- and two-year-old stallions. In front of her is a very distant landscape with fences and a few trees. The foreman, with his eyes on the animals, describes what they are able to do and what they will be able to do.

"Those two," a familiar voice cuts right across him.

She shows no surprise at all. The voice is powerful, at most a little hoarse.

"You mean those two?" She laughs with her face averted and points.

"Yes," comes the voice. "What do you think?"

"I like them fine."

"Right, then the question is what that guy wants for them."

"Let me go and sit down at the table with him."

"Ask for the papers first."

4

The young horses are delivered, radiant with promise. Lucie puts them in the loose house and subjects them daily to the lunge, the whip, and her voice. Shortly afterward she takes in two lodgers for payment, the pedigree mare Batoon and her pitch-black foal, a filly less than a month old. April is coming to an end, the birch is in bloom, from the hedge next to the house a whole swarm of lemon butterflies rises. Everywhere in our area the houses are being cleaned up. If you look down the road you can see them whitewashing the walls left and right and painting the woodwork in the coach-green color that is still favorite here. Lucie's lost a bit of weight, but apart from that is the same as always: ginger coloring, a pallor that asks questions and doesn't answer a single one. At the Wednesday market the women buy curtain material and linen at this time of year. Lucie buys a duvet one morning. I get too hot in my sleep, she explains to the stall-holder, I sweat, I think that I'll just take a silk duvet. That night I hear them talking together again.

She: What do you think?

He: Could certainly do with a coat of paint.

She: But I can't do everything, this year I'll just do a bit.

He: The front of the house? The window frames and doors at the front?

She: I think I'll start with the fascia —

He: That's so high.

She: — because it's been in the wind.

He: It's too damn high, Lucie!

She: What difference does it make? You know perfectly well that I've a good head for heights.

He: That's true.

I can hear from their drawling voices they've been lying there talking like that for a good while. They lie and talk quietly under the duvet, and their familiarity takes them to the edge of sleep and beyond.

Perhaps a week later an enervating incident takes place. It's halfway through the morning. Lucie is standing at the countertop making up a shopping list when she hears a horse whinnying from behind the house.

"My God," she says. "That must be Batoon."

In the fraction of a second it takes her to leap to the door at the back of the house, her gray mood, her daily increasing sadness that she's still alive, has changed to a kind of fatal shock: This horse's bellowing is something she's heard only once before in her life, at the age of eleven, when Koops's barn burned down in the middle of the night on the other side of the road. On reaching the field, she sees the mare rearing and understands the panicked screams of the animal. The black foal is gone. It must have slipped away under the rails of the fence.

Foals are often born out in the field at night. If there are other mares around, they will accept the newcomer tenderly and cheerfully. But they find an unknown foal very spooky. Mares can be thrown completely by a strange youngster simply because it is unfamiliar. At this moment Lucie jumps over the electrified wire of the paddock. And you can see her running through the sand where the black foal is be-

ing chased by two or three mares that are completely en-
tranced by its frightening innocence. The animal breaks
through the fence, with the mares in pursuit. They will try
to chase it and then run it down at a furious pace.

"Whoa there! Come here a minute!"

Twice in succession her hands fail to get a grip on its
coat, which is smooth and soft. But when the black ghost
shoots around the back of the house, Lucie manages to take
advantage of the position of the coach doors to anticipate
the arc of the foal across the barn, and with a tight throat
and her arms spread wide to prepare herself for its run. All
this is taking place right next to the dung heap. And it is indeed on the dung heap, on top of it, that the foal comes to a
halt and abandons itself to the mercy of Lucie, who has
leaped on its back. Paying no attention to anything else, she
takes the head in a hold and spreads herself out completely
over the thrashing legs and body.

She lies like that, not moving, letting her heart calm
down. She can smell the dung and feel the animal's body and
hear the mares still running around. Suddenly inconsolable,
she calls everyone in the house one by one, and falls exhausted.

Help arrives like magic. It has misleadingly begun before she realizes it. At a certain moment Lucie lifts her head
up and from under her elbow sees one of the mares being
grabbed by a halter by a man. She hears the whip cracking
among the horses and then, before her head has completely
cleared, a voice.

"Come on, then, you bastards! Damn it, calm down!"

Shortly afterward Joseph and Lucie are taking the
mares to the patch of meadow that about eighty yards farther on comes to a point at the willow wood. Then they put
Batoon and her foal in the stables. They check that the foal

is unharmed, rub it down, and give the mother some extra food. When the job is finished, they sit down on a fodder box between a couple of young red-blossomed chestnut trees that stand like parasols at the edge of the cornfield. It's going to get warm today. Under a cloudless sky that stretches far beyond the last visible properties, Lucie turns her head to have a good look at him at last.

He is young. She puts him at thirty at most. Impressed by his smooth-shaven face, his hooked nose, the eyes that again have the passionate seriousness that immediately won her over many years ago, her eyes glide toward his clothes. He's wearing a Moroccan leather jacket with embroidered sleeves that she hasn't seen before.

"I'm glad you're back." She sighs.

He looks contentedly from the farm to the potato field on the other side. "I always liked coming here."

"If you only knew how much I've missed you."

"I felt at home at first glance, it's unbelievable."

"For the first time I was wondering where the hell you'd got to."

"I saw right away that you're not one of those women who's always walking around yelling."

A few flies, sun, not a sound anywhere. Lucie and Joseph sit talking perfectly at ease. The two voices carry a long way. She looks filthy, with smudges across her face. He on the other hand looks cool and clean. There's a flat gold chain around his neck.

"I'm so sorry," she suddenly blurts out.

"Sorry? Stop it now. The dead don't like sorry."

"I've always stayed so terribly angry about it. She'd ironed your shirt. If you ask me, she'd even starched the collar and cuffs."

"To hell with her!"

"Now I'm ashamed. I shall be sorry for all eternity that I didn't forgive you."

He shrugs his shoulders. Indifferently he says, "Well, do it now."

"Can I still do it?"

He brushes his cheeks with his hand and appears to think. "Not really, no. You exchange forgiveness when you're alive."

"Well, but . . ."

"But what?"

Silence, and still the flies. He looks at her a little teasingly from the side.

"Come on, give me a kiss!"

She gives him a kiss on the cheek.

Then he reminds her of his talents with his dark cunning eyes.

"There's so much that can't be done, Luce. For Christ's sake, you know I sometimes smuggle things over the border!"

She presses her chin against his chest and breathes in deeply. When she relaxes and exhales, she feels something oppressive flow out of her and then flow back, already weakened, and then flow out of her again.

"You always smell so good," she murmurs, relieved to the depths of her soul.

With a grin he says, "To be honest, *you* don't at all right now."

She leaps up. She looks in dismay at her smeared clothes and notices the flies.

"Why don't you go and get washed?" he says.

You gave him the space. You gave him the opportunity to do what he wanted and you followed him without taking a step.

After summer workdays you sat under the trees in a state of sweet drowsiness. Although no one was talking to you, there *was* someone talking to you. Although no one was reasoning with you, you drew fantastic conclusions. Thinking is actually listening. Why should you not transfer the adventure of the mind to the hearing? Tell me! I'm the extension of your prehistories. Blow your top, lie, swear for all you're worth. I'm your sacred vessel. With the help of your unique tone and your very personal meter I am gradually filling up. When Joseph was gone, Lucie found her way to his soul purely by ear. Just leave the windows open, let it rain, the sun makes a checked pattern behind the garden gate, in everything that happens there's something of you. The separation didn't mean much to her.

She starts on the painting of the house in the first week of May. Two children help, but when they're at school she continues by herself, working hard but carelessly. Perhaps she's tired. No less than five times she leaves the blowtorch on the wood for too long and has to grab the garden hose in a hurry. In the evening she forgets to take the ladder off the front of the house. In order to paint the fascia she climbs onto the roof via the hayloft. She walks so nonchalantly over the rungs that you wonder if she knows what she's doing. On Friday something really does happen: She is lying on one elbow, on a bale of straw that's been taken out of the stack, near the ladder, her face chalky white, a shiny bruise on her cheek. Now and then she closes her eyes and opens them again. Then she looks right through me as if from a mirror and with the face of someone who's far from awake. I get cold shivers down my spine.

"Come on, take your shoes off!"

From the direction of the outside pump Joseph arrives with a dripping cloth, which he wraps around one of her ankles after taking off her shoes. Again it is immediately striking how handsome he looks. Morocco leather jacket. This time a hat of fox tails as well.

"It's already stopped hurting, you know," she says. She holds out a hand, lets herself be pulled up by him, and again looks at the roof where her paintbrushes are still waiting for her behind the fascia.

And so a moment or two later the two of them follow each other up the ladder into the gutter and then via the tiles up onto the ridge. Where they sit down. Just like that, and obviously so familiar with the situation that it strikes me as something they've prearranged. And then when I hear him launch into some story or other and when she listens, blinking as she always used to, a peace comes over me, a boundless carefree feeling that I only knew when I was a child, in the village, still in bed at daybreak.

"From *that* direction," he says. His voice sounds imperious. "We came from *that* direction."

"Where?" She peers. She wants an answer. "Where then —"

He gestures. "There."

And then I see it too. The landscape has suddenly shifted. The clouds have lurched and a couple of birds dive down headlong at a strange angle. Where the Twente countryside had been, there is now a river flowing from south to north, a wide waterway with a town on its right bank with towers and double towers behind Gothic walls.

"Deventer," I hear him say. "I assure you that it was five or at most six days' journey."

It's 2:22 P.M. and clear weather. Along an eastern access road, which is so well maintained that you can certainly imagine needing only a scant week to travel from Westphalia to the Hanseatic town on the IJssel, a group of at least two hundred horsemen approaches. They are men, women, and children on unusually fiery horses. They are surrounded by packs of dogs. At their head rides a man with a fierce, haughty appearance. He wears a hat of fox tails. It is Joseph Andrías, Duke of Egypt.

5

That last part of the journey, Lucie, was a stretch with scores of windmills. None of us had ever seen anything like it. The city gate was already in sight, a stone gate at the end of the road which rose slightly there. Then there was that industrial area, grain and oil mills, a wind was blowing, the sails demanded every bit of our attention, our thoughts were whirled around and around. Up to then the area had been green. With streams and ditches along which black and white cows grazed without any supervision. A hospitable region. Geese and teal were dead easy to catch. Well, then: Surrounded by the raging sails we held a final council."

Six horsemen went on ahead. Clever, shameless, and dressed in expensive clothes, they galloped posthaste to the Noordenberg Gate, where they arrived on the dot of twelve. The guards were amazed by their regal appearance.

"Make haste," ordered Joseph. "Notify the town council. Announce our arrival!"

Following their own instinct, his group was already turning into Bisschopstraat. Immediately they felt the pulse of the town. At the spot where the Schipbeek emerges into the IJssel, they found the old merchants' houses. When they got to the Bokkingshaven, they stood staring silently at the ships. They turned around and rode behind a tall church in a direct line from Assenstraat, Sandrasteeg, Halvesteeg, and Bruynsteeg to the north side to emerge via the Graven near another very old church. A curious crowd was growing. The people looked at the outsized horses and felt the need to talk about life to the foreigners who were carrying gold-handled whips. The streets filled with the smell of tantalizingly exotic things. Joseph Andrías's group looked with interest at the houses with the wavy gables.

"Imagine, Luce, in the warehouses you saw ceilings with blue skies and gleaming gilded suns!"

They rode in procession across the Brink, where despite its being afternoon a roaring trade in dried fish was still being done, and then decided they might as well enter the town hall, on the corner of Tolstraat.

"Where exactly do you come from? Where are your lands?" asked the two burgomasters who approached them in the chamber. Tax-collectors and masters of guilds made pleasant faces. Respect spoke from their souls. Such horses, this gold, this lofty way of behaving: The Duke of Egypt could certainly make claims in Western Europe.

"I didn't answer at once. I wanted to encourage their respect and curiosity. They looked at the gold of our accessories. Then I said: 'History knows us under many names, gentlemen, and assigns areas to us in all points of the compass. The oldest mention of us you can find in one of our patriarchs from Ionia, called because of his blindness Ho me horon. He, a man of many words, had heard and retained something about our descent from the Sinti who lived on Lemnos. Centuries come, and go again, but long before the birth of the Divine Son another narrator, also a great Greek but with Carian blood, alludes to the horse-rearing Sigynnes in the river basin of the Danube. What is a people, a race? Our descent is manifold, to mention a single country of origin is misleading. It is said that the Atsingani, who were magicians and performed with the bear, are among our ancestors, but don't take that as the last word. We have been associated with those rescued from Atlantis. Are we Syrians by origin? Canaanites? My dear sirs: Of the facts, which are full of gaps, I can't keep from you those about India, because along the upper reaches of the Indus our language is understood, understood and spoken to this day. Because of the limited time, I shall ignore here the mountain people of the Sakas who fought Mithridates, and will say nothing of the Rajputs, all of whom were kings' sons. So as not to take up your time unnecessarily, my information will race quickly from our presence in India at the time of the Parthians to our exodus after the arrival of the Muslims. This is what happened: Our two hundred thousand horsemen and five thousand elephants fought on the side of the Rajputs against Mohammed of Gur, a rogue but a creditable general, and won the first battle. The second was under a godforsaken star. So it happened, and so it was to continue: some of us escaped via Afghanistan to Europe and we settled in Lower Egypt.'"

Silence. But the words lingered and demanded expansion. The aldermen wanted to know what happened next. Thereupon Joseph Andrías changed his voice because he wanted to appeal to the virtue of the heart and to Christian, evangelical virtue. This is well known: Hospitality to wandering pilgrims, that's number one, and number two is death to everything Turkish in the Balkans and far beyond. He told the town council of Deventer that they, Egyptians, had been converted to Christianity generations before, and had been driven out by the Turks on account of their faith.

"And we wandered for seven years, just imagine, if you can, it isn't pleasant: seven years of enduring banishment." And he continued about the generally very bad roads, the cold and the wind, that would put you completely out of sorts if you didn't simply take those things for granted in order to do penance for your sins. . . .

Oh, he spoke like a man of principle. The burgomasters offered the six princes, offered the people outside the gates, shelter without hesitation.

Here Joseph starts grinning. He casts his cunning look at Lucie, who sits there as impassive as usual. "They didn't even ask for our papers!"

She takes it as a joke. "Which, of course, you had!"

He takes her hand, she can still feel his rather forceful, lively fingers and, like that, in the languor of the afternoon, they look out over the streets where people already feel like celebrating. The sun is warm. The wind timeless. A bunch of children tries with sticks to catch a young goose that has found its way into the stinking window of a cod-drying shed, and the two follow his escape into the shiny green trees along Rijkmansstraat where the prosperous citizens of Deventer live.

"Yes! Indeed. Never had such a nice passport before!"

Wait. Joseph Andrías made a theatrical gesture, pushed aside the lining of his jacket, and produced a letter. Before opening the document, he looked around the council chamber. Those present fell silent as though enchanted by a secret performance.

"We, Sigismund," he read aloud, "by the grace of God King of Hungary, Bohemia, Dalmatia, Croatia, and other territories," whereupon there followed in forceful terms the charge to do everything to help the Duke of Egypt and his people in all lands of the Holy Roman Empire, hence also in Deventer. And the letter was passed around open afterward. It was the king's hand, definitely.

"Let them all in! Prepare the Wantshuis!"

To be on the safe side someone asked Joseph, "How many of you are there?"

"Two hundred."

"Book the Köln inn as well!"

"Well, Lucie, that's what happened. The gates were opened and our people filled the town with their horses and dogs."

The festive atmosphere immediately continued. While the Egyptians rode to the Wantshuis and installed themselves among the piles of woolen and cloth fabrics, while they watered their horses in the courtyard and lit their cooking fires in the square in front of the deanery, the town took out its accordions, its prize pigs, its flags, and straw was strewn on the Brink in advance because nobody doubted that the following day there would be horse trading. It became dark in the streets. That night, by the light of wax candles, you could meet brightly dressed women who spread your hand open and looked at it and then prophesied something light and happy for you from the lines.

The morning began with the tolling of bells. And with the clip-clop of hooves — heavy native working horses and riding horses so tall, black, and impatient that they can only be associated with immortally beautiful stories — they made their way to the Brink.

"Good God, Joseph, those coldbloods! Look!"

"You're telling me, wonderful nags. We bought four."

"Do you remember Ulaleen?"

"The grandmother of Bellaheleen?"

"Yes."

"She was standing by the gate when I drove up in 1963."

"You came past the orchard. You parked next to the barn. By the gate there was a heavy horse with broad hooves."

"She may well have had something in her of these primeval types, don't you think? Hard, willing, slow. It was a wonderful breed, Luce, then, from the country around

Deventer. But they made us laugh, you know. They'd pulled the teeth of some of the very young mares."

"To sell them as mature horses, I suppose."

"Yes. Yes, and in order to palm them off onto us as mares who could already carry a stallion."

Horse trading in the far distance. Sun, wind. By about noon the bustle and the money result mainly in music. The Egyptians populate the pubs and pavements around the square with large-scale exuberance. Their strange singing voices, the shuffling of their feet and hands, their eight-stringed fiddles, are answered by the astonished but scarcely hesitating people of Deventer led by six young master carpenters with drinking and guild songs. And in the afternoon there are equestrian games. At full gallop farmers' sons, who have managed to round up their stallions like pedigree animals, spear a ring hung over the road with a poplar branch, which they stick out like a lance. And the Egyptians make everyone think by jumping on their horses over three beet carts placed next to each other, while another group make their decked-out stallions step to the side and backward to the music of the carillon in front of the Lebuïnuskerk.

Wonderful images. Which take up two whole days. Absorbing them is not difficult, reporting on them is, because the moment called "now" is timeless and hence a piece of "forever." Here is a town in which for once the people quite calmly leave the doors of their houses open, in which they sleep when they feel like it and eat when they feel like it because the firmly anchored residence has been overcome by the most powerful of all intoxications, a life within life in which everything is a little different. You can find the dark Egyptians everywhere. They tell good fortunes. They do business. They accept smoked herrings, straw, beer, and twenty-ounce loaves as presents from a town that has been admonished by its king and bears the eagle in its coat of arms. They tell anyone who will listen about the situation in the far corners of the world, but in reality they are announcing their departure. They're leaving, and if anyone asks where to, they will roll their eyes and see land, hills, and seas. For convenience, however, they will answer: We're going to the holy relics in Saint-Laurent-les-Mâcon, we're making a pilgrimage to Aachen, we are on our way to the Abbey of Saint-Adelbert in Egmond. . . .

That morning when the town is completely unsuspecting because it's living in the present, there is a harsh wind. Suddenly the Egyptians are riding through the streets. They are already approaching the Bergkerk when they're noticed, by a begging student from a Latin school, and make for the gate. A great crowd, suddenly realizing what's happening, has gathered to look at them and wave them goodbye with feelings of intense loss. The people see the six familiar men riding in front, in their middle, dark, watchful, and with an indescribable atmosphere of good humor, their leader. They look at the flickering of the gold on his chest and his hat of fox tails, but none of them looks at him at such length as the farmer's girl, a sturdy lass with watery eyes and that high-Gothic, ginger hair, who knows that her life will have no further meaning at all if . . .

"Take me with you!" she cries with the same extreme act of the heart with which she caught his glance.

The wind has meanwhile risen to a single gust. And yet he has heard her voice.

Bravura, a trace of haughtiness in his eyes.

"All right! Come on, then!"

A huge horse is driven into the crowd. At a pat on its neck it stops. Then someone doesn't hesitate for a moment to reach out with both arms.